MY GENTLEMAN SPY

SASHA COTTMAN

To Dean and Laura

Chapter One

GIBRALTAR 1817

Hattie Wright sucked in a deep breath before slowly letting the air back out. The long drop over the side of the ship to the water below was a heart-rending distance.

What had seemed a plausible idea only a minute or two before; now revealed itself to be nothing short of madness.

She wondered how hard the water would be when she finally hit it. Had she overestimated her strength as a swimmer and was she fated to drown before she could make it back to shore?

Worst of all, were there sharks lurking in the murky depths below?

She lifted her gaze from the deep green of the bay and looked at the small town of Gibraltar a quarter mile across the water. Soon it would be out of sight and the *Blade of Orion* would be on her way to Africa.

Earlier that morning, with her fiancé holding her firmly by the hand Hattie had made the short journey up the gangplank and onto the ship. All the while her heart had been beating a loud tattoo within her chest.

No. no. no.

Gibraltar was the last stop before they embarked on the long journey down the West coast of Africa to their destination of Sierra Leone. When her parents first announced their mission to Africa, she had tried to convince herself that this was her destiny. Her parents were resolved in their mission to bring the word of God to the people of Freetown and she as their dutiful daughter was to accompany them. Reverend Peter Brown, her recently acquired fiancé, was just another part of the grand plan. One which had been laid out for her.

She rubbed her finger across the deep scowl line which sat just above her nose. She was by nature a person who worried about all manner of things. The impending journey to Africa had her lying awake every night.

Long before the ship had left London Dock a nagging doubt had sparked and grown within her mind. Was this what she truly wanted for her life? Once she was wed to the dour Peter, all choice would be gone. Her life would be set in stone.

And what of the friends she was being forced to leave behind. How would they survive without her?

She looked back at the ship's deck. Apart from the crew there were no other passengers up on deck. Her mother would no doubt, be busy rearranging their tiny cabin for the second time that morning. Hattie knew her mother well. A place for everything and everything in its place.

Her father and Peter would be locked in one of their never-ending conversations about how they were to set up the ministry on the edge of the African jungle. Every day on the journey thus far they had spent hours poring over paperwork and the building plans for a new church. A church in which she and Peter would be married.

Everyone was busy with their own priorities. No one would come looking for her until it was too late. By the time they did she would be long gone.

She looked down once more at the water lapping against the side of the ship. Soon the *Blade of Orion* would be far from port and the opportunity to change her life would be lost. She either accepted her future as the wife of a missionary or she jumped.

2

The chill wind ruffled her light gold hair. Her pounding heart reminding her in its heavy beat that she was still very much alive. But would she be so when her body hit the water far below and she sunk deep beneath the waves?

The ship's leading hand bellowed out orders to set out the sails. Sailors on the deck quickly scrambled up into the ropes. As the hive of activity swirled around the deck, she was grateful no one appeared to have noticed her presence.

Her conscience which had until this morning vacillated between acceptance and rebellion finally made up its mind. The truth was, she counselled herself if she were to die shortly, it would be the better death. Quickly drowning in the Bay of Gibraltar would be preferable to a long living death as Peter's wife in the dark heart of the African continent.

In the short period they had been engaged, Peter had revealed to her the kind of husband he would make. There would be little laughter or happiness in their marriage. Duty would be the only constant.

A tiny voice in the back of her brain whispered, urging her on.

"You have to move."

For every second that she delayed, the opportunity to determine her own future slipped further from her reach. Even now the swim to shore would test her endurance to its limits.

She slowly began to make her way along the deck to where the gangplank, having been raised, was now stored. The end of the plank still jutted a good eight feet out over the side of the ship. Not much, but it at least afforded her the semblance of a chance that if she went into the water from here, she could be clear of the ship and its dangerous wake.

Hoisting her skirts, she climbed up onto the long wooden bridge. Dropping to her knees, she crawled out past the edge of the ship and over the water. At the end of the gangplank she sat down and swung her feet over the side.

In the middle distance, Gibraltar was slowly, but certainly slipping away.

It was now or never.

"Lord if you grant me this boon I shall remain your devoted servant always," she vowed.

After a final glance back over her shoulder at the deck of the ship, Hattie took a deep breath and dropped over the side.

Chapter Two

W ill Saunders leaned back against the rock wall of the Port of Gibraltar and closed his eyes. The warmth of the sun seeped deep into his bones. For all that he longed to return home to England, he knew it would be the warm weather of Europe he missed the most once he left.

All those long years spent in Paris as an undercover operative for His Majesty's government now seemed a lifetime ago.

Yet it was only last month that he had finally packed up his things, given notice to his landlady, Madame Dessaint and vacated his lodgings in Paris. Treating himself to a farewell tour of the now peaceful cities of lower France and Spain he planned for his journey to end with a boat trip back to London.

London.

He shivered at the prospect of facing the forthcoming English winter.

"Oh well it has to be," he murmured. His fingers caressed the warm stone sea wall of the dock.

For five years he had been away. Years which had seen him change forever. The young man who had slipped into Paris in the summer of 1812 was long gone. Too self-assured bordering on arrogant, he had quickly learned the truth of life as a spy. Living on the knife's edge, knowing that at any moment there could be a knock at the door and his mortal existence would be at an end.

A spy's greatest hope was that when it did come, death would be quick. Only those whom fate had completely abandoned were faced with arrest and the inevitable journey to the scaffold and an audience with Madame Guillotine.

Will opened his eyes. The bright sun had him blinking hard to focus. He put a hand to his chest, feeling the strong beat of his heart. He sighed, grateful that he, unlike so many others, had been fortunate enough to escape that terrible fate.

If the damp weather in England was the worst he had to deal with for the rest of his life, he would be blessed. He lifted his head from the wall and sat upright, before indulging in a long, tension releasing stretch.

The wind from the sea blew through his linen shirt and chilled his still damp skin. A short while earlier, he had taken a leisurely swim in the harbor. Seated now on an upturned wooden crate at the bottom of a series of steep stone steps he could hear the local Spanish traders as they beckoned for all comers to buy their wares at the Friday morning market which was taking place in the town square above.

He rummaged around in his leather satchel, which sat on the stone paving next to him, and pulled out a small knife and an orange which he had purchased earlier that morning in the market. After peeling off the dimpled skin of the succulent fruit, he stuffed a piece of the orange into his mouth. A smile crept to his lips as he relished the sweet citrus juice. With his thumb he wiped a stray trickle of juice from his lips.

"That is good," he murmured.

Days from now he would be home in England, and back in the rarefied air of London high society. These simple days would be pleasant, but ever distant memories to cherish as he tried to re-establish himself within the *haute ton*.

Letters from his parents and family had offered all manner of assistance once he had made known his intention to return home permanently. His brother and sisters would no doubt make every effort to see him well set once more.

He missed his family. How much he missed them had been brought home during his brief summer visit back to London earlier that year.

Instinctively he reached for his left hand, his fingers searching for his wedding ring. They touched only skin, and the ridge where once a ring had been. He flinched momentarily before remembering his recent decision to take it off.

Yvette was dead.

Three years and eight months. He had stopped counting the days, but even now he was unsure as to whether he was truly ready to move on. To finally accept that his wife was gone. To allow the ghost of his guilt to rest in peace.

A movement on the horizon caught his eye. A ship which had left the nearby dockside only a short while earlier, turned portside. He recalled seeing the last of the ship's passengers scramble on board the *Blade of Orion*. She was a sturdy, though not overly large sea going vessel. He sent a silent prayer to those on board, wishing them a safe journey. She was bound for Africa.

Only the brave and steady of heart made the perilous journey to Africa. Apart from the countries which bordered the Mediterranean Sea, the African continent was largely unknown. Many had left Europe seeking their fortunes in that vast land, only to be never heard from again. Africa was known as the white man's graveyard with good reason.

He was about to turn away and put his boots and jacket back on when something else caught his attention.

He could see someone crawling along what appeared to be the raised gangplank of the ship. Will frowned at this rather dangerous occupation. The life of a sailor was fraught with peril. As he put a hand up to shade his eyes from the bright morning sun, he squinted to get a better look.

As the person reached the end of the gangplank they sat down. Will's breath caught in his throat at the sight of long skirts draped over the edge of the plank. It was not a sailor; it was a woman.

"What the devil are you up to?" he muttered.

The words had barely left his lips when to his horror, the woman dropped over the side of the ship and fell into the water below. She disappeared beneath the waves.

For a moment Will stood rooted to the spot, struck motionless as his brain struggled to accept what his eyes had just beheld. From where he stood, he could see no one else on board the ship had seen the woman fall.

The crew continued about their business of preparing and setting the sails, oblivious to the crisis which was unfolding. He frantically called out to the ship, but his voice was carried away on the wind.

The woman was now alone with her fate. Only he could possibly save her.

Coming to his senses he tossed away the remainder of his orange. He stripped off his shirt and flung it down on the stones. He hurried down to the edge of the dock. Reaching the water's edge, he dived in. Coming up for air, he began to swim toward the ship, praying against all hope that he could reach her before she drowned.

&.

The impact of the water punched the air out of Hattie's lungs so hard that she feared she would lose consciousness. Salt water filled her mouth and eyes.

She flayed about for what seemed an eternity, bordering on the edge of panic as her limited vision filled with swirling skirts and foam. Finally, she caught a glimpse of light above her and realizing it was the sun began to swim toward the surface.

Breaking the surface of the water, she sucked in a huge lungful of air. Her momentary relief dashed by the sight of the ship which filled her entire vision.

Death stared her in the face. Even if she had been able to scream, no one could have heard her above the roar of the waves and the ship. Any moment now the ship's wake would pull her under and she would die.

"Dear lord," she muttered.

She turned and began to frantically swim away, hoping against all hope that she could by some miracle survive.

She soon found the going to be tougher than she could ever have imagined. Hattie had never had to swim in boots and skirts before. The weight of her clothing threatened to overwhelm her efforts to make good her escape.

Lifting her head, a break in the waves afforded her a brief glimpse of the dockside. So tantalizingly close.

Get clear of the ship and then float. Come on Hattie, you are not done for yet. You shall not die this day.

Knowing that the greatest enemy of any swimmer was fatigue she rolled over onto her back and began to kick strongly away from the ship. Slowly, but surely, she gradually built a safe distance between her and certain death.

As the *Blade of Orion* slowly drew away, the first tangible sense of relief pricked her brain. Her drop over the side of the ship had gone unnoticed. No one up on deck was running about and pointing to her in the water.

Best of all she had survived. So far.

"Next time I jump over the side of a ship, I shall remove my boots first," she chided herself.

With the ship now sailing away, she gathered her thoughts. Her first task was to make it to safety. She would deal with the rest of her predicament once she was back on dry land.

With her head pointed toward the town, continuing to swim on her back made sense. It allowed her legs to partly float and take some of the weight of her boots. Every so often, she would stop, turn around and once she had reconfirmed her bearings continue to swim toward the shore.

The rhythmic strokes of her arms helped to calm her panic. As she drew closer to the dockside, hope sparked in her heart.

"I'm going to make it," she sobbed.

A scream erupted from her mouth a second later as a firm hand took hold of her downward descending arm.

She fought vainly against the stranger, but he was altogether too strong for her. He wrapped his arm around her shoulder and pulled her toward him. With her back against his chest he began to swim toward shore.

"Stop struggling or we shall both drown," he bellowed at her above the noise of the waves.

She caught a glimpse of dark hair and a naked torso. Where had he come from?

The thought that only a lunatic would be out swimming in the middle of the bay briefly crossed her mind, but at that moment all that really mattered was that they were swimming toward land.

He was also right about not fighting him. If he was prepared to do the lion's share of the work then she stood a much better chance of making it safely to shore. Accepting his assistance, she relaxed against the stranger's chest and attempted to aid him in his endeavors by kicking as best as she could in her water-logged boots.

Working together they finally made it to the water's edge at the dockside. Several local dock hands came down and helped them both ashore.

As soon as her feet touched solid ground, Hattie's legs buckled from under her and she fell heavily to her knees. The soft flesh of her hands smacked hard against the stone paving of the dockside.

"Ooof," she groaned.

Her dark-haired savior bent down and putting an arm around her waist, lifted her to her feet.

"Swimming in boots is never a good idea," he said.

"No," was all the reply she could muster.

With his arm still wrapped tightly around her waist, he guided her up a nearby short set of stone steps. The curious dock workers followed. Reaching the top, he sat her down upon an upturned wooden crate. He dropped down beside her. After reassuring the dock hands that the two of them were safe, he waved them away.

While she did not understand anything of the words the men were muttering as they headed back down the steps, Hattie suspected they were not kind. No one in their right frame of mind would willingly leap over the side of a ship.

From years spent listening to the firebrand preachers who visited her local church she knew the look and tone of disapproval well.

Women should be obedient, and know their place in the world.

She lifted her head and looked out to sea, just in time to see the *Blade of Orion* round the nearby head of the south mole of the harbor and disappear. Her head and shoulders slumped.

She was free.

"It's gone," the stranger remarked.

He reached out and placed a comforting hand on her upper arm.

She flinched involuntarily, before remembering where she was.

"Thank you. That was an incredibly brave thing you did. I owe you the deepest debt of gratitude."

"London?" came the reply.

Hattie turned to look at the stranger properly for the first time. Her heart which was only beginning to calm down from the strenuous swim, began to thump once more in her chest.

Dark hair. His sodden black trousers clung tight to his strong muscular body. No boots. No shirt.

She had never seen the fully naked upper torso of a man before, it left her breathless.

His gaze followed hers and a sheepish look of embarrassment appeared on his face.

"My apologies. I forgot about my attire. Now where did I leave my clothes?" he said.

He leaned over and picked up a bundle of cloth which lay nearby and after a brief struggle with it, managed to pull it over his head. The sleeves of what she now knew to be a shirt proved to be a more difficult proposition. After several unsuccessful attempts to put his arms into the damp twisted sleeves, Hattie was forced to render assistance.

"Here let me help you," she said.

If the stranger had thought that by donning his shirt he would add a little modesty to the situation, he had not counted on what the linen would do once it touched his wet body. The shirt quickly stuck to him, affording Hattie a second look at his hard, masculine body.

Her quiet appreciation of his body was interrupted when the remains of the seawater which had lodged in the back of her throat shifted and quickly brought on a violent bout of coughing.

Finally, she heaved and the rest of the vile seawater came up from her stomach and was deposited on the flat stone ground. She got to her feet. The stranger followed suit. Her patient rescuer gently rubbed her back.

"Come on cough it all up. If you don't you will be laid up in a sick bed by the end of the day," he said.

Finally, she held up a hand. The spasms were gone and she could breathe deeply once more.

"Thank you," she said.

He stepped away and stood silently looking at her, eventually drawing her gaze to his face.

The words handsome devil immediately sprang to Hattie's mind. A devil with grey eyes of a shade she had never seen before. In the bright light of the sun, she thought them almost silver. Then he blinked and when she looked once more she saw there was a warmth and softness about them.

"What did you say?" she stammered.

"I said to get all that sea water out of your stomach," he replied.

"No before that."

"I said London. Not quite Park Lane, but at least west of Covent Garden. I have a particular talent for picking accents."

Hattie shivered. The wind blowing through her wet clothes was mostly to blame, but something else stirred within her. With the *Blade of Orion* now out of sight, the gravity of her situation hit hard. She put a trembling hand to her chest. Her situation was perilous.

She was over a thousand miles from home, with no possessions and no money. Her parents and fiancé were bound for Sierra Leone, oblivious to the fact that she was no longer on board the ship. And yet here she was, standing with a stranger, discussing the intricacies of her provenance.

"Oh, dear god, what have I done?" she muttered.

Will stepped forward and after placing a gentle, but firm hand on her shoulder posed the obvious question.

"May I ask you something?" he said.

This man had just risked his life to swim out into the harbor and rescue her. Of course, he had questions.

"Yes?"

"I won't attempt to judge; I just need to know if what just happened out there in the harbor was an accident or if you intended to jump from the ship."

Hattie winced. Lying was not something which came naturally to her.

"I jumped," she replied.

"I thought so. I was watching you before you fell and it didn't look from where I sat that it was an accident. Your movements seemed quite deliberate in the minute or so before you went over the side. So, may I now ask why you jumped?"

She met his gaze. His grey eyes held a kindness which beckoned to her. Made her want to reveal her deepest inner thoughts to him. Only to him. A man whose name she didn't even know made her want to share all the secrets and dreams she kept hidden from the world.

And what was the truth? That Harriet Imogen Margaret Wright who had been a dutiful, obedient daughter all her life had suddenly been possessed of the overwhelming need to seize her own future. That she had taken a literal leap into the unknown.

A small spark in the back recesses of her mind gave her pause. She could sense that beneath his veneer of kindness, he hid a strength of will. If he chose to wield that will against her, it could easily over-power her own.

Having only just been saved from a possible watery grave, she was in no mood to tempt fate twice. Yet his question demanded an answer.

What then was she to tell him?

"My name is Sarah Wilson," she replied.

The real Sarah Wilson, her maid was still on board the ship. But since her maid had eagerly signed up to become part of the mission to Africa, there was little chance she would be suddenly appearing on anyone's doorstep to poke holes in Hattie's story.

"I was engaged to be married. My fiancé told me we were going on a trip to Spain, and it was only when we got to Gibraltar that he told me we were headed to Africa. I tried to reason with him, but he became unkind," she added.

Shut up Hattie. Don't make the lie any bigger than it needs to be.

"I see. And that is why you jumped overboard?"

She nodded. Keeping her mouth shut was the best thing she could do right now. Lies were hard enough if you had been granted time to come up with a convincing one. Making things up as she went along made the task nigh on impossible.

He remained silent for a moment. Hattie could almost hear his brain processing her words. He turned away, and with his hands clasped behind him, he looked out into the harbor in the direction of where the *Blade of Orion* had gone.

A chill of recollection slid down her spine. The memory of watching her father standing looking out the window of his study the moment before he suddenly announced her engagement to the Reverend Peter Brown crashed through her mind. At this moment, she wished she could be back home in England and in her father's study. Anywhere but here.

The stranger turned and faced her. She pushed the image of her father from her mind.

There was a kindness in the stranger's countenance which she had not seen in her father for a long time. Unlike her father, she sensed this was a man she could reason with to have her voice heard. A man she could trust.

"Do you know anyone in Gibraltar?" he asked.

Hattie shook her head. She knew few people outside of London, let alone England.

"William Saunders at your service Miss Wilson," he said, adding a graceful bow.

He offered her his hand and she was compelled to take it. For someone who had just been in the cold sea, his hands were surprisingly warm. Yet, she shivered at his touch.

She shivered a second time before letting out a loud sneeze. A flash of dismay passed over Will's face.

"There is little point in me helping to save your life, if I let you sit here and catch your death of cold. You must come back with me to my hotel and get those clothes dried off."

He tightened his grip of her hand, revealing his offer to be more of a command. The recklessness of her actions now laid themselves open to her sight. She was alone in a foreign country; and within minutes of leaving the protection of her family she was being asked to accompany a man back to his hotel. Tears pricked her eyes. How long would it be before something terrible befell her? Before she was utterly ruined.

She tore her hand from his grasp.

"I don't think that is a very good idea Mr. Saunders, we have only just met. I am from a respectable family, and as such you must understand that I am not the sort of girl who goes anywhere with a strange man," she replied.

Will softly chuckled. "I've oft considered myself a little odd, but never strange. Though my sister Eve may have something else to say about the matter."

He walked over to a nearby leather satchel and after rummaging around in it, pulled out a card. He handed it to her.

Mr. William Saunders Esq, 28 Dover Street, London it read.

As Hattie read the card, relief flooded her heart. She knew of the Saunders family; they were very respectable members of the *ton*. Her mother had attended several functions at the Saunders' house in Dover Street. She had met Evelyn Saunders the year of her coming out, but could not recall an older brother. The family were connected to the Duke of Strathmore. Rich and powerful.

If this gentleman was indeed William Saunders, then she was as likely to be safe with him as anyone else. He would understand the predicament she was in and the risk to which her reputation was currently faced. A small mercy had been bestowed.

"You live in London?" she asked.

"As of next week, yes. That's my father's house, where I shall be residing until I can secure a new abode for myself. I have lived abroad for the past few years," he replied.

"I assure you Miss Wilson you shall be perfectly safe with me. As a gentleman it is my duty to take care of young ladies such as yourself and make sure they come to no harm. Let me at least escort you back to my hotel and see that you are settled."

Hattie looked once more at Will's calling card. It was not as if she had a lot of other options to call upon. Beggars were not offered the luxury of choice. She offered him her hand.

"We need to get you into some warm dry clothes and soon, your hands are like ice," he said.

Chapter Three

T he walk up the stone steps and into the town concentrated Will's mind. What could have possessed Sarah to make her jump ship? While he was prepared to accept that her fiancé was likely a blackguard, he also suspected she was holding back much of the truth. From the way she spoke, he deduced that there was an actual fiancé somewhere in the story. What was not so certain however, was whether he was the real reason behind her fleeing the ship.

The *Blade of Orion* had been in port for at least several days, during which the passengers would have had to disembark and stay somewhere in the town. Why hadn't she sought help from the authorities while still onshore? Gibraltar was full of British naval personnel, anyone of whom could have been called upon to come to her aid.

He chanced a look in her direction.

She was pretty; in a keep you happy in bed in the middle of winter way. Her warm brown eyes alone could capture a man's soul. Her face, while not beautiful, still held the promise of laughter, which to a man of Will's experience was far more alluring. Beauty often failed to live up to its promise.

Her full lips were meant for long luxurious kisses. Instinct told him that whomever married Sarah Wilson would never feel the need to stray from the marital bed. She was a woman to cleave onto and be grateful for, for the rest of your life. If he had been asked to describe her in a single word he knew what it would be. Lovely.

Her fiancé had lost a special woman, though from the sound of the cad, he would likely never come to that realization.

With her sea soaked clothes still clinging tightly to her body, Will found himself appreciating the soft curves which were on display. Her ample breasts stretched the seams of the gown's water shrunken bodice.

He checked himself. It had been a long time since he had allowed the thought of a woman's body to pervade so strongly into his mind. For the past few years he had buried those thoughts and desires deep in the black hole of loss.

Grief was a thick, dark blanket to the joy of life. Once the sharp heat of it ebbed, it offered protection to the heart.

What am I doing?

For the first time since the death of his wife, Will was forced to accept that the girl walking beside him stirred his longing.

"So, we shall get you to the hotel, and you will be fine after that?" he asked. He was testing her, seeing how long she could hold her story together.

"Yes, yes of course. Thank you, Mr. Saunders," she replied.

When they finally reached the top of the stairs which led to the entrance of the largest of the handful of hotels in Gibraltar, Will stopped and held open the door. Hattie stepped inside and he followed.

On the climb up the hill, he had silently evaluated her situation. He doubted she had any money. If she had thought to take some with her before leaving the ship, those coins were more than likely now resting at the bottom of the harbor. If his theory held true, then it was only a matter of time before she would be forced to admit the truth of her predicament.

As they reached the front desk of the hotel, which doubled as both reception and an extension to the tavern bar she stopped.

He could see she was ill at ease. The constant wringing of her hands gave her away. When she cracked the smallest knuckle on her left hand, he knew it was time to act.

His sister Caroline had the same nervous habit, one which made him grit his teeth every time he was forced to bear witness to it.

What sort of man are you? What could you possibly achieve from making her beg you for help? Will Saunders, you are a better man than this. She is not some operative you need to bend to your will. Offer her your full assistance.

He waved the hotel's head porter away and taking hold of Hattie's arm steered her away from the front desk.

"You don't have any money, do you?" he asked, once they were out of earshot of the hotel staff.

She winced. Her reaction confirming his assessment of her lack of skills as a liar. In his old life he would have viewed this as a character flaw, but in the young woman before him he knew this to be a sign of her true character and breeding.

It was refreshing to meet someone who did not practice deceit as part of their normal day to day existence.

She pulled away and turning on her heel headed for the door.

Will who until that second had thought himself a canny predictor of the reactions of others, suddenly found himself wrong footed. Any other woman would have thrown herself on his charity. Called all societies dictates to the fore, but not this girl.

He watched in amazement as she screwed her courage to the sticking place and walked away. She was not going to ask for his help.

She was so like Yvette. So bloody stubborn.

Stop her you fool.

"Sarah!" he called out, but she did not react.

She moved faster than even he expected. By the time he reached the door, she was well out into the street and headed for the nearby town square in which the market was being held. He ran after her.

Taking a firm hold of her arm he stopped her in mid stride. When he saw her tears, Will instantly felt lower than a gutter rat's paw.

"It's alright, I won't leave you," he said, trying his best to offer reassurance.

Hattie's face said it all, she was in dire straits. Whether it was of her own making or not, it did not matter. He had to help.

"I just want to go home," she sobbed.

His senses sprang to attention. A soft tingling in his left ear, which rapidly became a sharp ringing warned him that they were in danger. His gaze shifted slowly from Hattie to their nearby surroundings.

The people around them in the market place began to shoot disapproving glances his way.

It did not take a genius to realize that the locals had assumed he and she were a couple.

From the loud clicking of tongues and whispered *bestia* it was also obvious that they held him responsible for her current miserable condition.

Hattie's hair was an unkempt disaster, plastered all over her head. Her clothes, though slowly beginning to dry, made her look like she had been dragged backwards through a hedgerow. She looked at best untidy, at worst mistreated.

A heavy knock on the shoulder from a passing stall holder revealed the depth of enmity beginning to build amongst the crowd. Will was the villain of the piece. If he did not bring the situation under control, and fast, he was likely to find himself on the receiving end of a solid fist or two.

"Alright, alright. I will take you home. Just please stop crying," Will pleaded.

The local women who had gathered to stand behind Hattie looked to one another. Will caught the glimpse of a donkey whip in one woman's hand and sizeable pieces of rock in the hands of several others.

The buzz of the crowd rose in pitch.

Their adopted daughter however did not appear to comprehend what was going on around her. Hattie's head dropped and she stared at the stone paving. Unwittingly she held the crowd and therefore both her and Will's safety in the palm of her hand.

"They want to know if everything is alright," he explained.

"What?" she replied, when she finally looked at him.

He took a step forward, intent on speaking more privately to her, but the crowd murmured its disapproval.

"*Bien bien,*" he said, taking two overly long steps backward, hands help up in surrender.

Hattie's gaze fell on the nearest of the women. The woman's finger was pointed at Hattie's disheveled gown.

Hattie looked down at her gown and frowned. "Oh, I see."

As she attempted to straighten her skirts, a bright patch of red appeared on her cheeks. Will's heart went out to her once more. The poor girl was embarrassed at the bedraggled state of her clothes in front of these strangers.

The creased and partly shrunken gown refused to yield to her attentions. Nothing she did to make it appear more presentable made the slightest of difference. White sea salt lines had begun to appear on the few dry patches of the bodice.

Finally, with a sad huff, she gave up. Her hands hung limply by her sides.

The crowd, which was rapidly increasing in size coalesced into a single angry beast, and growled. The ringing in Will's ear rose to a deafening clang. It was like a bell being tolled inside his head.

Realization of the crowd's mood finally dawned on Hattie's face. She turned to the crowd and pleaded.

"No, no it's not his fault. He is trying to help me. He rescued..."

"Come darling," Will interjected.

While it was all well and good for her to attempt to paint him to be a savior, it did not further their cause if those gathered in the town square got the wrong idea. Her Spanish was likely non-existent and he for one did not think the townsfolk were in any mood to listen to his explanation, no matter how eloquently or fluently it was given.

There was also the matter of exactly what he would say to the townsfolk if he was given any kind of hearing. He would be a dead man if they thought he was trying to accost an innocent stranger.

She, in turn would fare little better. The well-meaning people of the town would likely make every effort to have her back on board the *Blade of Orion* before it reached the next port.

"If you ever wish to see England again, you had better come with me now. If your new friends discover the truth of your situation, they will involve the local authorities. You do not want that to happen. Your fiancé has legal rights over you in this part of the world. They will hand you over to him," he said.

He knew whatever lies she had told him so far would not stand up to any serious scrutiny. She looked once more at the assembled throng and to Will's utter relief accurately read exactly what the situation needed.

She took several stuttering steps forward and threw herself headlong into Will's arms.

The crowd cheered and applauded this delightful development. Love had triumphed all obstacles. Several of the women wiped tears away as they tucked their rocks back into their aprons. One even ventured a kiss on the cheek of a nearby man. Several bystanders laughed at the sight of the kiss, while Will prayed it was the woman's husband.

Watching this byplay unfold, Will took his cue. He bent down and placed a chaste kiss on Hattie's cheek. Her melodramatic gesture of forgiveness demanded the fullness of his acknowledgement.

The act of creating an impromptu facade was second nature to him. Spies were always having to think on their feet. Lives usually depended on it.

The townsfolk mumbled their disapproval. This was not the submission their hearts and minds craved from the wicked husband who had hurt his beautiful young wife. Truth was sitting quietly in the gutter at this point nursing a sore head. The crowd was making the love story up in its collective mind as it went along.

Will saw the pleading looks on the faces of several old senoras and knew a kiss on the cheek was never going to pass muster.

He looked down at Hattie and whispered.

"Forgive me."

He bent his head and set his lips to hers.

Chapter Four

A s Will's lips met hers, Hattie's heart leapt. This was an unexpected development and one which she quickly decided was not unwelcome.

His kiss at first tentative, soon deepened much to both hers and the crowd's delight. As he speared his fingers through her hair pulling her close to him, she found herself praying that the locals had plenty of time on their hands. She for once in her life was in no hurry to be anywhere else.

Warm, tender lips touched hers, inviting her response. Opening her lips, she welcomed Will's attentions. As his tongue swept into her mouth she felt her knees begin to buckle.

Oh, this is heaven.

He was skilled in the art of kissing, but not in the calculating way she had heard was the hallmark of men of his class. And most certainly not like the horrid, hard kisses Peter Brown had forced upon her. His cold and often harsh attempts to kiss her were a world's difference to this delightful encounter.

The tenderness within Will Saunders was natural and freely given.

The noise from the crowd and the market disappeared, leaving only them and the heady delight of their kiss. She tasted the sharp citrus tang of orange on his tongue. Her mind whispered thoughts of sunny climes and long nights under starry skies. A life, if given half the chance, she would take hold of with both hands and never let go.

A sigh escaped her lips as she imagined what it would be like to call this man her very own for all time. She indulged herself in the pleasant fantasy that she was indeed his wife.

That he would take her home to a place they shared that was full of love. And once there he would lay her on their bed and make passionate love to her. He would be hers and hers alone.

"Miss Wilson?"

She opened her eyes. Will was still holding her close, studying her.

How long had she been standing there, eyes closed, lost in the kiss? And when had he released her from his lips?

"Oh. I am so sorry. I got caught up in the moment," she stammered.

Her fingers instinctively touched her lips. They were still warm from his kiss. Disappointment stirred in her heart as they rapidly cooled. Her disappointment was compounded by the fact that he had called her by someone else's name.

The boisterous swell from the crowd filled her ears once more, returning her to reality. She turned.

A smiling and thoroughly appreciative market crowd stood behind her. There were few dry eyes among the women. Even the old, craggy men sitting on the stone steps of the nearby church wore grins.

The young lovers had won over the hearts and minds of the locals.

Will leaned in. "While the situation is still in our favor, I suggest we head back to the hotel. I should like to discuss matters further with you, but somewhere a little more private," he said.

He offered her his hand and without hesitation Hattie took it. Why she felt so safe with this stranger was something she could not understand. But she knew that a man capable of kissing a woman in such a passionate way, a man who could make her soul stir to life would never seek to cause her harm.

❧

And so, it was that within an hour of having leapt from the side of the ship, Miss Hattie Wright, in the guise of Sarah Wilson, was under the protection of Mr. William Saunders Esq.

She had also been thoroughly kissed by him in public.

After making enquiries, Will managed to engage the services of a local dressmaker who quickly put together a small selection of ready-made clothes for Hattie. The hotel arranged a maid.

Will silently congratulated himself for having so skillfully attended to the needs of a young lady of his class. His mother would be proud. Whether the wardrobe Hattie now had at her disposal was the latest of London fashion he was not certain. Anything however was better than her ruined dress which was beyond salvation.

While Hattie was upstairs changing in the room he had arranged for her, Will sat downstairs in the small alcove which served as the hotel's lobby.

He attempted to read a copy of *The Times* which had arrived that morning by ship from London, but his mind refused to give it any real attention. He folded the paper in half and put it down.

Thoughts of Hattie refused to leave his mind. Her long flaxen hair, though tangled and stuck to her head, was an enthralling color. He had once owned a Palomino horse with a similar luxurious mane. He suspected once it was dry and thoroughly combed, his new companion's hair would shine in the sunlight in much the same way.

"Who are you?" he murmured.

When he had called out her name in the market earlier that morning, she had not reacted. Only when he reached out and took hold of her arm had she registered his presence. Her real name was clearly not Sarah Wilson. What or whom she was hiding from was bad enough for her to have taken on a false name.

She was an enticing conundrum. Well-bred by the sound of her accent and manner of behavior, but with an undertone of the common touch. The way she had addressed the villagers and even the hotel staff stamped her as someone who did not look down upon those of a lower social class.

As for her fiancé, Will wondered exactly what sort of a man would lure a girl away from her family and drag her half way across the world to Africa. That aspect of her story still did not ring true to his mind. Therein lay the heart of the lie.

Just who had she been with on board the *Blade of Orion*?

He licked his lips, surprised at how dry his mouth had suddenly become. His heartbeat increased as the familiar rush of the game began to course through his veins.

The thrill of the chase had been part of why he had volunteered as an undercover operative for the British government. He knew that his motives had not been entirely patriotic or noble. The lust for danger ran strong in his family's blood.

Right from childhood delving into the deepest, most secret places of others minds had been his special skill. Slowly extracting the truth was a long game of which he was the master.

By the time he was done with her, he would know all her secrets. He would take his time. After he had gained her confidence and trust, she would willingly tell him everything he wished to know. She would reveal all.

He absentmindedly rubbed his fingers across the stubble on his chin. He did not quite fit the image of the well-bred London gentleman, something he would need to address if he was to gain her trust.

Recalling that moment outside in the marketplace, when he had held her in his arms and kissed her senseless, Will's wish list began to take form.

Names and places were one thing; they could be so easily checked and verified. It was what lived within her soul he desired to know. Kissing her had been more than just a diversionary tactic. He had thoroughly enjoyed it.

And from her groans of delight, so had she.

He wanted to know all he could about her. A woman possessed of the courage to leap over the side of a ship into a dangerous and unknown future, was a woman he needed to understand.

Control, don't you mean?

The sudden thought pulled him up short. He had tried to stop Yvette from putting herself in danger more times than he could recall. Resourceful and stubborn, she had extracted herself from peril countless times.

All, except the last time.

He closed his eyes and leaned back in the chair. He had promised himself he would only think of Yvette twice a day as he tried to rebuild his life. Once on rising and once when he went to bed. He had held her memory tight within his mind.

Yet today he had thought of another woman. Lustful thoughts which had led him to kiss her without holding anything of himself back.

Forgive me.

They had both known the danger. A pact made early on in their marriage still held. If anything was to befall the other, the survivor was not permitted to spend the rest of their life wallowing in grief. It was only this binding promise which had kept Will from the edge of insanity during the dark days following Yvette's death.

He could imagine the conversation he would have had with his wife regarding his new charge. Yvette would be intrigued by this young woman and already have made several lists of pertinent questions.

Why had she jumped from the ship?

"I don't believe the story about a sudden trip to Africa. Her tale has more holes than the Paris catacombs," he muttered.

If she is telling the truth, then why should she feel compelled to give you a false name?

He opened his eyes and sat upright, a sly, knowing grin threatened at the corner of his mouth.

Getting to the matter of Sarah's real identity was the key to the entire mystery. Solve that piece of the puzzle and the rest of the pieces would soon tumble into place.

A shiny coin slipped into the hand of her maid at an opportune moment was in order. At some point her mistress would make a slip and unwittingly reveal more than she realized. A lady's maid looking to supplement her income would be the perfect agent.

A short time later Hattie, descended the stairs. Will rose from his chair with a sense of satisfaction. His money with the dressmaker and hotel staff had been well spent.

Gone was the drowned rat with straggly hair and ruined clothes, in her place was perfection. An emerald gown with white lace trimming the bodice and skirt clung to her well- proportioned body. The hint of cleavage which the gown afforded was a refreshing change from the stiff, high necked grey creation she had been wearing when he had fished her out of the harbor.

He had been at a loss for words to describe her attire when first he stood beside her at the dock. Dull had been the first one which sprang to mind. Dowdy had been the second.

Her new attire revealed her to be younger and prettier than he had at first thought her.

His gaze took in the soft curls which kissed the sides of her cheeks. Light brown curls showed golden highlights as the sunlight caught them. He was grateful that the local fashion did not include the bonnet. He disliked the new fashion that many English girls had adopted of wearing their bonnets tightly over their heads, so hiding their natural charms.

He dipped into a bow.

"Miss Wilson, I am at your service," he said, as an easy smile came to his lips.

The sheepish grin he got in return would have melted the heart of any man. He corrected his first thought. She was not perfection; no, she was something else. More alluring than perfection could ever offer.

"Mr. Saunders. I cannot begin to express my gratitude for all that you have done for me. How can I ever repay you?" she replied.

His heart sank. The last thing he wanted was for her to feel a sense of obligation toward him.

"Your safe return to England will be all the reward I shall ever need," he replied.

Inwardly he cursed himself for being too self-assured and smooth with her. He feared she would only now see him as someone who felt a sense of duty to help her, nothing more.

It was a school boy mistake; one he knew he should never have made. With the war against Napoleon now over, it was clear his unused skills were becoming rusty.

As Hattie took a seat in a shady spot near the window, Will caught the attention of a hotel servant and headed over to speak to the man.

"Two glasses of Malaga wine and whatever hot dish the chef can rustle up in a short time *por favor*," he said.

Returning to her side, he took the seat opposite.

"Considering your early morning swim, I expect you might be more than a little hungry. I have taken the liberty of ordering us some food and drink."

Hattie looked down and gently spread the skirts of her new gown. He heard her uncertain intake of breath as she did.

"Why are you helping me? You don't know me and yet you have purchased new clothes for me, and put me up in a hotel room. You could have easily, as you say, handed me over to the local authorities and let them handle the matter. You owe me nothing Mr. Saunders."

She lifted her head and met his gaze.

"Why?"

The voice of his mother whispered in his mind.

Because you have always imagined yourself as a knight in shining armor, Will. Seeking out the next damsel to rescue and protect. It is one of your most noble traits, and of those you have many.

No matter how uncomfortable he felt about it, Adelaide Saunders could read her eldest son better than anyone. Wherever she was right now in England, he suspected a secret smile was already on her lips.

He shrugged his shoulders. "Because at some point in their life, everyone desperately needs a friend. Someone to protect them from the harshness of the world. I would suggest that you have reached that particular point," he replied.

The hotel servant brought over two glasses and poured a generous amount of wine in each before making himself scarce.

"To your good health Miss Wilson, and your safe return to your family" said Will. He handed Hattie a glass, then raised his own in toast to her.

She looked down at the glass and for a moment hesitated.

"When we get back to England you must allow me to reimburse you for all your expenses. I insist," she said.

She raised the glass to her lips and took a sip. At the first swallow she began to cough. Hattie hurriedly put the glass down.

Will frowned.

"I take it you are not a regular imbiber of wine?"

"No, my father considers it liquid evil and to be avoided at all costs. We have not partaken of wine in our house for quite some time. My father turned the lock on his wine cellar a number of years ago and threw away the key," she replied.

Will took a sip of his wine, mentally filing away that small revelation. It added nicely to the picture he was beginning to build of her.

Religious parents, who had not always been puritans. That part of her story he was inclined to believe. Her story could be as simple as having run away with her fiancé only to have changed her mind. Will suspected it was not.

He watched as she picked up her glass once more and took a second hesitate sip of the wine. Bravery was not in short supply when it came to this young woman; and she clearly did not hold the same views as her father when it came to alcohol.

"I promise not to tell your parents that you have sat and drank wine in a hotel with me," he reassured her.

A scowl appeared across her brow and she shifted in her seat. It was only the slightest of moves, but it was enough. Will pushed his toes hard against the inner sole of his boots. She had just given him one of the classic tell-tale signs of a lie.

"What do you mean?" she replied.

"I mean when I return you to their protection. I will of course be accompanying you back to London and making certain of your safe return to the loving bosom of your family."

At that moment he caught the sound of wine catching in her throat. She stifled a cough. The noose created by her lies was slowly tightening around her neck.

Careful now, don't get her guard up too soon. Draw her out.

"I couldn't ask you to do such a thing. It is such a long way back to England. I am sure a gentleman such as yourself has better things to do," she replied.

She moved more obviously in her seat. Will pointed one foot in the direction of the door. A look passed between them. She would not get a step ahead of him again, and they both knew it. Whether she liked it or not she was going to have to endure Will's hospitality.

The hotel servant reappeared with a large platter in his hands and placed it on the table between Will and Hattie. She looked down at the food, but did not touch it. Will sensed her unspoken discomfort. She felt threatened.

Will picked up the platter and offered it to her.

"It's Calentita, Gibraltar's favourite dish. It is not unlike a baked pancake. It's very good. Nothing too ostentatious about it, so I am sure your parents would approve," he said.

No matter her own self will, Hattie's stomach quickly turned traitor and grumbled. Will smiled. Food always won out.

She took a square piece of the Calentita and popped it into her mouth. Will followed suit. Rescuing her from the harbor so soon after his early morning swim had meant missing breakfast. The half orange he had eaten down at the dockside was the only food he had managed to eat all day. It was only now, as the smell of baked chickpea and olive oil filled his senses did he realize that he too was ravenous.

"It is good," she said, before helping herself to a second piece.

They sat in silence for a time, eating and partaking of the wine. When Will ordered a second bottle of the wine and Hattie readily agreed, he sensed she was finally beginning to relax.

Whether she realized it or not, Will had commenced the subtle game of winning Hattie's trust and getting to her truth.

Chapter Five

Hattie allowed her maid to assist her for as long as it took to unlace her gown and take the pins out of her hair. Desiring solace, she politely dismissed the young woman once these tasks were done.

As the door to the room closed, Hattie felt the weight of the world descend upon her shoulders. Outside the sun had now set. There were only a few hours left in what felt like the longest day of her life.

Alone for the first time since earlier that morning, she sat on the side of the bed. Her fingers gripped the edge of the mattress.

She had done it.

Screwed every inch of her courage and then some to the sticking place. Where the line between bravery and recklessness stood was a matter for conjecture. What she did know for certain was that her bravery had its limits, and today she had touched the sharp outer edges.

If William Saunders had not come to her rescue, she had no idea where she would be right now.

Several glasses of wine during the afternoon had calmed her nerves, but as night approached the effect of the wine began to slowly wear off. Fear now crept into her mind.

Loud voices in the corridor outside her room, had her scurrying across the floor and locking the door before hurriedly retreating to the sanctuary of her bed. She was in a strange country, far from home and unfamiliar with the local language and customs. Who knew what went on in these foreign places?

Her parents and Peter had made sure she did not venture from the guest house at which they had stayed for the short stopover in Gibraltar.

"The monkeys of the Rock of Gibraltar are known to bite, and a fall from the top of the Rock would surely kill," her mother had cautioned.

At that point, Hattie had been too wrapped up in her own turmoil to make mention to her mother that the place where they were headed had lions and tribes of cannibals.

Now she was alone and her parents were a half day's sail from Gibraltar. The only person she knew within a hundred miles was William Saunders.

It was not as if she did not trust him. Only a cad with a death wish would swim all the way out into the harbor to rescue a stranger on the off chance that he could then betray her. She would bet every penny that she owned, which for the moment was none, that he was indeed the gentleman hero she believed him to be.

The Saunders were a good family of the *ton*. She had to count her blessings for having met Will.

Yet instinct cautioned her to keep as much of herself hidden from him as she could. The less he knew of her, the less likely it was that he could interfere with her slowing evolving plan.

"I must get home."

With Will having secured passage back to London on a ship leaving in two days' time, she would only have to keep up the façade of mistreated fiancée Sarah Wilson for two weeks. She knew enough of the background of the real Sarah Wilson to make a half convincing story. She hoped that Will would not be too deeply concerned with the intricacies of her life to press for anything more.

"Keep the story simple and you won't trip up."

Once they reached London, Sarah Wilson would simply disappear and Hattie Wright could go into hiding. Will would be gifted with the intriguing tale of the young woman he had rescued from the depths of Gibraltar Harbor. It would make for an entertaining dinner party story.

In time he would forget her.

She looked at the lady's travel bag which sat on the end of her bed. Will was a man of means. Not only had he purchased her three new gowns, he had also managed to find a boot maker with a ready-made pair of boots to fit her. Her own salt water stained leather ones were stuffed full of paper and drying in the window. Gibraltar was not cold enough to warrant a lit fire in the middle of October.

A knock at the door stirred her from her thoughts. She looked at her own recently washed and dried thin muslin shift. Will's sensible shopping had not extended to a nightgown nor a dressing gown. She crossed the floor and put an ear to the door.

"Hello?" she called out.

The door handle rattled.

"Let me in," Will commanded.

"No, I am not decent. I don't have any suitable night clothes," she replied.

Curses drifted in from the other side of the door. She glanced around the room for something to cover her state of undress. Seeing the bedclothes, she hit upon an idea.

"Just a minute," she said.

She quickly pulled the blanket from off the bed and wrapped it around herself before reluctantly unlocking the door and opening it fully.

Will stepped into the room. His nimble fingers closed and locked the door before she had time to blink.

"I wanted to make sure you are alright. That you have everything you need," he said, refusing to look directly at her.

She stifled a grin. For the first time since she had met him, Will seemed ill at ease. He shuffled his feet and kept his gaze downward toward the floor.

It was nice to see that he had a vulnerable side. She had had more than her fill of men in recent days who were cocksure about themselves. The chink in his armor made him even more of a hero in her eyes.

"I am fine, thank you Mr. Saunders. More than I expected to be after the events of today," she replied.

Will cleared his throat.

"I must also apologize for the encounter between us in the market square. I had concerns about the crowd, but that does not excuse me for taking such liberties with your person. I should have apologized as soon as we got to the hotel. Please forgive me. I promise it will not happen again."

The sting of disappointment pierced her heart. Then reminding herself of where she was and the impossibility of them being anything more than temporary acquaintances, she forced the emotion away.

Of course, he had regretted kissing her, he was a gentleman. From the little she knew of men, they never kissed gently bred women that way. And from the moment they had first spoken with one another, he had rightly guessed she was from a good family.

"I understand the need for what you did Mr. Saunders. Apology accepted," she replied.

They shared an awkward silence for a moment. Will stared once more at the floor, while Hattie picked at her fingernails. The sea water had left the skin of her fingers rough and split.

"Is there anything else?" she asked.

Will's head shot up.

"Yes. Make sure you lock the door after I leave. This is one of only two places in Gibraltar where you can purchase liquor after dark. The downstairs of the hotel tends to get a little rowdy and full of inebriated English sailors later in the evening. I would not want one of them to accidentally stumble into your room. If you have any problems during the night, I shall be right next door. Do not hesitate to call upon me if you so need."

"Thank you, I shall make certain the door is locked when you leave," Hattie replied.

As soon as Will left, she locked the door. Then after hearing the bellowing of men from down in the street below her window, she dragged the dressing table across the floor and blocked the door.

"Better safe than sorry," she murmured, climbing into bed.

Within minutes Hattie was sound asleep. The long swim in the harbor coupled with the rest of the day's events had finally caught up with her. If a riot had broken out downstairs, she would surely have slept through it.

Back in his room Will paced the floor, his mind in a whirl. Had he been suddenly possessed of a kind of madness? Not only had he gone to the room of an unmarried woman, but earlier in the morning, he had kissed that same girl in public. The kiss they had shared was far more passionate than had been dictated by the situation. Worse still, he had enjoyed every second of it.

He stopped and checked himself. Since Yvette he had not laid hands on a woman. The temptation to take solace in the company of one of Paris' ladies of the night had taken him to the edge more than once. Instead, he had held fast to his grief and guilt, allowing long lonely nights to concentrate his mind.

Yet the first time he had held the girl he knew as Sarah in his arms, he felt the unmistakable stirrings of desire flare. He had wanted her in every way.

Perhaps today was the day when he would wake from the nightmare of Yvette's death and begin to move forward with his life. It had taken all his resolve to finally leave Paris behind for good.

He rubbed his hands over his tired, sun browned face.

"You did a good deed today William of the House of Strathmore, leave it at that."

He slowly stripped off his jacket and cravat. The use of a valet was something he had been forced to forgo during his years in France. Having a man servant would have been difficult to explain when he was supposed to be living undercover as a simple shipping clerk.

Making a mental note to call for a bowl of hot water for his razor first thing in the morning, he sauntered over to the window.

Out of the window he could see the dark shadow of the giant Rock of Gibraltar. It dominated the landscape. You could not look anywhere without it being in view. The town of Gibraltar itself hugged the narrow strip of coastline to the west of the limestone monolith. It was so unlike anything in his native England.

He had spent enough years away from home to be comfortable with being in places foreign and unusual. The changing of coins and often illegal crossing of borders was just another of life's challenges he had learned to meet.

His mastery of the Spanish language was more than fair. He spoke French, the mother tongue of his father, like a native-born son.

He was well experienced in the life of an expatriate, a life he had chosen to lead. The girl in the room next door on the other hand had suddenly and unexpectedly found herself a long way from home, with only him to protect her. Seeing her safely back to England was now his solemn duty.

He put a hand up against the cold glass of the window. The night outside providing a dark backdrop. Staring at his reflection he made a vow.

She was one woman he was not going to fail.

He stepped away from the window as fatigue began to get the better of him. He normally slept fully naked, but tonight he thought it prudent to leave his trousers and shirt on. When the difference between life and death could be measured in seconds, time wasted in getting dressed could be crucial.

The hotel manservant who had serviced his room all week, and received generous daily tips in return, had left a bottle of port on the narrow white table to the left of the door. Will abstained from his usual night cap. Tonight he needed to sleep lightly.

From his travel trunk he withdrew a small pistol and loaded it. He then took out a dagger. Deadly sharp and with a handle that had been crafted to fit his grip to perfection it was a weapon that brooked no discussion. The blade gleamed steely silver in the candlelight. More than once it had run red with the blood of another man. He prayed neither weapon would be necessary tonight.

Lying back on the bed; pistol and dagger within easy reach, he closed his eyes. The sound of the sea drifted in through the window bringing a calm balm to his mind.

Within minutes he was asleep, dreaming of wet boots and long flaxen hair.

Chapter Six

For someone who was many miles from home and with an uncertain future, Hattie slept well. The only time she woke during the long night was when the revelers from the hotel's bar spilled out into the streets in the hour before dawn and started singing a loud sea shanty. At the sound of the less than Sunday hymn like tune, she rolled over in her bed and stuffed the pillow over her head.

Her father, wherever on the high seas he was would be horrified to know that his daughter was sleeping above a tavern. She chortled softly before going back to sleep.

The morning however, found her in a more somber mood. Somewhere in the jumble of her dreams Hattie had seen the grief-stricken faces of her parents. She woke, sure in the knowledge that her parents believed her dead.

"How stupid could I have been? How selfish," she cried.

While she had been sitting drinking wine with Will and enjoying the delights of the local cuisine, her parents were likely beside themselves with grief.

No one had seen her jump from the ship. For all they knew she had fallen overboard somewhere far from land, never to be seen again.

Seated on the edge of her bed, she hugged herself as sobbing shudders of guilt wracked her body.

No matter what she thought of her parents' decision to take her to Africa, they did not deserve this cruel punishment. Worst of all, there was nothing she could do to alleviate their pain. A letter sent on the fastest ship would still take many weeks to catch up to them. She had made a rash decision and left others, including Will, to pay for it.

The damage was done.

When her maid knocked on the door a short while later, Hattie reluctantly allowed her in. The last thing she wanted to consider was which one of her pretty new gowns she was going to wear that day. The most she felt she deserved was to wear her old salt stained gown and get about bare foot.

Dressed in the plainest of her new gowns, she sat in front of the dressing table while her maid set her hair in a simple style. The maid had the good sense not to mention the tear stains on Hattie's face and her bloodshot eyes.

There was a knock at the door, and Will's voice drifted in from the hall. The maid quickly opened the door and Will stepped into the room.

He took one look at Hattie's face before turning to her maid and pointing toward the hall.

"*Te importaria?*" he said.

The maid scurried from the room and closed the door behind her.

Will came to Hattie's side and looked at her reflection in the mirror. There was no hiding the fact that she had been crying. He put a gentle hand on her shoulder.

"Don't tell me you sat up all night thinking of your heartbroken fiancé and decided that he wasn't such a bad chap after all. That perhaps you had misunderstood his intentions and you should have stayed on the boat. If that is the case, I would suggest it is a little late for tearful regrets," he said.

Hattie's tears began to fall once more. Not only had she caused her parents' untold misery through her actions, but because of the lies she had already told Will, she could not share her troubles with him. She was now trapped in a thickening web of lies.

"I didn't leave a note to tell my parents I was leaving with Peter. We eloped. My parents must be sick with worry as to my whereabouts," she explained.

It was as close to the truth as she dared to tell him. And in a way, it was the truth. Her parents did not know where she was and, they would be left with the obvious conclusion that the very worst had befallen their daughter.

"We shall be back in England within the fortnight. I am certain that your safe return will overcome any anger or possible recriminations. Besides, any letter you wrote and sent from here, would probably leave on the same boat as us so you are just going to have to bear up and be patient. I promise to speak to your father and explain things on your behalf," Will replied.

Distressed though she was, Hattie noted the undercurrent within his words. Will was probing yet again. Seeking the truth in her story. Seeing if he could prise a little more of it from her lips. Though he did not know it, Will had given her the first hope for making amends with her parents. The first chance of redeeming herself in their eyes.

As soon as she was back in London, she would pen a letter to her parents in Freetown. She would explain it all. Her reluctance to marry Peter Brown. The certain knowledge that she was not cut out to be the wife of a missionary. And finally, the truth which had been the eventual catalyst for the drastic choice she had made.

That she was not prepared to abandon her friends in the filthy, rookery of St. Giles. Vulnerable friends who even now could be in deadly peril. It was because of them that she had finally found the courage to jump ship. She had found her calling with the weak and vulnerable of London, she owed it to them to go home. To continue her work.

She wiped away the tears, acknowledging that there was nothing she could do to ease her parents suffering until she got home. With time, perhaps they would understand and forgive her. Will was right, until then she would just have to make the best of things.

She reached out and touched the sleeve of his jacket.

"Thank you" she said.

"Good."

They silently stared at one another in the reflection of the mirror for a minute longer, before the soft voice of Hattie's maid came from outside in the hallway. Will looked toward the door.

"May I attend to the *senorita, Senor*? Your *prometida* may wish to finish dressing," she said.

"*Prometida*?" Hattie whispered.

Will turned and gave her warm smile.

"It's Spanish for fiancée, which considering your current predicament is probably the best thing you can pretend to be until we arrive back in England," he replied.

❦

Will waited patiently downstairs in the main dining room of the hotel. The rooms of the Seawinds Hotel were too small to be able to partake of breakfast privately.

Prometida.

The word had slipped quickly off his tongue when Hattie's maid entered the room.

"Yes of course, my *prometida* would like to finish dressing. She had a terrible nightmare, but is recovered enough now. Aren't you my sweet?" he said.

When he placed a chaste kiss on Hattie's cheek the maid giggled and blushed. The stunned look on Hattie's face had made his bold move worth it.

She had shared something of her real self this morning. He had no doubt that whoever and wherever her parents were, they were in great distress over their missing daughter. There was a deal of truth in her lie.

Her maid had in her mistake, handed him the perfect solution to their masquerade. By claiming her as his fiancée Will could pull her into his version of the story. If a false story was to be created around them, he would be the one framing the picture.

"Mr. Saunders?"

He looked up and saw a vision of loveliness which filled his heart with joy. While Hattie's day gown was a simple pale cream, the jacket she wore over it was a magnificent deep crimson. She wore a matching crimson ribbon in her hair.

His heart lifted when he saw a smile come to her lips. The tears were gone and he saw hope shine in her face.

Rising quickly from the table, Will took hold of Hattie's hand and placed a kiss on it. As she tried to pull away, he gently rebuked her.

"It would not do to show any form of displeasure with me in public. Don't think for a moment that the whole staff of the hotel are not currently discussing us and the little scene in your room earlier. I expect your maid could not get down those stairs fast enough to run and tell anyone who wished to listen that the English lady and gentleman must have had a disagreement, and that you had been crying."

The small 'o' which appeared on Hattie's lips and the relaxation of her hand was encouraging. He leaned in close and murmured in her ear.

"And do not call me Mr. Saunders, we are supposed to be engaged. I am William. Will to all my friends and family. If you continue to address me in such a formal fashion, you will give the game away."

Hattie nodded her head.

"Will," she replied.

Over a breakfast of coffee and sweet buns, he did his best to form a more familiar bond with her. He chuckled at her puzzled face when she saw the paucity of their breakfast.

"They adhere to the Spanish way of things here for a lot of their customs. A small breakfast, followed by something a little more substantial later in the morning. The main meal of the day is partaken after midday," he explained.

"That's odd," she replied.

"Not really. People rise early here, get some work done and then after the midday meal they go and have a long sleep to avoid the afternoon heat. Notice how tired you were yesterday by the time you went to bed? The heat of the Spanish sun saps all the energy out of you," he said.

As he sat and watched her, Will was once again reminded of his late wife. Hattie and Yvette shared some very similar mannerisms. The first time Hattie screwed up her face at the bitter coffee, Will came close to tears. Yvette had always liked to take the first sip of her morning coffee before declaring it undrinkable and heaping sugar into the cup.

He slid the small pot of sugar across the table, and with a flourish removed the lid.

"A large spoonful always takes the bitterness away," he said. He hastily coughed, clearing the lump which had formed in his throat.

Hattie took several more bites of her sweet breakfast roll before sitting back in her chair. The coffee she left untouched.

"So, what now? Do I just keep to my room until the boat back to England sails?" she asked.

No matter what the truth was behind her lies, he found himself becoming fonder of her every minute. He liked that she was able to see the bigger picture of their situation. The leap from the side of the ship, was he suspected, a complete aberration of her normal behavior. That she was not by nature a risk taker. In that she and Yvette differed greatly.

"I was thinking about that while I was waiting for you. Are you someone who enjoys the outdoors or the countryside?" he replied.

She sat silent for a moment, before finally replying.

"I do like to get out and walk in the fresh air," she said.

Anyone else would have added further details of their life. Of the parks they regularly visited or their favourite place to ramble, but not her. If she had been one of his young, still in training operatives, he would have applauded her effort. She had given him an answer, but only just enough.

Her body language however still gave her away as an amateur. A good spy should be able to utter the words and appear relaxed. Hattie had unconsciously stiffened her back.

"Good. Then I think we should agree to use the time we have remaining in Gibraltar to its best advantage. The boat leaves on the tide tomorrow night, so we have time today to venture across to the base of the Rock and to visit the cave of St Michael. I visited the cave earlier in the week and I must say it was well worth the effort. It would be remiss of me as your host not to show you the caves.

But first, I think we should make the trip up to see Europa Point. We can go later this morning. In the meantime, we can visit the local town shops and purchase any other items you might need for the sea voyage home," he replied.

Chapter Seven

The last thing on Hattie's mind as she swam ashore the previous morning was to spend her time in Gibraltar as a tourist. Her parents and Peter had determined it best she remained at the guesthouse during their stay. Sightseeing was a frivolous waste of a young woman's time.

To her surprise and utter delight, Will had other ideas. He took on the role of amusing and engaging host with thinly veiled relish.

After purchasing supplies for the boat trip, including several books, Will hired a local guide to show them the sights. It was late afternoon when they finally reached Europa Point, the southernmost tip of the European continent.

"Our guide says be careful where you step, the donkeys don't mind where they leave their fresh droppings" said Will.

Before she could say otherwise, Will had placed his hands either side of her waist and was lifting her down from the small cart which had brought them along Europa road.

On the trip up from the town, Will had given Hattie a quick lesson in the history of Gibraltar and the Rock.

"Pretty much everyone in this part of the world has ruled Gibraltar at some point. The Moors took control in the eighth century, finally being thrown out in the thirteenth. Between then and when the British took control last century, the Spanish fought amongst themselves to rule. The Spanish of course would like to have it back, but I can't see that happening any time soon."

"What about the locals, what do they want?" Hattie replied.

Will paused for a moment, then answered. "To be honest, I think they are happy to keep things just as they are. That way they get the best of both worlds. The British spend money here with the naval military presence and shipping, while Spain is only a short distance away for food and supplies."

Keeping up the pretense of being an engaged couple, Hattie slipped her hand into Will's arm and let him escort her across the short stony patch of ground from the cart to the edge of Europa Point.

The guide whom Will had hired in the town, stood with his hands on his hips and surveyed the view out to sea. His donkey being less interested in the view wandered over to a nearby clump of wild jasmine and began prodding the leaves with its nose.

"*Lo que es una magnifica vista,*" the guide exclaimed.

Hattie and Will came and stood beside him. She nodded her agreement. It required no translation to understand what the ruddy faced man had said. The view spoke for itself.

Miles and miles of ocean stretched out before them on three sides. Far below them, the blue of the sea was broken only by the reflection of the hot sun as it shone a bright ribbon across the glass like surface of the water. Will pointed off into the distance, to where Hattie could see a line of mountains on the opposite side of the water.

"Those are the Rif mountains of Morocco. The tall mountain is Jebel Musa, otherwise known as one of the Pillar of Hercules. This is an ancient land. We are standing on the southernmost tip of Europe and over there is Africa," he said.

Africa. The massive continent that had once held her future now lay in view across the thin stretch of water that was the Strait of Gibraltar. It was so close, that she felt she could reach out her hand and touch the mountains.

She looked down at her new boots. They were coated in the fine limestone dust of the Rock. Dust from the European continent.

SASHA COTTMAN

When she looked back again across the water, she smiled. There was no pull in her heart to make the journey. The dark land did not beckon unto her to come into its embrace. And with that she let go of much of her fear.

She knew where she belonged. Home in England.

Will caught her smile and raised an eyebrow.

"At least you can say you have seen Africa, albeit from a distance. What do think?" he said.

"I think I would like to go home," she replied.

They stood for a little while longer silently taking in the view. The only noise to be heard was the cry of seagulls on the wind and the occasional grunt from the donkey.

Finally, the guide spoke and Hattie turned. As she did her jaw dropped. Towering above them was the Rock of Gibraltar in all its magnificence.

From the town and the harbor, the pinnacle of the Rock had been hidden from view, but here at Europa Point, she had a clear view of the immense height of the limestone monolith.

"It's amazing. I've never seen anything like it before," she said.

Will gave her an encouraging grin. He was not an easy man to discern. At times he was friendly and relaxed, like he had been since they left the town earlier. But at other moments, she sensed he was not by nature a happy man.

Watching as he bent down and picked at a small clump of seaside daisies, she considered him again. There was an inherent sadness about him, but she suspected it had not always been so. Perhaps he had suffered a terrible loss in his life, one which had left deep scars. She could not explain why she felt this about him, finally forcing herself to accept that it was only a hunch.

"Yes, the Rock is a true wonder of nature. Nearly one thousand, four hundred feet high," said Will.

He handed her a small bunch of daisies which had pure white petals and golden centers. Hattie accepted them with a shy smile. She held the flowers close to her heart. It was lovely to receive such a spontaneous gift.

"We saw it from the deck of the ship as we came into the harbor,

48

but it was early and with the low morning rain clouds we couldn't get a clear view. My father."

Hattie stopped herself just in time.

She was about to tell Will how disappointed her father had been at his first sight of the Rock, when she realized what she was doing. The carefully constructed lie she had managed to maintain for the past day had nearly unraveled like a loose thread caught.

"Your father?" he replied.

The sunny disposition he had displayed moments earlier disappeared. His eyes became hooded, his face a study in wariness. She was reminded of the lion she had once seen at the Royal Menagerie in the Exeter Exchange. A dangerous wild beast ready to strike out at any moment and tear her to pieces.

Hattie looked down at the bunch of flowers in her hands, while frantically searching for something to say. Anything.

"Yes, my father. He has always wished to see Gibraltar," she finally replied. The stems of the flowers bent in her tightly held hands.

One thing she had learned since meeting Will was to keep her lies small. Any embellishment appeared to present him with the irresistible challenge to try and poke holes in her story.

He did not believe her, of that much she was certain. She was at a loss to understand how he came to choose which aspects of her fabrication he would try to challenge. There was a strategy in play, but she could not see it clearly in her mind.

He had not pressed her regarding the major parts of her lie, yet he seemed intent to work at its inconsequential edges. Edges which she knew were fraying by the minute.

"Perhaps you shall travel here with him some time. Retrace the steps of your grand adventure. But first we must get you safely back to England," he said.

The lion retreated.

As she looked at him, Hattie was possessed with an almost overwhelming desire to confess everything to Will. In many ways it would be so much easier if he knew. This continual game of trying to read one another's thoughts and emotions was exhausting.

She hated lying. It went against everything she believed in. But telling Will the truth of her situation would mean handing him total control. With nothing left to negotiate with, she would be at his mercy. Once again powerless to determine her own life.

"You said you had climbed to the top of the Rock," she replied.

If he was able to read her as well as she suspected he could, Will would know she wanted to change the subject. He had succeeded in cracking open a little more of the door to her secrets, now he would be content to let her become comfortable once more. Then he would press her again for answers.

How long she could continue to play this game, she was not sure, but with luck by the time Will had finally put the pieces of the puzzle together she would have slipped from his grasp.

"Yes, I ventured up to St Michael's cave earlier in the week. It is a steep walk up from the town, but we can visit it on our way back down from here. I doubt we shall have time tomorrow. I have some business matters to attend to in the morning before we sail," he replied.

Her mother had warned her about the monkeys that lived on the Rock. The wild Barbary monkeys were said to be dangerous and prone to attack without provocation.

"I am not certain if I should go. What about the monkeys?" she said.

He reached out and took hold of her hand. The look he had given her when he asked about why she had jumped from the ship reappeared on his face. It was a look so full of honesty, Hattie felt a tear spring to her eye.

"Yes, you should, and do you know why? Because years from now, when you are old and reflective of your life, you will look back upon your brief stay in Gibraltar and remember the choices you made. That you were brave. You will not be disappointed with the cave. I promise I won't let the monkeys hurt you. Trust me."

She pulled her hand away. Fear held her back. Many times, Peter Brown had shown her a small kindness only to then reveal it as nothing more than a means to bend her to his will. She would keep her own counsel.

And yet.

His deep grey eyes held the promise of warmth, of the strong bond of friendship and more. She was torn in a thousand directions as to what to do.

༜

The guide brought the donkey and cart over to where they stood. Will could tell Hattie was unsure as to what to do.

"A short stay at the cave. If at any time you feel uncomfortable, you only have to say the word and we shall leave immediately. Agreed?" he offered.

"Agreed."

He silently congratulated himself on having won her over, but knew he had to tread carefully. She was as skittish as a young colt this afternoon.

On the road back down from Europa Point, he did his best to make small talk.

"Did I tell you that the ship I have secured passage for us on board for our journey home is a sister ship to the *Blade of Orion*? It's called the *Canis Major,* and while I am led to believe it is a little smaller than the ship you arrived in, it should still suit us fine."

Having made up her mind to accompany him to the cave Hattie appeared content to sit quietly and take in the view out over Gibraltar Harbor. After rambling on about the Spanish and how goods travelled back and forth between Spain and Gibraltar, and getting little in return from her, Will decided it was better to say nothing.

At the cave of St Michael, the guide showed them the path. Will took hold of Hattie's hand and led her up to the entrance of the cave. At the entrance a man sold them two tickets and a grass torch. Will lit it as he and Hattie walked slowly into the cave.

Her hand gripped his. He turned toward her, offering her a reassuring smile. The light from the torch was reflected in her eyes. She was afraid, but she was with him. He would keep her safe.

Several monkeys sat just inside the cave's entrance. Will shooed

51

them away. When it was clear than neither he nor Hattie had any food, the monkeys ambled away.

"Is everything alright?" he ventured.

Hattie looked away from the retreating monkeys and back to Will.

"Yes. I was just thinking of the monkeys. They are rather tame, aren't they? I did see some at the Tower of London once, but they were quite aggressive," she replied.

"Yes well, these ones can be nasty when the mood suits them. I would caution against attempting to pat any of them. Come let's venture into the cave, then we shall go and find some supper. I am famished."

He led her deeper into the cave. The torch soon became the only source of light. Hattie squeezed Will's hand more tightly.

He lifted the torch and Hattie gasped as she beheld the whole subterranean world that spread out before her. She had never imagined that such a place could exist.

"Oh," she murmured.

"That was my very same reaction when I saw the caves earlier this week," he replied.

The roof of the main cave towered many feet over their heads. Huge spear like stalactites hung down from the ceiling, while stalagmites rose in tower like formations from the floor of the cave.

"It's wonderous. How far back does this cave go?" she said.

"Well there are ancient myths that it is a gateway to the underworld, but I expect it goes back quite some way. No one has really made a concerted effort to explore deeper into the lower chambers for fear of never being seen again," he replied.

Hattie released her hold of Will's hand. Her fear of the monkeys and the cave were gone, she felt emboldened enough to explore a little on her own. The cave was empty of other tourists. Will was right, it was like something from Greek mythology. She half expected an ancient god or a monster to appear at the back of the cave

Reaching the nearest stalagmite, she put her hand against it.

"It's wet!" she exclaimed, pulling her hand away.

Will laughed.

"The water from the roof has to go somewhere."

He pointed toward the roof of the cave.

"The rainwater seeps into the limestone on the top surface of the rock outside and over many years makes its way down into the cave. That water you just touched could be thirty years old."

Hattie looked at her hand, and shook the water from her fingertips. Will clapped his hands in delight.

"You look just like my youngest sister Caroline does when the cat has licked her hand. It is the funniest sight you will ever see," he chuckled.

Hattie snorted. Her family cat Brutus was more likely to take a piece out of your hand than give you a friendly lick.

"So, do you have many siblings?" she ventured.

She knew she was treading on dangerous ground asking about family, but she knew enough of her former maid's family history to be able to rattle off a few names without too much hesitation if Will decided to turn the tables and ask about her own family.

A wistful look appeared on his face.

"I have two sisters and one brother. Evelyn, who we call Eve, is in her early twenties. Caroline who is three years younger. And Francis who fits somewhere in the middle, though at six feet four he struggles to fit in anywhere. I am especially looking forward to getting reacquainted with them."

The joy in his voice when he spoke about his family brightened Hattie's mood. It had been a long time since her whole family had been together and exchanged kind words with one another. It was nice to hear of other people who still had loving family relationships.

Another group of tourists entered the cave and began to look around. The private moment between them was at an end.

The sun was sinking slowing in the west and the air rapidly cooling when they began to make the slow descent back down the mountain and into town. They had spent several hours in the cave walking around seeing the various limestone formations. Will had shown her one which had been cut across the top and had growth rings like a tree.

He was an excellent guide, warm and engaging. By the end of

their time in the cave, Hattie felt a small tendre beginning to bud for Will.

The excitement which continued to course through her veins, had her quietly asking if they could walk back into town rather than take the cart. Will paid their guide and sent him and his donkey on their way as they left St Michael's cave

Hattie was exhausted when they finally reached the town square, but her soul felt alive. The day spent with Will was a world away from the strict and dull existence to which she had become so accustomed over the past few years.

"Let's find somewhere private for us to enjoy some more of the local cuisine. I don't know about you, but I am starving," he said.

When he turned and looked at her, Hattie's gaze immediately settled on Will's lips. Only a matter of a day ago he had held her in his arms and given her that swoon worthy kiss.

A blush burned on her cheeks and she lifted a tentative finger to feel it's heat. Turning away, she hoped he had not seen her moment of temptation.

They found a tiny cantina a few streets away from their hotel. Stepping into the cool stone building, Hattie felt the exhaustion of having been out in the late afternoon heat descend onto her shoulders. She would sleep well tonight.

The walls of the cantina were painted white. A collection of mismatched chairs and tables filled the room.

"There is no one else here,' she said.

"Most of the local population here will be resting in their homes until after sunset, we are just a little early. In an hour this place will be crowded to all four walls," Will explained.

He ushered her over to a table in the corner. She thought it odd when he took the seat with its back to the wall, leaving her to take the one opposite. She knew enough of society's rules to know it was not the proper thing to do when out in mixed company.

While she pondered his behavior, Hattie watched as Will took a slow account of the room. His lips moved ever so slightly as he did so. Turning, she looked in the direction of his gaze.

She glanced briefly back at him before turning away once more.

Had Will been counting the steps from the table to the door? She did a rough count herself and turned back to him, convinced of her theory. What sort of a man needed to know the exact number of steps from his seat to the front door; like herself, Will too had his secrets.

"No one stays in their homes in the evening here. They dress up and promenade. A bit like the five o'clock crush at Hyde Park in London during the social season. Have you ever been?" he asked.

"No," she lied.

Only the upper crust of London society made the journey to Hyde Park in the afternoon. If she had said yes, it would have given him the perfect opening to ask whom she knew among the *ton*. She was not setting foot on that slippery slope.

The owner of the cantina brought them over a bottle of wine and some fresh olives before disappearing into the kitchen to cook the fish Will had chosen from the simple menu painted on the whitewashed walls.

Hattie took a sip of her wine. She had forgotten how much she used to enjoy the simple pleasure of a glass of wine at supper. Her brother Edgar had an expert nose for a good bottle of red wine.

She missed the nights when seated around the table with her parents and brother she had enjoyed the light heartedness and simple pleasure of their company.

"So?" said Will.

She looked at him and she saw a now familiar look appear on his face. His Spanish Inquisition look, she dubbed it. The relaxed Will of the afternoon was now replaced with the Will who was full of uncomfortable questions.

"Pardon?" she replied.

Whatever line of questioning Will was about to embark upon, she knew he was intent on tripping her up.

Disappointment that their easy friendship of the afternoon had been set aside stung her. She didn't like people who played games, and it hurt to think that Will's friendly demeanor in the cave had somehow been an act. An act to make her relax and trust him enough so that the next time he questioned her, she would slip up and reveal more of her truth.

"You were saying that your father considers wine to be the work of the devil. Yet you do not seem to share that same opinion. That must be an interesting tale to tell."

Hattie stared down at her wine glass. What was she to say? That her father and mother had had a sudden conversion to a puritan sect of the church and had renounced all matters that they considered evil. Of the schism it had caused in the family, resulting in her brother and his wife severing all ties?

No. She would not betray what her parents believed in. Whether she fully agreed with their choices over the past few years, she still owed them some loyalty. The work they had done in saving lives and changing futures was beyond reproach.

"I don't think it is my place to tell my father's story," she replied.

She lifted her head and straightened her back. Hattie had a capacity for stubbornness which her mother had oftentimes mentioned as being a serious fault in her character. Even Peter had noted that once they were married, she would have to put her willfulness aside and obey him.

Will slowly blinked as he sat back in his chair. His face showed no emotion. Under the table Hattie nervously cracked her knuckles. She hated the silent, guarded type of male. To her they were always harboring ill thoughts and wishes.

"Of course," he replied.

When the tavern owner came over with a large platter containing a lump of goat cheese, fresh tomatoes and the cooked fish, Hattie sighed with relief.

The arrival of the food had the effect she hoped it would. Will immediately ceased his interrogation of her and picked up a tomato. He cut it in half and handed a piece to Hattie.

"Coffee that's what we need," he said, waving the tavern owner back over to their table.

"Have you lived in this part of the world for long?" she asked as soon as the tavern owner had disappeared back into the kitchen.

She could swear she heard Will mutter touché under his breath. The tables were being turned on the inquisitor.

"Not long. I tend to travel about a bit," he replied.

Hattie concentrated on the task of displaying a disinterested air, much the same as the one Will appeared to have mastered.

"Oh. So, what do you actually do Will?" she replied.

He slowed his chewing, but other than that, showed no outward sign of discomfort.

Hattie gritted her teeth. She knew enough of the Saunders family to know Will was most certainly not a man who dealt in any sort of trade. It took serious blunt to be able to be a member of the *ton*. And his uncle was the Duke of Strathmore.

Two can play at that game.

"I am in the very dull trade of import and export. I travel regularly to Spain to source goods," he replied.

Hattie cracked the knuckles of her other hand. This was becoming a game of lies she knew she could not win. She looked at Will. He sat smiling at her, the challenge to continue to play written all over his mirth filled face.

She yawned.

"I am exhausted, it has been a long day out in the sun."

Will nodded, and yawned as well.

"I suggest we eat and then get you back to the hotel. We have a long day ahead of us tomorrow."

❧

After returning to their hotel and seeing Hattie safely back to her room Will decided he needed to go for a walk. A long walk.

He took the path which led from the town further along the beach and down to Rosia Bay, one of the few places on the western side of the Gibraltar peninsula that had an accessible beach.

There he kicked off his boots, rolled up his trousers and walked in the cold sea water. The sun had long set below the horizon. A golden glow lit the coastline. Somewhere nearby a local band was playing. A chorus of singers accompanied the music. The night felt magic.

The day spent with Hattie had been one of constant revelations, both about her and surprisingly himself.

She had suffered at the hands of some rogue; her fear was real. What he could not grasp was why she was not prepared to trust him.

"Am I that much of wolf?" he muttered.

He stuffed his hands into his jacket pocket, unable to shake the nagging thought in the back of his mind. There was something else about her, something unexpected.

Staring out to sea, watching as the local fishing boats headed out with the late evening tide, he sensed the truth of the effect she had on him.

He had known her all of one day; he did not even know her real name. Yet desire stirred in his blood. Every time this afternoon he had looked at her, he had been gripped with an impulse to take her into his arms once more and kiss her senseless. To run his hands over her hips and pull her hard against him.

He let a whoosh of air out of his lungs, feeling himself go hard at the mere thought of her. How was he going to survive two weeks on the ship back to England with her? He could not stay locked in his cabin the whole time.

If he was not to go mad in that time, he had to uncover all that he could of the mystery woman he had pulled from the sea. Make her reveal all her deepest secrets to him.

First thing he had to do was to discover her real name.

Then he would make her his own.

Chapter Eight

Leaving the hotel early the next morning, Will headed for the Port of Gibraltar shipping office which was situated down at the waterside.

Before they sailed this day; he was determined to get to the bottom of who Sarah really was; he was no longer convinced that it was purely the former spy in him that was driving him to get to her truth.

He knew enough about shipping movements to know that the shipping register in the port office would give him the vital information he sought.

The *Blade of Orion* had stayed in port for several days from his recollection. The passengers would have had to register with the local Gibraltar authorities as they came ashore. Names and places of origin would be in the registers.

He wandered leisurely up to the small grey wooden building that was the shipping office and opened the door. The Quartermaster in charge was a bald, rotund gentleman who looked to Will as if he could do with a decent night's sleep. He fitted his naval uniform more by chance than design. Another ale or large pie and the gold buttons on his regulation blue jacket would be fit to burst. Standards since the end of the war with France had most surely slipped.

The Quartermaster shuffled over from behind his desk to where Will stood at the long wooden counter. As the Quartermaster reached the counter, Will got an unpleasant sample of the odor of stale sweat and bad breath. He took a half step back.

"Only ship's captains and people on official naval business are allowed in here, sir," he said.

Will noted that the 'sir' was added in as a mere afterthought.

With no emotion on his face, Will slid a folded piece of paper across the counter toward the Quartermaster.

Then he waited.

It took only a moment for the Quartermaster's demeanor to change. He stopped reading and looked up at Will. A bead of nervous sweat slid down the man's cheek.

He straightened his back and adjusted the front of his jacket. It didn't do anything to make him look any better, but it gave Will all the understanding he needed.

"How may I help you sir?"

Will took the precious letter, personally signed by King George, and put it securely back in his jacket pocket.

"A few minutes alone with the shipping register for the past week, if you would be so kind," he replied.

He was promptly ushered into a nearby office. The Quartermaster tidied some papers on the desk and made space for Will to sit. He then scurried off, returning as quickly as his portly legs could carry him. In his hands he bore a large green book which he placed on the desk in front of Will.

"Take as long as you like sir. Would you care for a glass of port sir?"

Will waved him away. Only navy personnel drank at this hour of the day.

Will opened the book and began to turn the pages. At the top of the page dated some six days earlier, he found the listing for the *Blade of Orion*. He began to search the passenger list. It did not take him long to find the travelling party which best matched the description of his suspicions.

Mr. and Mrs. Aldred Wright of London

Miss Harriet (Hattie) Wright of London
Reverend Peter Brown of London
Miss Sarah Wilson of York

He sat back in the chair and stared at the list of names.

There had been a Sarah Wilson on board the ship, that much was true. But his Sarah Wilson spoke with the accent of someone born and bred in London, not with the distinctive accent that a Yorkshire girl would be hard pressed to hide. He would bet his last penny that the real Sarah Wilson was still on board the *Blade of Orion* and on her way to Africa.

That left only one other possible name.

"Miss Hattie Wright. Pleased to meet you," he muttered.

He took a notebook and pencil from his jacket pocket and wrote down the names of the travelling party. He was strumming his fingers contentedly on the desk when the Quartermaster returned some ten minutes later.

"Did you find what you were looking for sir?" he asked.

Will stood up from the desk and closed the book. With a flourish he presented it to the Quartermaster.

"Yes; thank you, I found exactly what I was looking for."

Chapter Nine

Heading back to the hotel, Will spied down at the dockside, the *Canis Major*, the ship he had booked passage on board for Hattie and himself for the return journey to England.

He thought of the piece of paper in his pocket. It was odd to think of Sarah now being Hattie. Yet somehow the name better suited her. The time would shortly come when he would confront her about what he had discovered at the shipping office. That conversation though would have to wait until they were well out to sea. Will was taking no chances.

As he drew closer to the ship, his heart sank.

It may have been a sister ship to the *Blade of Orion* but that was where any similarity between the two vessels ended. While the *Blade of Orion* had been a sturdy, well-kept ship; the *Canis Major* was well past its best days.

The top of the portside of the ship, below the chains, had originally been painted a deep blue color, with gold detailing. In places patches of the paintwork were still evident, but for the most part it was either badly peeling or completely gone.

The figurehead on the bow of the ship looked like it had once been a gold painted dog holding a shield with stars picked out in red. Now half the dog's head was missing, as was one of its legs.

Will began to reconsider the wisdom of sailing in such a vessel. He walked alongside the ship until he reached the gangplank. As a crew member walked past him, carrying a large barrel, Will stopped him.

"Is the captain on board the ship?" he asked.

The sailor nodded in the direction of a small table, at which sat a white-haired gentleman furiously writing in a ship's manifest. He appeared well dressed which gave Will a flicker of hope. He headed over.

"Good morning. I understand you are the captain of this vessel," said Will.

The captain looked up, sized Will up in an instant and got to his feet.

"I am. Who wishes to know?"

Will shot out his hand, and the surprised captain was left with little choice but to take it. Will's time as an undercover operative had taught him the value of an easily offered handshake, over that of a gold coin. Men by nature wanted to trust likeable men.

"I have passage booked on board for my fiancée and myself. Do you still intend to sail with this evening's tide?"

The captain nodded.

"If we can get all the cargo loaded on board by midday, then yes."

Will looked up at the deck of the ship and could see it was already heavily laden with barrels and crates which the crew were lashing tightly together with heavy rope.

"You have quite a cargo there. Won't it be a little tight for the passengers to move about on deck?" he asked.

The captain shook his head and pointed toward the rear of the deck.

"There is only the two of you, so we won't be needing much deck. This ship wasn't meant to do the run up to London until next week, but one of the company's other boats hit a reef off the Canary Islands last week and tore a hole in its side. We must take as much of the cargo as we can on this trip. Every cabin apart from your one and mine is full of cargo."

Will frowned, unsure if he had heard the captain correctly.

"Did you say there is only one cabin for the two passengers?" he replied.

"Yes, and you were lucky to be able to get that. But don't worry, there is ample room for the both of you. That's of course if you still wish to sail with us today, I have plenty of takers for your cabin if not."

Will looked back at the ship, and the captain snorted.

"Don't be fooled by her rough edges, she is a sturdy vessel. I'm retiring to a wife and a little cottage in Dorset come the end of the year. I wouldn't be setting out in anything that would send me to a watery grave before then. My wife would kill me."

Will took heart. Cramped though the ship might be, if it got them both safely home, he was prepared to endure a little discomfort.

And much as it was not ideal, he knew he had little choice. It could be another week before he was able to secure passage on the next ship to England. He was not going to risk waiting around in Gibraltar. If the local port authorities got wind of who Hattie really was they might decide to take her into their protection. As far as he was concerned, he was the only man who would be protecting her.

"Your ship will do just fine, thank you. My fiancée and I shall be ready to board early this afternoon."

He turned on his heel and headed along the waterfront to the series of stone steps which led back up to the town and the hotel.

He would find a strong coffee and some breakfast before he broke the news to Hattie that she would be sharing a cabin with him for the duration of the journey home.

Chapter Ten

Will had resigned himself to having to make do on board the ship. Making do, transpired to be a lot more difficult than he had expected.

As soon as he and Hattie got on board that afternoon and went to their cabin, Will knew the trip home was going to be an interesting one.

The cabin would have been cramped for one person. With two it was more of a crush. With nowhere else on board to store their luggage, Will's travel trunk had been dragged into the space between the bed and the end wall. The space it took up effectively cut the small writing table against the other wall in half. The chair at the table was now jammed in hard between the trunk and the edge of the table. The travel bag Will had purchased for Hattie sat on top of the table.

Between the table and the bed there was enough room for the pair of them to stand, but do little else. It was a tight squeeze to reach the back wall of the cabin.

The only redeeming feature, was the bank of double windows along the back wall of the cabin; the warm light and view of the sea beyond gave the illusion of more space.

As he closed the door behind him, Hattie turned to Will.

"Whilst not ideal, I can understand that you and I shall have to endure the cramped conditions if we are to make it home. What I do not understand is where the two of us are supposed to sleep," she said.

On his trip down to the dockside earlier that morning, it had not occurred to Will that one cabin, also meant one bed. While the bed in question was sizeable and clearly designed to hold two people, sharing it with Hattie was an impossibility.

"I shall go and speak with the captain. I am certain he will have a spare hammock in the crew's quarters in which I can sleep. In the meantime, just unpack your things and make yourself at home. I shall come and get you before we sail, so you can say your final farewells to Gibraltar."

As the London bound ship finally drew away from the dock, Will let out a large sigh of relief. He had managed to get Hattie on board the *Canis Major* and in a matter of days, she would be back in England.

He looked down at his hands as they held onto the ship's rail, surprised at how tense he had been until the moment the gangplank was finally raised.

On the walk back to the hotel earlier that morning, he had considered Hattie's situation. From the snippets of information, he had thus far managed to garner during their short time together, he had what he considered to be a reasonable estimation of matters.

Mr. and Mrs. Wright, he deduced were her parents. Hattie's slip of the tongue at Europa Point had not gone unnoted. Her father had seen the Rock of Gibraltar as they sailed into port.

The real Miss Sarah Wilson was likely a maid or another missionary. When Hattie had been forced to come up with a false name, she had used the name of the first person who came to mind.

As for the last member of the travelling party, the Reverend Peter Brown, Will had his bets placed on him being the fiancé Hattie had been so desperate to escape from.

That left Will with an unexpected problem.

Who was left in London for Hattie? He could not return her to England and simply let her walk off the boat and disappear into the unknown.

"I can't say I'm not happy to see the back of this place," Hattie remarked.

Will turned as she reached the top of the steps and came to stand beside him. She surveyed the town of Gibraltar as it slowly slipped away. He meanwhile studied her.

She had taken the news of their travelling situation without a hint of displeasure. Had things been so bad with her family and fiancé that she was willing to undergo any form of discomfort just to get home?

As the ship cleared the head of the harbor, the wind began to pick up. A sudden gust had her staggering on her feet. Instinctively he reached out and took hold of her arm.

"Thank you, Mr. Saunders," she said.

As she leaned over the ship's railing to get a better look, he continued to hold fast to her arm. The last thing he needed was for her to topple overboard. In the back of his mind was also the notion that she may jump. Foolish though it was, he was still uncomfortable with his charge being anywhere near to the side of the ship.

"When did we go back to being formal with one another," he asked.

He caught the edge of a frown on her face as Hattie turned away.

"I don't know. It feels a little too familiar, especially now that we are among other people," she replied.

Considering that they would be spending the next week or so sharing a cramped cabin on board the ship, remaining on such a formal basis seemed odd. He had decided that continuing the façade of being an engaged couple was the safest option. He had to convince her to call him Will.

"Just remember the crew think we are a betrothed couple, you might want to show me a little more friendship, if not affection," he cautioned.

If she did, there was a good chance her mask would slip a little and he would be granted a further glimpse of her true self. He wondered just how much of that she had already revealed to him.

Whatever her truth, he had to know more of it before they reached London. While they were on the boat, she could not hide easily from him or the multitude of questions which were currently swirling around in his head.

Will pursed his lips. He was a patient man when the mood took him, but Hattie was surprisingly testing his mettle. He reached out a hand and gently brushed his fingers against her cheek.

She shivered.

"It's cool in the sea breeze," she said. His touch had been so light, she had not seemed to notice.

Her Spanish made cotton gown gave her little protection against the chill of the sea wind. Will quickly unbuttoned his greatcoat and offered it to her. When he had purchased several new functional day gowns for her, it had not occurred to him that she would need a coat. Gibraltar was not exactly a place for heavy English wool overcoats.

"Thank you," she said, slipping her arms into his oversized coat. The coat went all the way down to her feet. It looked a little ridiculous, Will found it utterly charming.

She is getting under your skin.

"Well you shall not be cold up on deck if you make sure to wear it," Will observed.

Fortunately, he was returning to England with all his belongings and somewhere within his travel trunk a second wool coat was stored.

With the ship now clear of the harbor, the captain turned the ship's bow northward. Hattie looked back over her shoulder toward the south, toward Africa. The mountains of Morocco slowly became a tiny speck in the distance before finally disappearing.

She sniffed back tears and wiped her eyes with the palm of her hand.

"Regrets?" he asked.

She met his gaze.

"None," she replied.

Conflict wracked Will's brain. If he was to return Hattie safely to her family, he had to know who in London would take this young woman in and offer her a home. Her parents were on their way to Africa, and no matter the circumstances of her leaving them, he still owed them a duty to ensure he delivered her into the hands of someone in England who cared for her. His questions demanded answers.

The view from the ship's deck soon became one of repetition, the blue ocean stretched out for miles on the portside with only a thin brown line of land on the starboard. Within an hour they had both retired to the cramped cabin. Hattie curled up asleep on the bed while Will squeezed into the seat at the tiny writing desk and continued to make notes for his first few days back in London.

He had a few personal belongings with him in his travel trunk, the rest of his possessions had been shipped home the day he left Paris for the final time.

Having lived in lodgings for several years, he had not required much in the way of furniture but upon deciding he was moving permanently back to England, Will had set about purchasing enough elegant and expensive pieces of furniture to fill a house. When he got to London, he intended to rebuild his life. A wife and family lay ahead in those plans.

When Hattie finally stirred from her slumber, Will decided it was time to confront her.

ॐ

She knew it was inevitable. The only thing which truly surprised her was that Will had left his questioning until this late into the sea journey.

From the moment they had stepped on board, she had been waiting for him to press her further about her origins. About her family.

As she opened her eyes she could see him seated on the chair facing her, his hands held tightly together in front.

"Hattie, we need to talk," he said.

"Yes."

The word was out of her mouth before she realized what she had said. Will had called her by her real name, and she fool that she was, had answered him.

Her sense of gratitude that the door of the cabin had a lock was instantly diminished by the sight of Will holding the key in his hand. Any hope for escape was effectively blocked.

How had Will discovered her real name?

The only sign of emotion he displayed at her response was to sit back in the chair and let out a low whistle. His face remained implacable. From his outwardly indifferent demeanor, she knew this was not the first time he had sat someone down and interrogated them. The tale of him being a merchant was a convenient lie.

What had he said about his time on the continent? She wracked her brains. For all her evasiveness, he too had managed to reveal little of himself or his past.

"Good. Well at least we have established your real name," he said.

"How?" she replied.

He stood up from the chair, and put the key in his coat pocket.

"This morning I went to the shipping office down at the dockside. When you and your parents came ashore you were all registered with the local port authority. It didn't take long for me to find your name among the list of passengers from the *Blade of Orion.*"

Hattie pushed her back up against the cabin wall. While it did little in a physical sense, it at least helped her to mentally create distance between them. Hot tears came to her eyes and her hands started to shake. She felt herself on the verge of losing control. She clasped her hands together and sucked in several deep breaths.

Hattie looked down at her tightly twisted hands. What was she to do now?

"What do you want?" she finally replied.

He met her gaze. An unexpected softness appeared on his face. The same warmth shone in his eyes as had done at St Michael's cave. She gritted her teeth, refusing to allow herself to be fooled by his act once again.

"I want the truth Hattie. As I have said before, I cannot help you if you refuse to let me do so. I do not need to know it all, keep whatever secrets you feel you need. But after all that I have done for you, I deserve some explanation."

She sat and stared at her hands while she contemplated his words.

They were at sea. The next landfall was England. If she did tell him the truth, there was little he could do between now and when the ship reached London. For all that he had done for her, he really did deserve the truth. Or some of it at least.

"What do you want to know?"

"Good. May I suggest a good place to start would be an explanation of how it was that you came to be floating in Gibraltar harbor," he replied.

Hattie climbed off the bed, and walked over to the window. Under the window was a small padded wooden bench. It would be the sort of place to sit and read a book on a long sea voyage.

She sat down, relieved when Will made no indication to move from his spot closer to the door.

Where exactly was she to begin? For such a longtime, her life had been about serving others. No one had ever asked for her story.

"My parents underwent a religious conversion several years ago. My father renounced much of our privileged life as being wicked and not worthy of the path he had chosen to follow. I have spent much of the past two years working in the rookery of St Giles trying to help those less fortunate than us.

About a year ago Papa met the Reverend Peter Brown and his whole focus shifted. Peter Brown convinced my father that the poor of London were not enough. His plans were grander. Rendering earthly assistance meant nothing, when there were thousands of souls they could be converting. That's when they hit upon the idea that a mission to Africa was what their life's work would become."

Speaking the words out aloud made her father and Peter Brown sound cold and calculating, but it was the truth. They now saw their work as being all about numbers. The number of people they could bring under their spiritual guidance in Sierra Leone was what drove both men on.

"And you and your mother went along with the plan; but somewhere along the way you decided to take a different path. When did you first realize that you did not want the same as them?" asked Will.

Her mother, yes. All Hattie's life her mother had done as her husband instructed. Her parent's marriage was a practical one. Even when her father had taken Hattie out of the London social scene in the middle of her first season, her mother had said nothing to stop him.

For herself, she had hoped for a time that the mission to Africa was a plan on paper at worst. But as the day of their sailing drew ever closer a fear began to grow within.

Reverend Brown began to pay her special attention. Her parents were oft to remark on his fine character, recommending him to her.

She had ignored the obvious signs; and thrown herself into her work. Eventually even she could not ignore the clear plans of others.

Hattie closed her eyes as tears began to run freely down her face. She had been a part of a family, yet had been so alone.

Will rose from his chair, but she waved him away. If she was to tell her story, it had to be on her terms. She was surprised by the slow anger which began to simmer in the back of her mind as she talked about her father and Reverend Brown.

When her father announced her engagement to Peter Brown she feared the battle was lost. Daily her willpower has been assailed with plans and pronouncements for their combined futures. She had come so close to capitulating.

"The day my mother told me my cat would not be coming with us. That was the day I knew," she replied.

A nervous titter escaped her lips. It was absurd to think that it had taken the impending loss of her mangy cat Brutus for Hattie to finally see sense.

"They expected me to give up everything. My home, my life and everything I held dear. That was two months ago. I've been trying to find a way to avoid going ever since."

"I panicked the morning we set sail from Gibraltar. Reverend Brown had pressed my father to allow him to share my cabin and my father had agreed. I knew if I didn't jump, then I would likely be pregnant by the time we reached Sierra Leone. Once we arrived, there would be nothing left for me but to become his wife."

Hattie felt nauseous. It was not the motion of the boat. She had seen the life which had been set out for her and known it was a life of misery and loneliness.

Ignoring her protests, Will pulled her into his arms and held her tight. She felt the warmth and comfort of his embrace. Her heart desperately hoping that someone finally did understand.

"Thank you. I know that took an enormous amount of courage to tell. Thank you for trusting me enough and allowing me to finally understand."

Chapter Eleven

Will Saunders was not by nature a violent man, but he knew there were men who only responded to violence. Years as a spy in France had taught him that uncomfortable truth. Men had died under his hand.

Hattie's father and former fiancé were fortunate that they were many hundreds of nautical miles away at this moment, otherwise Will feared he would have done violence against them.

Holding a sobbing Hattie in his arms, he was overwhelmed with pity. This poor girl had been nothing more than a pawn in a bigger game being planned and played by those who should have protected her. He did not know who he hated more at that moment. Reverend Brown for having made the presumption that Hattie would make a comfortable wife, or Aldred Wright for having considered his daughter as nothing more than something to offer up to another man in marriage.

She had been given no choice but to do their bidding. No say in her life. Reckless though it had been, she had done the only thing she could by fleeing from them.

When her tears eventually ceased, Will sat Hattie back on the bed. He resumed his seat opposite.

With her parents and fiancé out of her life, Hattie was in a precarious situation. Will now faced a difficult decision. Did he let things lay as they were, or did he press her for more information?

He gritted his teeth. The next few minutes could change everything between them.

"So, Hattie, what other family do you have in London?"

❧

She slowly raised her head and met his gaze.

If Will thought she was unaccustomed to the way of liars, he had never done business in the rookery of St Giles. While Hattie was not particularly strong in the art of lying herself, she still knew enough.

St Giles was the home of every thief, conman, and criminal worth his salt in London. She had dealt with many of them over the years; some lessons had been well learned.

While the newspapers regularly wrote articles demanding the rookeries of London be cleared, the authorities did nothing about it. Her father had a theory that if they did clean out the sordid slums, then the poor and criminals alike would be forced onto the streets of London. The rich of St James parish would not take kindly to having beggars and pickpockets living in the streets outside their homes.

Will's attempt to comfort her had been real, he was not that calculating. She knew however, it was only a momentary interval in the long game he was playing. It was time for her to move one of her own pieces on the board.

"My Uncle Felix has a house on Argyle Street. You could take me there," she replied.

She sat and waited. Watching as Will processed her words. The dark line on his brow relaxed just enough to tell her he believed her.

"Good. So that is where I shall take you once we make shore. What number is your uncle's house?" said Will.

"Oh, I am not sure. I think it is number seventy- five."

"On the right or left of the street as you come from Oxford Street?"

"Right. It's a white four-storey town house."

75

Will was still trying to pick holes in her story. Fortunately; she was telling the truth about the house and its location.

"Number seventy- five you said. That would make it the corner house?"

She frowned. Her uncle's house was in the middle of a row of houses.

"No, its four doors from the end of the street."

"Yes of course that would make it number seventy-five. I have friends in the corner house and they are in number eighty-one."

Hattie held her breath, desperate not to show any sign of relief that Will believed her. The truth was, she was not lying. Her uncle did have a house on Argyle Street. His permanent residence was in London.

Who then was she to quibble over the fact that her Uncle Felix was currently serving with the British envoy to the United States of America in Washington, and had been absent from England for four years.

There was a knock at their cabin door and Will answered it. As he stood and turned his back toward her, Hattie let out the breath she had been holding.

The first mate stood at the door, cap in hand. Will had requested to speak with the captain regarding his sleeping arrangements.

"I shan't be long," said Will.

As the door closed behind him, Hattie punched the air. She had won a small, but important victory. She had given Will the name of a family member and an address where he could take her once they reached London.

Her uncle was real and she knew enough of his house to be able to give Will a convincing story that a home could be found for her there. She had bought herself some valuable time. Time in which she could come up with a plan to disappear from Will Saunders' life.

Chapter Twelve

W ill returned to the cabin a short time later in the oddest
of moods.

His meeting with the ship's captain had not gone well. The ship
was heavily laden with goods and there was not a spare hammock to
be had with the crew.

Added to that problem, was the fact that the captain did not know
his crew, having picked them up only recently in the West Indies.
There were some of them he considered untrustworthy, others down-
right dangerous.

"Even if I had somewhere for you to sleep Mr. Saunders, such as
in my cabin, I would not offer you that accommodation. Your fiancée
may be in danger from the crew if she is left to sleep in your cabin on
her own," the captain explained.

The lock on their cabin door was nothing special. The same key
fitted most locks on board the ship. Will would have to sleep in the
cabin with Hattie.

That news pushed another thought to the forefront of his
concerns. What was he to say to Felix Wright when he returned Hattie
to London?

He had retrieved her from out of the sea. Been semi naked in front

SASHA COTTMAN

of her. And to top it all off had spent the best part of two weeks sharing a private cabin with her onboard a ship.

If her uncle was any sort of gentleman, he would demand the obvious. Will would have to marry Hattie.

He stopped outside the cabin door. It would not be the first time he had married out of sense of duty. His initial reason for agreeing to marry Yvette was to help build a false identity in Paris.

He had been a rash young man. Yvette was beautiful and strong willed. Lust and adventure had overruled any reservations he may have had about marrying the French undercover agent. Her father had also had a firm hand in the decision.

He had quickly learned not to regret his decision. Yvette was a sensual woman. She soon won Will's heart, and in time he had owned hers.

While Hattie was different from the vivacious Yvette, she was possessed of her own unique charm. He had little doubt that with time, they would come to a comfortable arrangement. There was even the chance that they could come to care for one another.

I am not a complete ogre, who knows she may fall in love with me.

The topic of marriage was for later, when they were closer to England. Between now and then Will had time to get to know a little more of the real Hattie Wright. Time in which to set the scene for the inevitable conversation.

Inside the cabin, he found Hattie seated at the window. She was watching the waves and the distant shore line that was the coast of Spain.

"Bad news I am afraid," he said.

"Yes?"

There was no point in trying to keep the truth from her. If she had worked the slums of St Giles parish, Hattie would know enough of the dangers of the street.

"The captain is not convinced that every man in the crew is of good reputation. I shall have to sleep in the cabin."

She shrugged her shoulders.

"That's perfectly alright. The bed is big enough."

Will frowned. Sharing a bed with her was not part of his plans, not yet anyway. Marriage first, then the sharing of the marital bed and the pleasures that came with it.

"I have some bedding, the floor should suffice," he replied.

She looked at the small gap between the bed and the rest of the furniture. It was a tight squeeze. Will would have little room to move about once he was down on the floor.

"Are you certain? It's not as if either of us is going to don our nightclothes. I am quite happy for you to share the other side of the bed," replied Hattie.

She was a practical minded girl, but Will suspected that Hattie was not overly familiar with the male form and what the effect sleeping next to a young woman could have on a man. Waking beside her in the morning with a raging erection was a real possibility he did not want to have to face. He did not want her to think he would treat her the same as Reverend Brown had clearly intended.

"While you may have been away from polite society for some time, don't think for one minute that it has become acceptable for an unmarried couple to share a bed. The floor will do."

With that the discussion was at an end. Will would have to hope that the gentle rocking motion of the ship on the sea and the sound of the waves was enough of a lullaby to put him to sleep each night.

Chapter Thirteen

Will paced back and forth along a short stretch of the cluttered deck. Every inch of the deck of the *Canis Major* was crowded with wooden crates and barrels lashed together with rope. There was little room to maneuver about the deck, let alone go for a proper stroll.

He tapped his fist against the side of one of the oak barrels, it was full. He licked his lips, thinking that a large glass of rum would be perfect right now. The crates stacked next to the rum, were marked *SUGAR. PINNEY ESTATE. NEVIS. FREE MEN PRODUCE.*

The former slave plantations in the West Indies were now being worked by free men, paid for their labor. It sickened him to think that at one point the *Canis Major* would have regularly shipped slave labor goods to England. Goods he and his family would have purchased and used. England may have won the war against a French tyrant, but it most certainly did not have a clean moral sheet.

The slap of a thick rope against his legs stirred him from his musings. He stepped to one side as two members of the crew pushed past him and lashed a rope around a stack of nearby barrels.

"Expecting rough weather?" said Will, half in jest.

"Yes," they replied in unison.

He looked to where one of the sailors was pointing his head. The clear skies of Southern Spain had disappeared. In their place was a near black cluster of storm clouds.

Within minutes he noticed a perceptible increase in the wind. The sails flapped loudly against the mast as the crew working in the ropes overhead struggled to bring them in.

Looking over the side of the ship, he could see the waves rising and falling in ever increasing tempo.

The ship's captain got Will's attention with a firm tug on his sleeve.

"Mr. Saunders, I suggest you might wish to retire to your cabin. The ship is heading into the North Atlantic and storm weather. It's going to be a rough night. The young lady may be in need of your comfort before long."

Will nodded. It was going to be a long night in the cramped cabin, the oncoming storm would only add another layer of discomfort for the two of them.

"The captain says we are sailing into a storm. It's going to be rough sailing through until the morning," said Will, stepping back into the cabin.

Hattie was sitting quietly on the bed a book in hand.

"I had noticed that the motion of the boat was getting stronger," she replied.

Will looked down at the floor. She had made up his bed while he had been out on deck. While Hattie had used all the blankets and the soft mattress given to him by the captain, it did not look particularly inviting. With the ship heading into a rough storm, he doubted he would get much sleep.

"Will they feed us?" she asked.

Food. He had not thought to ask. Hattie ever practical had.

"I shall make enquiries."

With that he disappeared back out onto the deck.

When Will returned a short time later, Hattie was seated in the same spot as when he left. He crossed to the bed and handed her a plate containing two apples, some cheese and four thick slices of bread. A small knife was stuck in the cheese.

"The extent of our supper I'm afraid. The cook and cabin boy are busy helping to secure the cargo below decks. There will not be any hot food tonight." he said.

"Better than many will eat tonight," she replied.

The words rolled off her tongue so easily that Will suspected it was a common saying in the Wright household.

"Come sit and eat something. I remember the weather on the journey here. Mama was terribly ill for several days as we crossed between the seas."

※

Will sat down in the chair opposite the bed and faced Hattie. There was a matter of inches between their knees. They both chuckled at how cramped the space was between them.

"We are going to be the best of dance partners by the time this voyage is over. Moving around one another will be second nature. Our bodies will be as one," said Will.

He had the manner of one whom she expected would be a skilled dancer. She had always enjoyed dancing in her younger years. Her brother Edgar had spent many hours patiently teaching her the waltz the year of her coming out. She had barely got to use all those lessons before her father determined that dancing was a sin and it was not permitted for his daughter.

Edgar. She had not thought of her brother for some time. The sudden memory shook her.

"Are you alright? My words about dancing perhaps came out a little askew. I meant we would move around the dance floor as one. I meant nothing untoward."

She looked up to see Will studying her, a concerned look on his face. He cared about her, that much was evident. There were certain mannerisms that gave his frame of mind away at times. Right now, he was worried he had offended her in some way.

"Yes of course I am. You just gave me a reminder of my old life. I sometimes forget my family life was not always this way. My parents used to love to dance when I was younger," she replied.

While she was prepared to talk about her parents, Edgar Wright was the one person she was not going to share with Will. The one person in London Will could take her to was also the last person who would want to see her.

She had treated Edgar and his wife Miranda terribly. Shunned them for not having taken up the mission of serving the poor. When the time came that she sent word pleading for his assistance to avoid going to Africa, Edgar had rightly abandoned her to her fate. There was no going back to being loving brother and sister.

She willed herself to think of the task at hand, of trying to eat before the storm hit. Pulling the knife from out of the block of cheese, Hattie proceeded to cut the cheese into bite sized portions. When she was done she wrapped some of the cheese up in a piece of bread and handed it to Will.

As he took it from her hands, their fingers touched. A frisson of heat raced up Hattie's spine. She shivered.

Will slowly withdrew his hand. Whatever she had felt, she knew he had felt it too.

They were as close as they could be without being on the bed together, yet she yearned to be even closer to him. His touch made her heart race.

She should not feel this way about Will. The struggle was real. Hattie tried to force the feeling away, to calm her turmoil, but it was too strong to fight.

In another time and place, she might have called this attraction love, but here and under the present circumstances she was at a loss to find the right word. Her body was sending signals she had never known before. It both frightened and thrilled her.

"Are you a good sailor?" she stammered.

He looked at the bread and cheese in his hand.

"Not particularly," he replied.

He took a bite of the sandwich and sat chewing it slowly. For the first time since she had met Will, Hattie sensed he was not entirely comfortable. The self-assured man of the world now revealed a vulnerable side of himself. She could tell he did not like it.

Hattie looked around the cabin, relieved when she spied a bucket in the corner attached to the wall by a small hook.

"So, what you are saying is that we may have need for that at some point tonight?" she said.

A pensive looking Will nodded and retrieved the bucket. He placed it on the floor next to the desk.

There was a knock at the door and when Will answered it, the first mate stepped inside. He doffed his cap to Hattie.

"Captain says to tell you to stay in your cabin until he sends word that it is safe to come out. There is a big swell building and we are likely to be tossed about a bit," he said.

Hattie's heart sank. It would be the ultimate irony for her to die at sea on the way home to England.

The first mate read her mind, and gave a reassuring grin.

"Nothing to worry about miss, we sailors travel these waters all the year round. With the ship getting thrown around, some of the cargo may come loose from the ropes. It won't be safe up on deck. Me, and the rest of the crew will be taking shelter soon to ride out the storm. By tomorrow morning it should have blown over and we will be making our way up the coast of Portugal. We should reach England in ten days after that. I'm sure your Mr. Saunders will keep you safe."

Will locked the door again after the first mate had left. He stood and surveyed the cabin before starting to take things from the top of the desk and putting them in his trunk. Hattie silently watched.

When he finally completed the task of securing the cabin, Hattie offered him some more cheese and sliced apple, but Will waved them away.

"It might not be a good idea for me to have too much food in my system as the storm hits."

Hattie hastily packed up the rest of the food, stowing the plate and knife in one of the desk drawers. Will retreated to his makeshift bed on the floor and lay down.

"When I said I wasn't a good sailor, what I meant was that I get a tad dizzy when the ship rolls up and down the waves. Silly for a grown man to suffer in such a way but there you have it," he said.

The ship gave a sudden, violent lurch, tossing Hattie back on to the bed. Before she could sit back up, a second wave hit the ship and forced her down again.

As the ship finally righted itself on the downside of the next wave, she rolled over and put her head over the side of the bed to check on Will.

He was rolled up in a ball in the corner, his hands were gripped tightly to his travel trunk. She muttered a word which would have had her mother turning red with embarrassment.

The floor was a dangerous place for Will to be at the best of times. With the ship now beginning a rolling pitch up and down the giant waves, the floor was quickly becoming a deathtrap.

"Will please, you need to come up onto the bed. If you stay on the floor you are going to be injured or worse," she pleaded.

He was no fool. Will scrambled to his feet, grabbed his blankets and was half way to the bed when the ship was hit by yet another wave and he was tossed back onto the floor. Will's head and the hard-wooden floor made sickening contact.

"*Merde!*" he bellowed.

Hattie clambered to her knees and put a leg over the side of the bed, but Will stopped her.

"No, stay where you are. The last thing we need is for the both of us to go bouncing off the walls and floor of the cabin. I shall come to you."

Getting to his feet a second time, he launched himself at the bed, landing inelegantly beside Hattie with a loud "Ooof".

She checked his face and head for any signs of blood, relieved when it was clear Will had not cracked his head open.

"When you have fallen from a horse as many times as I have you eventually realize that your head is a lot tougher than you think," he said.

Hattie moved across the bed and sat up with her back against the wall. Her feet were hard up against the side wall of the bed. Will did the same.

As the boat continued to pitch and roll, it felt like they were riding an out of control carriage. Hattie's stomach prayed for a set of reins with which to pull up the non-existent horses.

"If this is an indication of the night ahead, something tells me we are not going to be getting any sleep," Will said wearily.

She looked at his face and saw he had closed his eyes. Dark lashes kissed the skin above his cheeks, but his face was ashen. Pity replaced much of the fear she was currently feeling. With the storm likely to continue unabated for hours, Will was facing a tortuous night.

"If it's too difficult to sit up, then I suggest you lie down," she said.

"Yes," he finally replied. The weakness of his voice giving a clear indication of the growing depth of his discomfort.

With his large, masculine frame fully stretched out on the bed, Hattie was left with little option. She lay down on her side, her back facing toward his chest.

"Your bed is nice and soft. The padding is much better than mine," Will observed.

"Close your eyes and hopefully that will help to keep your head from spinning," she replied.

The full force of the storm hit the ship a short while later. With it came driving rain. The cabin door rattled as the fearsome wind challenged its hold on the door frame. Fortunately, it held fast. The bucket on the floor was not so lucky.

For the longest time Hattie lay awake, watching the bucket slide back and forth across the floor from door to bed and back again. When the ship encountered a larger set of waves the bucket was pushed all the way back hard against the side of the bed.

She reached down and swiftly grabbed a hold of it. With the bucket now in her hand she had solved one problem. The next question was what to do with the bucket. Holding onto it for the rest of the night was not an option.

There was a hook with a rope tie on the wall opposite, near the door. It must have been all of seven feet. She decided to risk it.

She slid one leg over the side of the bed and slowly sat up. Turning, she looked at Will. He was fast asleep, a soft snore rippled from his lips.

He really was a handsome specimen of a man. Her fingers ached to touch his hair. In his sleep it had become ruffled and a stray curl now sat on the edge of his fringe.

Her gaze dropped to his lips. Lips which she knew to be soft and warm. Lips her heart desired to possess forever.

"Oh, if only you weren't who you are and I wasn't who I am," she whispered.

She turned back to the task at hand. It was only a few steps to where the hook which would hold the bucket secure was nailed to the wall.

After a short period of sitting and counting, she began to perceive the patterns of the waves. Twenty counts for the ship to lean to starboard, ten seconds of stillness, then a further count of twenty for the ship to lean back fully portside.

As the ship began its next starboard lean, Hattie stood and with bucket in hand, quickly scrambled to the hook. By her reckoning she had fifteen counts to secure the bucket before she would need to be ready to make her way back.

Nervous fingers hoisted the bucket onto the hook and wrapped the rope handle round and round, securing it firmly in place.

She turned just as the ship set her staggering back toward the bed. She reached the bed and threw herself over the raised side. She had done it. The satisfaction of having achieved her goal, had her grinning.

"Well done," said a husky-throated Will.

"I thought you were asleep," she replied.

"I was, but as soon as you left my side, I woke."

Will threw the blankets over them and then wrapped a strong arm around her waist.

"Don't try and leave the bed again unless you absolutely have to, the safest place for the both of us is right here. You should try and get some sleep," he said.

They were in the middle of a ferocious storm in the North Atlantic, on a ship which was riding up and down huge rolling waves. But, with Will beside her in the bed, Hattie felt safe for the first time in a very long time.

As sleep finally took her, she slipped into a long warm dream of a man who always held her tight throughout the worst of life's storms.

When morning came, the storm had mostly blown out. Rain still lashed the decks. After a cursory view out the door, Hattie decided there was little purpose in venturing outside and she climbed back into bed.

ॐ

It was late morning before the deck was safe enough to venture out onto. The crew spent the best part of the morning checking the ropes and making repairs to the ship. Several crates of cargo had been swept overboard during the night and were lost at sea. Despite Hattie's efforts to rouse him, she was unable to wake Will.

"Sleep of the righteous," she muttered.

Only someone with a clear conscience could sleep that soundly. Finally accepting defeat, she put on Will's greatcoat and went in search of sustenance.

The ship's cabin crew, which consisted of the cook and a young lad of about fourteen stood silently at one end of the galley table as Hattie ate her breakfast. The cook, who wore an apron which had seen cleaner days, roughly cleared his throat.

"Would the young miss be wanting anything else?" he asked.

Hattie looked up from her contemplation of her hard-boiled egg. Both cook and cabin boy shifted on their feet. It was like watching a pair of dancing pigeons. As one moved to his left, the other followed.

"Yes, please. My fiancé is still abed. He had a terrible night. Could you please fix him some breakfast so I may take it back to our cabin?"

While Hattie waited for Will's breakfast to be cooked, she went and sat outside on the deck. Near the captain's cabin she found a small solid bench which was mostly out of the wind.

The sun was out and the storm clouds of the previous night had gone. The contrast of stormy night to blue sky morning was astonishing. Apart from the weary looks on the faces of the crew, and several tattered sails blowing in the sea breeze there was little evidence that the ship had been through a tumultuous night.

"Good morning."

She turned to see Will standing in the sunshine, a blanket wrapped around his shoulders. His hair was tussled from him having slept so deeply. She was heartened to see the natural color had returned to his face.

"You look a lot better than you did last night. Cook is making you some breakfast," she replied.

She looked at the blanket covering the warm masculine frame which she had slept against the night before and suddenly realized why he was wearing it.

"Oh, I am so sorry, I forgot I took your coat," she said.

The cabin boy arrived carrying two mugs of coffee. Will's face lit up.

"Coffee the elixir of the gods."

Hattie laughed. "I thought ambrosia was the elixir of the gods."

Will shook his head. "Not in my world. My brain does not function until I have had a strong brew of coffee in the morning."

The cabin boy scurried off to tell the cook that the gentleman passenger was awake and ready to take his breakfast.

Will sipped his coffee, watching as the boy disappeared back inside the galley.

"You shouldn't be out here alone. Remember what the captain said about not knowing his crew very well."

Hattie was on the verge of explaining to Will that she regularly walked the dangerous streets of London on her own, but decided against it. Memories of lying awake in the early hours of the morning while Will slept beside her were still warming her heart.

"Sorry. I forgot. The captain has been up on deck most of the time I have been out here, and I haven't wandered away from this vicinity. I won't do it again," she replied.

The truth was, she was so used to being in the violent and unsafe streets of the Parish of St Giles that she had become somewhat indifferent to all but the most obvious signs of danger. After the fourth time she had been accosted and robbed on the street in the early days of their mission, she stopped bothering to tell her parents. Risk came with the territory of giving aid to the poor.

"I just want to ensure that you get home safely to your uncle. I don't mean to be overbearing. If we can agree that you don't venture from the cabin without me, I will be content."

Hattie agreed. For what was only a matter of days, she was prepared to concede to as many of Will's demands as she felt necessary. She told herself it was purely for the sake of ensuring they both enjoyed a cordial and pleasant journey home. Her heart however was beginning to beat to the sound of a different drum.

With mugs of coffee in hand, they followed the cabin boy into the galley.

Chapter Fourteen

That night Will attempted to sleep on the floor of their cabin for a second time, but in the early hours, Hattie felt him slide in beside her. He wrapped his arm around her in a now familiar hold and from the gentle snores which soon arose from him, she knew he had fallen asleep.

Hattie lay awake in the night. The moon which shone through the cabin window bathed the room in a soft pearl blue light.

Eventually she lifted Will's arm from around her and slipped out of bed. Putting his greatcoat on, she crossed to the bench by the window and sat down.

In the bed, Will rolled over onto his other side, and slept on.

She smiled as she watched him sleep. He was a magnificent specimen of a man. Whenever he wrapped his arms around her, she felt butterflies flutter in her stomach. The woman who eventually married him would have a wonderful husband.

But Will Saunders was not for her. He was born and bred for the life of the *ton*. A world of wealth, fabulous parties, and self-centered people. That was the world she had left behind. Her life now had a purpose. Her work with the poor brought hope to people who otherwise had nothing.

Will for all his kindness would never understand.

When they returned to England they would go their separate ways. In time he would forget her. She knew however, she would never forget him. Never forget the first man who had held her heart.

She turned and looked up at the moon. It was close to a full moon. The moon's light shone on the white caps of the waves. They looked like tiny white lanterns dancing up and down in a never-ending bob.

"Can't sleep?"

Will had crept silently from the bed and now came to sit beside her.

"Just thinking," she replied.

"Of what?"

The memory of standing on the gangplank of the *Blade of Orion* slipped into her mind. The emotion she felt before she took the leap into a new life, stirred once more.

You were brave then. Why not now?

She softly chortled and feeling her cheeks blush red, turned away. Will reached out and touching her face, drew her gaze back to him.

"Of what, Hattie?"

Her gaze fell on his lips. Those soft, warm lips which had captivated her when Will kissed her that first day in the town square.

"Of what it would be like to be your lover."

She held her breath. Her gaze remained locked on his lips. She had been bold enough to say the words, but she was not possessed of the strength to meet his gaze.

Will took hold of her hand and raising it to his lips, kissed it gently.

"Do you realize what you are saying? I mean what being my lover would entail."

Hattie puffed out her cheeks. She had held onto the slim hope that this was one secret she would never be forced to reveal to him. But if she was to bring their relationship to the place she desired, she would have to be honest with Will when it came to sex.

Hattie rose from the bench and bending over placed a tentative kiss on Will's lips. She had never taken the lead before in a sexual encounter with a man, but her heart called for her to take a chance. The worst he could do would be to say no.

"Yes, I do understand. Will, I am not a virgin."

He returned the kiss.

"I take it the reverend decided he was entitled to liberties being your fiancé and took them before you left London."

She nodded.

She had been led to believe that love making was a beautiful thing between a man and a woman. She had seen the shared kisses and whispers between Edgar and Miranda in the months after they were wed. How Miranda's eyes lit up whenever Edgar touched her.

Girls at society balls had told her wonderful stories of secrets shared by their older married sisters of the joy of the marital bed. Of lusty husbands and moments of heady sexual pleasure.

When Peter had come to her room the first night, she had expected it to be a magical encounter. Instead it had been painful and degrading. When she cried, Peter had ordered her to remain still and be quiet.

His repeat visits had been just as horrid. She had submitted to him, but he had still used physical force to bend her to his sexual will.

"I know it would be different with you. You would be kind."

Will brushed a hand on her cheek and cupped her face in his hands. He pulled Hattie to him and took her lips with his.

Loving, tender lips touched hers. He was everything a young woman dreamed of in a man.

His cologne was a heady mix of spice and masculine woody tones. She luxuriated in its welcoming scent.

When Will speared his fingers through her hair, she felt heat race down her spine. His tongue slipped into her mouth. He teased and tempted her to respond. She returned his kiss with slow responsive strokes of her tongue.

Will rose from the bench and pulled Hattie firmly against him. She felt the hardness of his manhood against the side of her hip. Emboldened by the effect she was having on him, she reached down and rubbed the outside of the placket of his trousers.

Will groaned in appreciation.

He deepened the kiss and she was with him. This was the passion and the connection she had so longed for with a man. Two souls connecting and sharing the quiet of the night together.

He pulled away from the kiss and their gazes met.

"Are you sure you want this? I will understand if you had a moment of rashness and are now having second thoughts."

There was no doubt whatsoever in her mind. She knew exactly what she wanted, and it involved Will exploring every inch of her body with his hands and his lips.

"Yes. I am sure."

She caught the sigh in his breath. It would have been a most uncomfortable night for him if she had changed her mind.

Will kissed her once more. His hands held her by the waist, while she gripped onto his strong muscular arms. In the cramped cabin their heated bodies began to warm up the small space.

Though they had been sleeping in their clothes, Will was not wearing his jacket or cravat and under Will's greatcoat Hattie was dressed only in her gown with a light cotton chemise underneath. She slipped her arms out of the greatcoat and lay it on the bench.

Will made short work of the buttons on Hattie's gown, before slipping it over her head and draping it over the nearby chair. When he reached for the ribbons on the front of her chemise, she gently slapped his eager fingers away.

"Let me," she said.

She watched his eyes grow wide as she slowly, teasingly undid the bow and let the top of her chemise fall open. Her nipples puckered as they felt the kiss of the chilled night air.

She had never been naked in front of a man before. Her previous encounters in the dark with Peter had been conducted with her dressed in a neck to ankle nightgown. She felt wanton and desirable.

"Take off your shirt," she commanded.

She intended to be as equal a partner in this sexual engagement as she could. There would be no lying quietly in the bed praying for the encounter to be over. Her time with Will was limited, so she was going to enjoy every minute she could.

Will bowed his acquiescence. "As you wish my lover," he said.

At the sight of his hair dusted chest she reached out and touched him. She giggled.

"What?" he asked, placing his hand over hers.

She saw mischief dancing in the deep grey of his eyes as the moon was reflected in them. Mischief and the promise of much more. Her heart soared as her fantasies took flight.

"When I saw you for the first time after you pulled me from the harbor and you had no shirt on I was left speechless. I had never seen such a beautiful man. When you put your shirt on and your wet body caused the damp of your linen shirt to cling to you, all I wanted to do was touch you," she replied.

At the time she had thought the effect Will had had on her was because she had just had a near death experience. Now standing once more in front of him and his semi naked body, she knew it was something else.

Her words of appreciation were rewarded with a hot passionate kiss from Will. He cupped her face in his hands and their tongues began a slow dance once more.

Hattie let her hands drift to the placket of Will's trousers and began to work on the buttons.

The Hattie of a month ago would have trembled at her work, but here with Will her hands were steady. She was certain of her need for this man.

As he stepped out of his trousers and threw them onto the nearby chair her mouth went dry. In the moonlight she beheld him. He was magnificent. Every inch of him.

His shoulders were like those of a Greek statute, broad and muscular. As her gaze drifted lower, she saw more than she had ever seen before on a sculpture.

English gentleman he may be, but beneath that veneer simmered a power she longed to release.

"Before we continue may I note something? This encounter is very one sided at present. I am naked while you are still half dressed," he said.

Hattie reached for the straps of her chemise, and slowly slid it further down freeing her breasts fully to his sight. His manhood twitched and rose fully to attention. Her heart thumped loudly in her chest. This was how she had envisaged the moment of truth between a man and a woman. Mutual passion and desire.

Emboldened by his response, she pushed her chemise down over her hips and stepped out of it.

He kissed her once more and whispered. "Lay down on the bed."

She did as he asked. When Will knelt between her legs and placed butterfly kisses on the inside of her knee she shivered. He gently pushed her legs apart as he blazed a scorching trail of kisses up the inside of her leg.

When he reached the thatch of hair at the entrance to her womanhood, he pursed his lips and blew cool air onto her clitoris. When she shivered a second time, he chuckled with knowing delight.

"Close your eyes and give yourself over to me," he said.

The instant his tongue touched her, her hips bucked. He slid his hands under her hips holding them up, opening her more fully to his attentions.

"Sweet..." was all she could manage.

The torture he brought to her body had Hattie gripping the bedclothes in fisted hands. When Will slipped a thumb inside her wet heat Hattie's eyes flew open.

Gazing up at the wooden ceiling of the cabin she gave in to the ever-increasing pleasure Will inflicted upon her. Tension rose ever higher in her body. He was a master at the sexual worship of a woman's body.

She struggled to bring her mind back under control, this should not just be about her.

"What about you," she stammered.

From between her legs, she heard him mutter. "All in good time."

His tongue resumed its wicked slaving of her heat. Long skillful strokes worked around and over her sensitive bud. When the first throb of orgasm hit her, he released her legs and rose quickly over her body.

With one hard, deep thrust he filled her core, then withdrew and thrust home again. Hattie barely had time to register the change in their sexual engagement before her world fell apart in a shattering climax.

Will cupped his hand behind her head and pulled up to him, capturing her mouth. His tongue delved deep between her lips as she yielded up her mouth. He continued to ride her in an ever-increasing tempo of thrust and withdrawal. Her orgasm rolled on in waves.

"This is how it will always be," he growled.

He slowed his strokes, but even from her limited experience of sex she knew Will had not reached his climax. Withdrawing from her body, he sat back on his haunches and stared at her. She rose up on her knees and came to him.

"Tell me how you want me, how I can pleasure you," she purred.

She trailed hot kisses across his damp, sweat beaded chest. The heady taste of male rousing her once more to willingly give all that he could demand.

"On your knees, facing the wall," he replied.

As soon as she had done as instructed, Will came to her. He wrapped his arms around her body, taking both her nipples in his hands. He softly squeezed them, rolling the tight buds between his fingertips. When she whimpered, a groan escaped his lips.

He gently pushed her legs apart and thrust two fingers deep into her heat. Her body was still throbbing with pleasure from climax, but he brought forth her sexual need once more with his skilled stroking of her bud.

"Will," she said, the words a plea for him to release her from the torture.

He withdrew his fingers and her body welcomed his manhood once more. With hands gripped tightly on to her hips, he took her from behind. The position allowed a deeper penetration than before, the sound of their skin slapping against one another echoed in the quiet of the cabin.

"I want you to come a second time. I won't finish until you do," he murmured in her ear.

Even if she had been capable, Hattie could not refuse him. Will increased the tempo of his strokes, he knew exactly how to ratchet up the urgent need within her.

On and on he plundered her body until she fractured in a sobbing desperate cry.

How long after that moment it took Will to come, she wasn't certain. She was no longer in control of her body. He possessed her completely.

Her whole existence consisted of the sound of his groans and the deep pounding of his cock inside her still throbbing passage.

Her only thought when he did finally come was to be grateful that the crews' quarters were on the other side of the ship. His roar would have done a lion proud.

They slumped in a heated pile onto the bed, arms and legs entangled.

⁊⅊

Will woke several hours later. He and Hattie were still tangled together. Sometime in the night, he had managed to throw some blankets over their naked bodies. Hattie was warm. Her soft breathing told him she was lightly sleeping.

He leaned over and placed a tender kiss at the base of her neck. She stirred.

"Hello you," he murmured.

Hattie rolled over and sat up. The blankets fell, revealing her breasts. His gaze was drawn to their rose peaks. In the chill air, they quickly became hard little buds. Will felt his cock twitch. He wanted her again.

He pulled her to him and kissed her. She responded naturally to him, returning his kiss in equal tenderness and hunger.

When they eventually broke the kiss, he saw the signs of slight swelling on her bottom lip. In the heat of their passionate love making earlier, he had bitten her lip.

Don't be a rogue.

They had made love already this night, only a selfish man would ask it of an inexperienced woman to take him inside her once more so quickly. He would wait for Hattie to come to him when she desired his body once again. He lifted the blanket again and wrapped it around her.

"You don't want to get a chill my love."

Hattie reached out and touched his chest. Her fingers brushed across the fine black hair on his upper torso.

"What are those?" she asked.

He knew the question about his tattoos would eventually come. Tattoos were not something young unwed women were likely to have seen or even known about. Yet they were common among men of the upper social class in England.

In France, only the wickedly daring or those living outside the law were tempted to mark their bodies with ink. Yvette had been outraged when Will showed her the tattoo on his right shoulder, thinking somehow, she had been tricked into marrying a criminal.

The tattoo on his right shoulder was of a rearing horse with a crown overhead, standing over a cluster of three four-pointed stars. He watched Hattie's fingers as she traced the outline of the tattoo's markings.

"The Strathmore coat of arms. I got it in memory of my grandfather on my mother's side. I would have got one for my father's family, but being French my father threatened to disown me if I dared to put his family coat of arms in ink on my body," he said.

She touched the small black rose tattoo on his other shoulder.

"And this one?" she said.

Will cleared his throat. He had not mentioned his marital status until now, allowing Hattie to assume he had never been married. Informing people that he was a widower, tended to lead to awkward conversations. With Hattie, it was something he could no longer hide.

"This is for my wife. Yvette. She died."

Hattie withdrew her hand. She went to move away, but Will stopped her. Yvette was part of who he was, and Hattie needed to understand.

She would be his wife for the rest of his life, but she would have to come to terms with the fact that Yvette had held his heart first.

"What happened to her?"

He had practiced the lie of Yvette's death for so long, that at times he almost forgot the truth.

"She became ill and the doctors could not save her," he replied.

The lie was better than trying to explain how an operation in the streets outside the Great Arsenal in Paris had gone horribly wrong, resulting in the deaths of four British agents and two French royalist supporters. No one in polite society needed to hear how Yvette had been stabbed by an assassin and left to die on the side of the river Seine.

"I am so sorry."

"Thank you."

He moved to the back of the bed and sat up against the wall. He held his hand out to Hattie, smiling as she came to him. She lay back in his arms and rested her head against his chest.

There would be time enough in the future to talk of his past. To slowly reveal the truth of the life he had once led.

They sat silently together and watched out the window as the first rays of the morning sun heralded the dawn.

Chapter Fifteen

Like all good things, Hattie knew her time with Will would come to an end. She had granted herself this indulgence. Their affair had been all that she had hoped it would be, and so much more. Will was a passionate, tender, and generous lover. He had shown her pleasures beyond her imagination.

She now knew what a woman could experience with a man. If love ever did come her way, she would only ever yield her heart to another who could make her feel the way Will had done.

They were close to the end of their long journey home. The *Canis Major* was slowly making its way through the English Channel. Off the portside the English coastline was now clearly in sight. If everything went according to plan, they would be docking in London early the following morning.

Tonight, would be their last night together. One last day of living out her fantasy of being Will's woman.

Once they docked, she would go back to her old life. Back to helping the people who so desperately needed her. She had tried to put thoughts of her friends to the back of her mind, knowing there was nothing she could do until she reached London. Now as the ship drew nearer to the mouth of the River Thames, she began to wonder what she would find upon her return.

"Wool gathering again?" whispered Will.

She stirred from her musings. She and Will were lying on the bed, naked in one another's arms. A long afternoon of love making was drawing to a close.

"Just thinking of what will happen once we get back to London," she replied.

As Will placed a warm kiss on her nape, Hattie shivered. The air on board the ship had slowly been getting colder the further north they travelled.

She climbed off the bed, suddenly needing to put physical distance between them. Picking up her clothes she began to dress. She tried to ignore the huff of disappointment which came from Will as she left him. Will clambered off the bed and began to put on his clothes.

"I was hoping we could discuss that matter today, though we could easily have stayed in bed to do so," said Will.

Hattie worked on tying the ribbons on the front of her gown as a sense of foreboding slowly took hold. When Will came to her and took hold of her hands, she struggled to meet his gaze.

Don't say the words.

"It should be a simple enough matter to convince your uncle of the need for us to be wed. After we have secured his permission, we shall journey to my parent's home and inform them of our happy news. Rest assured my family will love you. My sisters will be delighted with my choice of new bride. I am certain you will become fast friends with Eve and Caroline. Francis will be like a white-haired pup, eager to do your bidding."

Her heart sank. What would Will say when he discovered her deception? That her Uncle Felix was not in London. Not only was he not in London, he was not even in England.

"I don't think we should be rushing into anything just yet," she replied.

Will growled. "I think time is of the essence. You and I have been sharing a bed for the best part of two weeks. I've lost count of the times you have given yourself to me. You may already be with child."

His words stopped her. She had not considered the risk of pregnancy. Surely it took longer than two weeks to fall pregnant. Her brother's wife had not fallen pregnant in six years of marriage.

"I don't feel pregnant. I would surely know if I was. So, as I said, we can wait," she replied.

The look on Will's face told her he was not happy with the direction the conversation was headed. He had mentioned marriage; and instead of throwing her arms around him and accepting his proposal, she was backing away from his offer and stalling for time.

Hattie picked up Will's greatcoat, deciding a turn on the deck might be the wisest thing she could do at this point.

"Where are you going? We haven't finished," he said.

She straightened her spine and met his gaze. If she did not hold fast, he would have her doing his bidding. She put the coat on and headed for the door.

Will reached out and took hold of her arm as she opened the cabin door.

"Stay. We need to resolve this. I don't understand why you are saying we must wait. It's almost as if you are saying no."

"Let me go. And I am saying no. I will not marry you Will," she replied.

She stepped out onto the deck. Will quickly followed her.

"No! What do mean no?"

Hattie pulled the greatcoat around her and kept walking. Will caught up and grabbed her firmly by the arm. She knew he did not mean to, but his grip was harder than necessary.

"Ow! You are hurting me! Let go!"

He softened his grip, but still held onto her arm. In his eyes she saw confusion and hurt.

"Come back inside the cabin," he pleaded.

The last place she wanted to be was alone with Will. He was a man not used to being told no, and therefore would do everything he could to bend her to his will.

"Let go," she ground out.

His gaze lifted from her, and settled on something over her shoulder. Hattie turned and saw a good number of the *Canis Major* crew, working on deck. They had all stopped their tasks and were watching the unfolding argument with keen interest.

Memories of the traders at the market in Gibraltar speared into her mind. Will had played the crowd and won them over. Could she do the same?

After all he had done for her Will did not deserve what was about to come. But, he had now backed her into such a tight corner that Hattie could not see any other way out.

I'm sorry.

"You cannot make me marry you! I know you only want me for my dowry. You are cruel and selfish," she cried.

A look of horror appeared on Will's face.

"Don't do this Hattie. These men are not simple market stall holders," he pleaded.

"No. No, I won't stay silent any longer. When we get to London I am going to tell my uncle exactly the sort of man that you are, you beast."

All movement on deck came to a standstill. The crew were rivetted by the unfolding drama.

Hattie pulled out of Will's grip. She staggered away toward the crew, doing her best to bring herself to tears. The first mate reached out and put a comforting arm around her.

"It's alright young miss, you won't come to harm," he said.

Will, hands clenched in tight fists, marched over. His breath was heavy and his stance ramrod straight. The master of the illusion was being beaten at his own game and he was livid.

"Gentlemen, you are being played by this young woman. Now if you would let her go, she and I can go back to our cabin and resolve this matter privately," he said.

Hattie leaned in closer to the first mate. She managed a sob for added effect.

"Mr. Saunders?"

As Will turned, Hattie caught sight of the ship's captain. The goings on out on the deck had now been brought to his attention.

'My fiancée and I are having a small disagreement. I am sorry that she has disturbed your crew and taken them from their work," explained Will.

Will was an intelligent man, and more than capable of talking himself out of any situation. Hattie also knew the captain liked him. Over the past days, she and Will had spent time with the soon to be retired old seadog. On several occasions they had taken supper in the captain's cabin.

As Will had judged the situation in the town, Hattie knew the stakes were high. She had to rise to the occasion.

"Disagreement? You wait until my uncle hears of the terrible things you have done to me. I will show him the bruises. He will see you for the wicked brute that you are, he will save me from you."

She buried her face in the shoulder of the first mate and wailed loudly.

"Help me, I beg of you!"

Two other members of the crew mustered behind the first mate's back in a clear show of solidarity.

"This is a bloody farce," said Will.

Hattie sensed the shift in the mood. Will had sworn in front of a young lady. Doubt of how much of a gentleman he was would now be in the minds of the crew. She sensed victory.

"Mr. Saunders may I suggest you and I retire to my cabin. The young lady can take refuge in your cabin until things have calmed down," said the captain.

Hattie clung tightly to the first mate. Her look of fear, quickly replaced by hope at the captain's words.

Will stared at Hattie for a good while. His jaw was set hard. Finally, he released his fingers from their tightly held fists and backed away.

"I can see that I won't get a fair hearing out here on deck."

Will followed the captain to his cabin. The first mate escorted Hattie back to her cabin.

"Will you be alright miss? he asked, opening the door.

She wiped at her face, brushing pretend tears away. She hoped he

SASHA COTTMAN

would not notice the mess that was the bedclothes, evidence of her and Will's occupation that afternoon.

"I don't know. There is still a full day before we dock in London. Who knows what lies he will tell the captain to get him on side. I fear what Mr. Saunders will do next."

"Is there anything the boys and I could do to help you?"

Hattie thought for a moment. She had regularly made deals with the market traders at Covent Garden when trying to secure food scraps for the local parish church. She knew that people were more open to helping others if they could see that they were getting something in return. The tight- fisted traders were happy to hand over rotten vegetables if their names were read out in church every Sunday, their benevolence on display for all to see.

Apart from offering herself, which was not an option under any circumstance, Hattie considered what else she had that the crew could possibly want.

"Do you have a lady waiting for you in London?" she ventured.

She had a bag full of gowns and lady's toiletries which Will had bought for her. While her gowns would not be fashionable enough for the ladies of the *haute ton*, they were still of excellent quality. Any sailor worth his salt would know he would be assured of an extra warm welcome home from his long sea voyage if he came bearing gifts.

"I have a lovely lass who will be waiting dockside for me," he replied.

Hattie smiled.

"Then I think we could be of mutual assistance to one another."

Chapter Sixteen

"Are you sure about this miss, your fiancé seems a decent enough man? He is always polite and friendly to the crew. Perhaps your fight this afternoon was just a little tiff. My missus and I have them all the time. We say things we don't mean, but we still love each other," the ship hand asked.

"Yes, I am sure. Being a gentleman in public is one of his more admirable traits, it is when he is alone with me that he is not kind. You heard him curse in front of me. I have never known those words to be spoken before I met Mr. Saunders. You finally got a glimpse of the heartless brute that he is, you can see why I must escape," replied Hattie.

Hattie stood on the side of the ship, rope tied firmly around her waist. She was not taking any chances of falling into the water. She could not wait to be off the ship and home.

A swim in the warm waters of Gibraltar harbor was one thing, taking a chance on making it ashore in the busy shipping lanes of the chilly Thames was quite another. Adding to the danger was the fact it was the dead of night.

"Well yes, he did yell at you and he seemed mighty angry," the man replied.

Will Saunders was a decent man. He had done everything he could to secure her safe passage back to England. He had not deserved the display of over dramatic tears and wailing she had put on in front of the crew earlier that day. He most certainly did not deserve to be abandoned by his lover in the middle of the night.

She had apologized to him in private, but Will rightly had refused to discuss the incident with her. When the cabin boy came later that evening bearing a bottle of wine as a peace offering Will had accepted the gift with a curt thank you.

The ship was moored a mile or so downstream of the docks. The docks were busy and piers were not always easily obtainable. The captain dropped the anchor a little after suppertime and announced they would have to wait for the morning tide before making it to a berth.

Hattie had used her time while Will was in the captain's cabin to good use. Once the crew knew she was willing to sell them her lovely possessions at deeply discounted prices, they were clambering over one another to give her their hard- earned coins. Coins she desperately needed.

She handed over the hairbrush to the cabin boy as the ship entered the mouth of the Thames.

After several glasses of the laudanum laced wine, Will fell into a deep sleep. Hattie had then broken his trust one last time and taken his greatcoat.

It would take more than a hundred mentions of her name at church on Sunday to make up for all the lies she had told him.

The sailor in the boat fell silent, his mind clearly on the lovely dress he had purchased for a handful of coins. His lady love would be well inclined to thank him properly when he made it home the next day. As for him, the matters of rich gentlemen and their ladies were not his concern.

As the row boat drew away from the ship, Hattie pulled up the collar of Will's coat and hid her face. Anyone who happened to glance over the side of the *Canis Major* at this point, would only see three crewmen going ashore and likely think nothing of it.

She could make out the lights along the river and hear the rowdy singing in the seaside taverns. A smile crept to her lips as she heard the words of a bawdy tavern tune. They were singing in English.

Once ashore, the sailors gave her hurried instructions as to how she could find her way to the west end of London. She was about to walk up a nearby dark laneway when the sailors having had second thoughts about her safety, went out into the main street and hailed a passing hack.

"Not the safest part of London for a young lady, especially one wearing an expensive fine coat and with coins in her pocket," they cautioned.

After thanking them for their kindness, she bade the two sailors farewell and gave the driver of the hack directions to her home.

Settling back against the soft leather of the seat she sighed. Hattie Wright was back in England.

She was home.

Chapter Seventeen

"What do you mean you cannot find her?" Will ground out.

He stood red faced, hands on his hips as he faced the ship's captain. It was taking every ounce of his self-restraint to keep his temper under control. The captain's visage in turn was a slightly whiter shade of pale grey. The young lady passenger had gone missing from the ship sometime during the night and the captain had no explanation.

"I sent the cabin boy to double check your cabin," the captain replied.

"After I had already checked it twice. I can assure you that my fiancée is not hiding under the bed clothes," replied Will.

It was a ludicrous statement, but in the cramped space of the cabin, it was the only place that Hattie could have been.

He raked his fingers through his hair in frustration. Where was she?

Memories of the previous night crashed through his mind. He had foolishly accepted the bottle of wine, never once thinking that Hattie would seek to drug him to sleep. The morning had brought with it the bitter aftertaste of laudanum in his mouth.

His anger at this point was not just directed at Hattie, but at himself. He had been well and truly played.

He had to give Hattie her dues. She had learned from their experience with the market crowd in Gibraltar. She knew the mind of the mob and had read the situation perfectly. The damsel in distress ruse had brought the crew very quickly on to her side.

And what had he, great spy and undercover operative done? Reasoned with her, called on the crew for manly support, no he had gone and lost his temper. He had shown himself to be the rogue she had claimed.

While he slept, Hattie had found a way to escape from the ship. When he finally woke long after the ship had docked, he knew she was gone. But how?

Will turned on his heel and headed back to the cabin. The ship was being offloaded and his travel trunk needed to be closed and secured. He would send it on to his parent's house while he remained at the dockside and tried to get to the bottom of Hattie's disappearance.

Inside the travel trunk, he finally got his first clue. As he went to close the lid, he caught sight of a small piece of folded paper wedged in one of the interior pockets. He pulled it out and read the short message written upon it.

Will,

You and I live in different worlds. Please know that I never wanted to lie to you and I will be forever in your debt. I love you with all my heart, our time together has been a dream come true, but you must let me go.

I love you

Hattie

A wave of anguish washed over him, leaving him to founder on a bitter shore. His instincts had yet again failed him when it came to Hattie.

What was it with this girl? He could not read her. Sometime during the night, Hattie had escaped the ship.

Worry creased his brow. If she had attempted to swim ashore with her possessions it would be a miracle if she was still alive. There were so many ships and boats moving up and down the river at any one time, she could have easily been towed under one of them.

He had brought her all this way, only to lose her within sight of home.

"Oh Hattie," he murmured.

The captain meanwhile made enquiries of the crew. The last person who had seen her was the cabin boy when he delivered the bottle of wine. No one else could shed light on what had become of her.

Will packed up the remainder of his things. As soon as he left the ship he would contact the Thames River police and ask them to search the waters.

If Hattie had come to grief while trying to escape the ship, he could only pray that her death had been swift.

As Will followed the crew carrying his luggage ashore he pondered what he was to do. They took his luggage to the nearby shipping office with instructions to send it on to his parent's house in Dover Street.

By rights he should have been accompanying his travel trunk, but he was in no mood for happy reunions.

Turning up the collar of his spare wool coat to keep out the early morning chill he headed down Pennington Street to the office of the Thames River Police.

The search took most of the day and it was late in the afternoon before Will finally gave up hope of finding a clue as to Hattie's fate. Hour after hour he had sat in the bow of a small police boat his gaze fixed on the dark brown waters of the Thames.

As the afternoon light began to fade, the police called a halt to the search and headed back in to shore.

"Once the tide has come in and then out again, the chances of finding a body are very dim indeed sir," said the accompanying constable.

It did not take the constable long to complete the regulation paper-work. A young woman had disappeared over the side of a ship while it was moored downstream in the river. The constable handed Will the report and Will wrote his name and parents' address at the bottom.

"If we find any pieces of her, we shall send word," said the constable.

He took the paper and placed it on the top of a dusty pile of similar looking documents. Will thanked him for the police time and effort, but not for his lack of tact.

Stepping back out into the street he stopped and looked at the long line of ships berthed at the dock. Under one of them, Hattie had more than likely met her fate.

Anguish swirled in his mind. Had he driven a desperate young woman to her death?

Groups of sailors passed him by, all headed for a nearby tavern. He was in dire need of a stiff drink. He fell in behind the sailors and followed them into the tavern.

Smoke and the raucous laughter from the crowded tavern imme-diately assaulted his senses. The tavern was not that big an establish-ment but it was packed to the gunwales with sailors, all in varying states of intoxication.

He finally managed to work his way to the bar and bought a tankard of ale. Following occupational habit, he found a corner in which to sit and quietly sip his beer.

The tavern wenches who came to offer him their company were given a coin and told to go and find friends elsewhere. He was about to tell the fourth girl in a row that he was not interested in her services when he noticed her gown.

In Gibraltar he had found Hattie suitable clothing to replace the clothes she had left behind on board the *Blade of Orion*. One dress he had taken a fancy to was green with a white lace trim. The very same dress it would appear that the young lady of nocturnal entertainment was wearing.

He pressed his boots hard into the wooden floor, working to bring his temper under control.

He pointed to the spot next to him and beckoned for her to sit down.

"That is a lovely dress young lady," he said.

She chuckled and showed a set of dark brown, misshapen teeth.

"Ain't it? My fella gave it to me when he got home from sea this morning. I am the luckiest girl in all the London Docks," she replied.

"That you are. May I ask which ship your chap sailed in on? I am a fancier of ships and would love to sail the oceans someday," he replied.

The charm offensive worked and soon Will was listening to the tale of a poor lass whose fiancé was evil and had threatened to cut off all her hair as soon as they reached land.

"And he said he would never let her see her parents again. Wot sort of fella does that to the girl he is going to marry I ask you?"

The undisguised disgust on her face had the blood boiling in Will's veins. Hattie must have spun the crew a long and lurid tale while he was sitting cooling his heels in the captain's cabin.

"And so, what happened to her?" Will asked, sliding another coin across the table.

The girl scooped it up and slipped it into her ample cleavage. Then raising her head, she met his gaze.

Will sensed she was wondering why a gentleman such as him would be interested in the story, let alone give an extra coin to hear more. Uneducated more than likely, but the eyes that studied him had the presence of intelligence.

"I happen to enjoy a good story, especially when it is told to me by such a pretty lass," he replied.

He pushed his half-finished tankard of ale across the table toward her.

To his relief she picked it up and took an eye wateringly large gulp. She burped and sniggered before wiping her mouth with the sleeve of her new dress.

"Well then, she convinced some of the lads of the crew, my man included, to row her ashore before the ship docked here. She traded all the stuff her horrible fiancé had bought her. I think everyone in the crew ended up with something. Even Eddie the cabin boy got a nice new hairbrush for his ma. While her fiancé was asleep, the crew lowered her over the side and helped her to escape."

Will took himself by surprise. His temper had returned to a near civilized state and remained there. A different set of emotions now rose to the surface and took hold. An odd mixture of relief and lust.

Lust for the chase.

Hattie had outwitted and outplayed him at every turn. Every time he thought he had gotten the measure of her, she had shown him a clean pair of heels.

She had made a fool of him. He was now hell bent on finding her. What he would do to her when he did eventually catch up with Hattie, he was not entirely certain. His body hardened, sure in the knowledge that it knew exactly what it wanted to do. Hattie was one drug he knew he would never be able to get fully out of his system.

The tavern wench sat staring at Will, a deep frown line on her brow.

"You're not going to hurt her, are you?" she asked.

Will had read at least one female right. The girl seated next to him had figured out his role in the story.

"No, I am not. I never did and never will. Believe me when I tell you every single one of us has been duped by a very clever liar."

He rose from his seat. He had what he needed. To linger any longer invited trouble from any *Canis Major* crew members who may still be in the tavern.

"You do look lovely in that dress," he said.

The girl downed the last of Will's beer and got to her feet. She stood for a moment smoothing her skirts. The dress fitted her like it had been made by a dressmaker with exactly the girl's measurements in mind. She turned and began to walk away, then stopped and turned back to Will.

"I wouldn't come here again if I were you sir. I have a gift for remembering faces and my man will know you came here looking for her."

Will nodded. He hoped his days of crawling through the under-belly of society were over.

Once outside the tavern he hailed a hack. As he climbed aboard, his parents address was almost upon his lips, but then he stopped.

How could he face his family and the expected joyful home coming? His mother would be full of questions regarding his recent travels on the continent. The tavern girl's revelations regarding the fate of Hattie had his mind in turmoil.

The reunion must wait. His parents and siblings deserved a cheerful and loquacious Will Saunders. His current mood was anything but. His emotions and instinct were locked in a battle for his attention.

There were a few things of which he was certain. One was that if Hattie had thought she had successfully slipped through his fingers she was sadly mistaken.

He also knew he needed a plan; and a good plan demanded an ally.

The path to finding Hattie and unlocking her secrets would begin at the home of the two people who understood the life of a spy as well as he did. The Earl and Countess of Shale.

"Duke Street," he instructed the driver.

Chapter Eighteen

"Do you have any idea what time it is?" asked Lord Shale. He was busily tying the sash of his dressing gown as he walked into the ground floor sitting room of the elegant mansion in Duke Street. Will noted the tussled hair and lack of footwear on his cousin's feet and frowned. He had dragged the earl from his bed.

Will looked at his pocket watch. It was almost midnight. A time when once he and Bartholomew Shale would have been in full swing stalking the streets of Paris conducting covert operations.

"Gotten old have we Bat?" he replied. Only the earl's closest friends were accorded the privilege of calling him by his old school moniker.

Bat raised an eyebrow. He knew Will well enough to immediately sense something was troubling him. Something of great importance.

"And a good evening to you too dear cousin. Can I take it from your demeanor and unshaven appearance that you did not have a pleasant journey home from the continent?"

Will snorted. It had been a long and trying day.

"Let me just say it was an interesting one."

"Then you had better tell me all about it. Have a seat," replied Bat.

Lord Shale and his wife Rosemary, had been undercover British agents working alongside Will in Paris. He and Rosemary were the only two people in Will's life who had known Yvette. Bat had been with Yvette the night she died, but a skillful poisoner had rendered him unable to save her. Lord Shale had barely escaped with his life.

Will then proceeded to tell Bat all but the very intimate moments of his time with Hattie. It was a rare thing for them to keep anything from one another. When Will was finished he sat and waited.

"And she gave you the slip. You have become soft my lad," chuckled Bat.

Will looked down at his generously filled glass of brandy. He pondered the statement for a moment before meeting Bat's enquiring gaze.

"The edges may have dulled a little I will grant you that, but this mission is far from over. Which is why your home was the first place I chose to go to once I knew Hattie was not dead. If anyone can help me get my head straight about this mess it is you," replied Will.

He set his glass down on the table, shaking his head as he did.

"I still cannot believe I let my judgement be clouded in such an appalling way."

He was disgusted with himself. The thought had been rolling around in his head all day, but to give it voice stung his stubborn pride.

Bat dismissed Will's words with a wave.

"And you are the first man in the world to allow a woman to get in the way of clear thoughts?"

His gaze moved to the doorway, in which a tall, raven haired beauty stood. Will followed his cousin's gaze.

"Rosemary." Will got to his feet.

Lady Shale gave him a warm kiss on the cheek before allowing Will to embrace her.

"Will, I'm so glad you are here. Finally, you are home. Adelaide sent word this afternoon that your luggage had arrived, but you had not. From the tone of your mother's note you had better have a very good reason for not having made it home tonight," she exclaimed.

Will grimaced.

"It wasn't the simple homecoming that I had expected, let me put it that way. I just need a night back in London to get my thoughts together before I face the family," he replied.

The clock on the mantelpiece chimed one. The cream silk dressing gown Lady Shale wore providing an added reminder that he was intruding on the earl and countess's slumber.

"My apologies, I lost track of time. I am keeping you both from your bed."

Bat rose from his chair and came to Rosemary's side. Will saw the sparkle in his cousin's eyes as he looked at his wife. A spark of envy lit in Will's mind as he watched Bat effortlessly slip an arm around her waist.

"You know anytime you need us, we are here. Always."

Beside him, Rosemary stifled a yawn.

"Come upstairs. We had the servants make up a room for you as soon as your mother's missive arrived. In the morning we can discuss things further over a decent English breakfast and come up with a plan to run your Miss Wright to ground. Sleep is what I daresay you need right now," said Bat.

"An excellent suggestion. Of course, by then my dear husband you will have debriefed me on all the pertinent details," added Rosemary.

She took hold of her husband's hand and a smile appeared on her face. Her husband would be shortly finding himself under interrogation.

"Good night Will, welcome home to England."

⁂

Upstairs in his room, William dropped down on the end of the bed and sat staring at the fire which had been lit for some time, judging by the warmth in the room. It was nice to have others thinking of his welfare once more.

He hadn't realized how big the hole of loneliness had been in his life. With Hattie's disappearance he was once more staring into the void.

He was tempted to take off his coat and climb in under the blankets, but he was still too restless. The day had forced him to face some uncomfortable truths.

He pulled the heavy counterpane off the bed and draped it around himself before taking a seat by the fire.

He closed his eyes, intent on calming his mind. Sleep however quickly took him and he slipped into a deep dream.

For so long the woman in his dreams had been Yvette, but another had recently taken her place.

Hattie.

He saw her standing looking out to sea from Europa Point. He smiled in his sleep remembering the way the sun picked out the gold highlights in her hair. Hair which kissed her shoulders and curled softly at the ends.

She turned and smiled at him, happiness evident in her face. He was her hero. He had saved her from a terrible fate and given her a new life. She held out a hand and his body felt light as he took it. Drawing her close to him he heard her whisper.

"I love you."

Will woke with a start.

He was still seated by the fireside, but the logs had burned down, leaving a golden glow of embers.

His mouth was dry and an erection strained at the buttons on his trousers. His body hungrily demanded the sexual release it had so recently rediscovered.

"You are under my skin," he whispered.

Sex was only part of the reason he wanted Hattie back in his bed. He wanted to know everything of her, possess both her mind and body. He had known her body, but she had held fast to what lay within her soul. When Hattie finally yielded up the truth she would be willing to give him her all.

"You my little minx are going to tell me everything."

And that included uttering the words that would make her his forever.

"Rest well my love, wherever you are tonight. Tomorrow you become my quarry."

Chapter Nineteen

"William!"

Will put down his satchel. The footman who had opened the door to the Saunders' family home in Dover Street moved swiftly to one side as Caroline Saunders launched herself at her older brother. She flung her arms around Will and held onto him with grim determination. He groaned as he felt the air in his lungs being squeezed out of his body.

"I missed you. Where have you been? Your trunk arrived yesterday. Mama is so very cross with you. Why didn't you come home?"

Caroline's words tumbled out, she didn't bother pausing to draw breath. Will's home coming was never going to be a quiet one. His first reception home earlier in the year had been marked with tears and long emotional hugs on all sides. When he had returned home in May it had been nearly five years since he had left England. Even his brother Francis, a young man renowned for his lack of emotional display had been in his own words a blubbering mess.

Now he was home for good.

As his father gently prised Caroline off her brother, he and Will shared a grin. Will offered his father his hand, which was promptly seized as Charles Saunders pulled his first born into his own welcoming embrace.

"So good to have you safely home *mon fils*, so good," he said.

"We were expecting you home yesterday. Mama sent notes to half of London demanding to know where you were," Caroline noted.

Will shrugged his shoulders, there was no point in going into details.

"The ship was delayed in the English Channel due to bad weather. I had a couple of errands to run after we docked, and by the time I had finished them, it was late. I stayed at Bat and Rosemary's house last night," he replied.

He felt obliged to explain the circumstances of his journey back to England fully to his father, but now was not the time. Now was the time for allowing his parents and siblings to rejoice in his return. To embrace the beginning of his new life back in London.

"Is mama out? The house is far too quiet," he asked.

He had not heard the excited squeal of his mother, which knowing Adelaide Saunders was most uncustomary.

Caroline rolled her eyes, at which her father gave her a disapproving glare.

"They are at Rosemount House paying a house call to Countess Rosemount," his father replied.

"Dearest sister, Eve has gone and got it into her muddled head that she wants to marry Freddie Rosemount. Daft idea if you ask me," said Caroline.

Eve was in love? Will paused, taken aback by this unexpected revelation. Nowhere in Eve's regular correspondence had she confided in him news of her heart. It would be disappointing to have his sister married and move out of the family home just as he returned. He had assumed that for at least the next few years he would be able to see the whole of his family whenever he visited home. Eve's pending engagement was a sharp reminder that during the years of his absence, his brother and sisters had grown to adulthood.

Eve, always thinking of her brother had obviously decided not to tell him of her future happiness. Not when she thought him still to be carrying a broken heart over the loss of Yvette.

A matter of months ago she would have been close to the truth, but things had changed in his life. A late summer visit in Paris from their cousin Lady Lucy Radley and her new husband Avery Fox had opened his eyes to the possibility of love once more.

The days spent with Hattie had made that notion now seem real. The ghost of Yvette was letting him go. Pushing him toward the happiness he knew his late wife would so earnestly wish for him.

"Well I hope he is deserving of her and makes her happy," replied Will.

Caroline raised an eyebrow. She had been all of fifteen when Will had left. In the intervening years Caroline had blossomed into a stunning beauty. Her maturity at times however lagged behind her looks. With luck he would still have time to see her grow into a sensible young woman before she too fell into the arms of love.

"I am not moving out of your old room. It's mine!" a voice bellowed.

Will looked up to see his younger brother, Francis waving at him from the top of the stairs. He hurried down to greet Will. His greeting consisted of several friendly whacks on Will's back and a bone crushing handshake.

Francis had been five feet eight inches tall to Will's six foot when Will first departed. Now at well over six feet four inches tall, Francis towered over his older brother.

Will placed a hand on the back of his neck, feigning discomfort. "Is it snowing up there?" he joked.

Francis, who possessed a shock of white hair, laughed.

"Very funny. I cannot help it if you are a short chap. You would have fitted in perfectly with all those little Frenchmen. Any wonder they never discovered who you really were."

Will chuckled. Whomever had started the rumor about Frenchmen being short in stature had never lived in Paris.

"Come now, let your brother get settled in and then you can tease him all you wish. He is not going anywhere," said Charles.

Will noted the happy pitch in his father's voice. It was good to be home and among family once more.

In his room, just down the hall from his old room, Will emptied the contents of his satchel and placed them on his dresser. As he closed the dresser drawer, his gaze settled on the wall.

The same familiar wallpaper covered the walls of the room. Red, white, and blue stripes covered most of the pattern. In between there was a stripe with a red rose and gold *fleur de lis* intertwined. It signified the union of the Scottish house of Strathmore and that of the French Alexandre.

Charles Alexandre, had changed his family name to Saunders not long after the bloodletting of *the terror* had started in his home region of the Vendee. His father, Francois, had been an early and vigorous supporter of the French Revolution. Then seeing the madness which eventually gripped his beloved nation at the hands of Robespierre during his murderous rule Francois returned to being a royalist. Following the Battle of Savenay which saw the uprising in the Vendee brutally crushed, Francois Alexandre had met his end under the blade of the guillotine.

After the violent death of his father, Charles turned his back on his country and became as English as he could. It was the English born and raised Will who eventually succumbed to the pull of Mother France and vowed to help rid her of yet another tyrant in Napoleon.

Outside in the street Will could hear the cry of the street sellers. It was odd to hear the sound of an east London accent outside the window. He was home, but forever a part of his heart would remain in Paris.

Earlier that morning he taken a stroll down Duke Street, and stopped at the nearest pie shop. The shopkeeper had given him a disapproving look when Will replied to his morning greeting with a polite *bonjour*. So, ingrained in the ways of French life, Will still often found himself thinking in his father's mother tongue.

Crossing to the window he looked down into the street. Wide and with well-maintained stone flagging, Dover Street was most unlike the tiny, narrow Parisian streets he knew so well. The houses had been so tightly packed together, a sure-footed man, or woman in

Yvette's case, could pass undetected over the roof tops. Many a time they had done just that to avoid the regular street patrols of the French army.

He was eager to see the rest of his family, sure in the knowledge that a few days at home would help to settle his mind. Bat had assured him that during that time he would make subtle enquiries as to the whereabouts of Hattie Wright.

"She let enough provable facts slip into her story, that we just need to follow the trail of breadcrumbs to find her," his cousin reassured him.

Chapter Twenty

W ill spent the rest of the day and the next settling into the family home. True to his word Francis steadfastly refused to relinquish what had once been Will's room.

"I can make him move rooms if you wish," offered Adelaide.

"He is fine where he is; possession is nine tenths of the law. It wouldn't be fair for me to come back after all this time and expect him to give up the room. Besides, I have lived as a lodger in a tiny garret, I wouldn't know what to do with such a large space," replied Will.

He gave his mother a kiss on the cheek. Adelaide reached out and took hold of his hand. She stood silently smiling at him for a good minute or so.

Will knew what she was thinking. All that mattered was that he was sleeping under his parent's roof once more. Her eldest son was home and the war with France was over.

"So, do you have plans for the day?" she asked.

Will had given Hattie sufficient time to find her way to her uncle's house. Time to enjoy the illusion of having given him the slip. This morning he intended to pay Felix Wright a visit and set Hattie straight.

"Just going to catch up with an old friend," he replied.

He hailed a hack out the front of the house, and made his way over to Argyle Street. Stepping out from the carriage, he paid the driver and with purpose headed toward number seventy-five.

Reaching the front steps, he stopped and checked that his waistcoat and jacket were straight. He had a speech carefully prepared as well as a plausible cover story to keep Hattie in her uncle's good graces. It was time to end the game and make a formal offer for Hattie's hand in marriage.

He knocked on the door. When the butler opened it, Will handed over his calling card.

"Mr. William Saunders for Mr. Felix Wright if he is at home," said Will.

The butler frowned.

"I am sorry sir, I don't understand."

A slight sinking feeling fluttered in the bottom of Will's stomach. He cleared this throat and attempted a second approach.

"This is Mr. Felix Wright's house is it not?"

"Yes sir, it is. Mr. Wright however has not been in residence for some time. He is currently attached to the British envoy in Washington, District of Columbia. That is in the United States of America," the butler replied.

Will ignored the man's attempt to show off his knowledge of world geography. He was too busy worrying about the sinking feeling which had started to make itself feel at home in the pit of his stomach.

"Oh, I do apologize. A friend gave me this address, she must have been mistaken. By the by how long has Mr. Wright been in the United States?"

The butler thought for a moment.

"Coming up for four years sir."

As the door closed, Will remained on the front steps. He was too angry to move. Hattie had lied to him even as he offered to take her home to her family.

The whole time they had been together on the boat. All through the long afternoons of passionate love making, she had been planning to make her escape. She had promised to not tell him any more lies.

"Deception by omission is still a lie, Hattie," he muttered.

For someone who claimed to be unskilled at the art of deception, Hattie was slowly revealing herself to be quite the artisan. Even Will was man enough to acknowledge that her lies were what hurt him the most.

He had shared some of his deepest secrets with her, confided the pain he felt over the loss of Yvette, yet Hattie in return had continued to live a lie. She had used him, and then betrayed him.

He gritted his teeth. He was done with being a gentleman. When he finally did run Hattie to ground, he was going to make her pay for her lies. For having so shamelessly stolen his heart.

Chapter Twenty-One

"Miss Hattie!"

The squeal of a young girl rang through the second floor of the dingy tenant house on Plumtree Street.

Annie Mayford threw herself against Hattie's skirts.

"You came back! You came back!"

Hattie wrapped her arms tightly around the youngster and let the tears fall. For weeks all she had thought of was the Mayfords, and how dire their situation would have become since her departure.

Mrs. Mayford, a middle -aged widow, struggled up from the rickety wooden bed where she spent most of her days and gave Hattie a hug.

"How are you?" asked Hattie.

Mrs. Mayford nodded slowly, the effort to speak beyond her. Her ongoing battle with the fatal disease of tuberculosis sapped her energy for all but the most vital aspects of life. She ate little; and in between violent bouts of coughing up blood, she slept.

"Are the boys here?"

Annie let go of Hattie's skirts and stepped back. Her face changed from one of happiness to one of outright anger. She held her hands fisted on her hips.

"Joshua and Baylee have become wicked since you left and joined the Belton Street gang. They are off with them right now."

Hattie and Mrs. Mayford exchanged a look of fear. The Belton Street gang were one of the most violent criminal gangs in the rookery of St. Giles. Joshua and Baylee were both terrified of the gang.

It made no sense. She could not comprehend why the two kind young lads would have joined up with such a bunch of cutthroats and villains.

The door to the small room which served as the Mayford family sitting room and kitchen opened and Joshua Mayford stepped across the threshold. He had a small sack in one hand and was dragging his brother Baylee behind him with the other.

At the sight of Hattie, Joshua stopped. Baylee crashed into his brother. The mute Baylee, made his displeasure known by lashing out at Joshua with his fist. Joshua in turn slapped his brother hard.

"Get off me you dolt!"

The uncharacteristic act of violence and harsh words took Hattie by surprise. The brothers Mayford were normally very close. It went without saying that Joshua was fiercely protective of his slow minded brother, who in turn worshipped Joshua.

"Baylee. I came back. I came to see you," said Hattie.

In the time she had known the family, she had been the only outsider Baylee had ever allowed to come near him. He trusted her. Whenever she came to visit their meagre accommodation, he welcomed her with open arms. She in return had always had an apple or two in her satchel for him.

She held out a hand to Baylee, but he shook his head. His face was contorted with rage. Tears filled his eyes. He grunted angrily at her.

Annie came over and took her brother by the hand.

"Come take off your hat and sit with me Baylee. Let me wipe your tears. Don't be mad at Miss Hattie. It's not her fault she went away."

Hattie looked back to Joshua, who was now busily emptying his sack of its contents. There were several apples, two scrawny carrots, and a lump of salted beef. It was the most food she had ever seen in the Mayford home.

"Welcome back Miss Hattie. Never thought to see you again," said Joshua.

He slid his cap off his head. His beautiful dark brown locks which Hattie had so often admired, had been shaved close to his head. His rough hair cut gave him a dangerous air. He stuffed the cap into the pocket of his dirty black woolen coat and sniffed.

"Nor I," she stammered.

Her heart was beating hard in her chest. This was not the reunion she had imagined. Life in London had not stood still in the time she was gone. She cleared her throat. She needed answers.

"Your sister tells me you and Baylee have become involved with the Belton Street gang. Is that correct? I thought you loathed them."

Joshua fixed her with a hard stare and then threw the sack into the corner nearest the door. He kicked the door shut.

"Well it's like this. Without the food you had been bringing us every day, we were going to starve. There wasn't a lot of choice in the matter. It's not as if there is a long line of fine ladies all wanting to hand over food to the likes of us. People like you are as rare as gold."

She clasped her hands together. The food problem was now solved. She was back in London and would be able to supply them once more with the food they needed. The boys could withdraw from the gang. Baylee could go back to sitting with his mother, and Joshua could care for Annie.

He read her mind.

"Don't bother telling me things can go back to the way they were. You know as well as I do that you don't just up and leave the Belton Street boys."

Hattie felt nauseous. Membership in the Belton Street gang was for life, death the only way out. She had prayed for the best, too frightened to think of the worst that could possibly greet her upon her return to the London slums. Losing two of her friends to the murderous crime gang was heartbreaking.

Joshua sighed. He put a comforting arm around Hattie's shoulder.

"It's good to see you again Hattie. Don't blame yourself. This would probably have happened even if you hadn't left. The gang has been trying to recruit us for some time now. I had to make some hard choices in order to feed my family. Joining the gang was the hardest of them all."

"Why are you and Baylee fighting? I have never heard you speak to him like that before?"

Joshua looked away, refusing to meet her eyes.

"He has to toughen up. If he doesn't he's going to die," he said.

Annie began to cry.

"They make Baylee fight. The crowd pays money to hear him grunt. The gang call him Bear, and everyone wants to fight the Bear," said Annie.

Hattie felt like she had been punched in the stomach. Hitting the water after the fall from the ship in Gibraltar had not hurt as much as Annie's shocking revelation. The Belton Street gang were using Baylee, a simpleton as a means of making money.

Joshua reached into his pocket and pulled out a handful of coins. He held them out in front of Hattie. The coins were few, but enough to cover the rent on their two squalid rooms for several weeks. No words passed between them, but he would know that she did not judge him for what he was doing. He was doing the best he could to help his family survive.

Hattie was also not foolish enough to think that her and Joshua's situations were the same. While she had been forced to sell some of her mother's precious small items since her return, she had options in her life. She could seek out her brother, or even Will Saunders to ask for their help if she so chose. Joshua Mayford had no such saviors on which to call.

"I think you should go," he said.

He put the coins back in his pocket. Hattie opened her satchel, took out the loaf of bread and the apples she had brought with her and handed them to Annie.

Without a word she left.

Chapter Twenty-Two

W ill's plans to seek out Hattie had to take second place to his family commitments. While he had managed to get his parents to hold off on a large welcome home celebration for the time being, he was still being pressured into attending social events.

A small gathering at a family friend's home presented the first opportunity he had to meet with the young man Eve had sent her marital sights upon. Frederick Rosemount, second son of Viscount Rosemount.

From across the ballroom, he spotted Frederick and Eve as they walked arm and arm in his direction. Eve's face was one of glowing happiness. She hung on every word that her young gentleman said.

"Oh dear. Prepare yourself for meeting the fabulous Freddie," muttered Charles.

Will scowled. It was unlike his father to find fault with others. It was concerning that he was not finding Eve's paramour to his liking.

"He can't be that bad," replied Will.

Frederick Rosemount strode confidently up to the two Saunders males and thrust out a hand to Will. Beside him Eve beamed with pride.

"William, well met. You must be so glad to be free of all those annoying, smelly Frenchmen."

Will laughed at the remark. There was not much else he could do. He had become immune to the many English soldiers still based in Paris who felt they needed to continually remind everyone about the outcome of the war. London was even worse. It was full of jingoistic Englishmen who did not understand the suffering and sacrifice that many thousands of the French had endured during the bloody revolution and then under Napoleon.

Freddie snorted his approval at his own joke.

Will glanced in his father's direction. Charles had forced a social grin to his face, but Will saw a sadness in his father's eyes. A new future for France had cost the family dearly. Charles would never be able to return to the land of his birth and claim his rightful inheritance.

"It's good to be back. Though it feels like I barely know this city anymore. I got lost this morning making my way to Strathmore House," he replied.

Changing the subject always seemed the best option in the face of such ignorance.

He had been hoping to find one or more of the Radley family at home, but none of his cousins had returned from the family seat in Scotland. The only member of the Duke of Strathmore's family not presently in Scotland, David Radley, was at his estate in Bedfordshire.

"So, what are your plans? Do you intend to go into business with your father and Francis, or perhaps run for parliament? My father is always going on about me taking up some form of occupation. Tiresome business. I would much rather be out with the four-in-hand club," said Freddie.

Will thought for a minute. At this stage he was not actually certain what he planned to do now he was back in England. The prospect of taking up the reins with his father had a certain appeal, but his brother Francis had shown a talent for business which Will knew he could not match. While Francis was more than capable of spending his evenings getting drunk and running amok with his friends, he also had the ability to be at work early in the morning studiously checking the shipping sheets of the goods Charles Saunders imported from South America.

Will had not previously considered a career as a politician, but his uncle Ewan Radley, the Duke of Strathmore had introduced him to various political figures during the summer and his interest had been aroused. The appeal of being in London and attending parliamentary sessions was to his liking. If Will knew one thing for certain about himself, whether it was Paris or London, he was most at home in the city.

"I plan to speak with his grace when he returns from Scotland, he mentioned a vacancy may be coming up in one of the local London seats before the year is out. I think I know enough of world events to be able to make a useful contribution in the House of Commons," he replied.

Freddie patted Eve's hand. She giggled.

"That will keep you tied down Will, old chap. Though you will need a wife before you seriously consider a career in politics. The electorate are never keen to elect bachelors to parliament, something about single men being untrustworthy. Frightfully tiresome business marriage, but I expect we shall all have to put our heads into the parson's noose at some point. A chap can't stay happy forever," said Freddie.

He tilted his head back and laughed, genuinely amused by himself. Will watched Freddie with barely concealed rage. Marriage was no laughing matter. He was not the least impressed by this young man and his cavalier attitude, especially when it came to the prospect of marrying Eve.

Will had never considered marriage to be a tiresome endeavor. He missed being married. Only when he had been with Hattie had he realized how empty his life had been.

Yvette had transformed Will from a selfish self-centered youth to the man he was now. He owed a lot to both his former and future wives.

At this moment however, his mind was more concerned about the man Eve had set her matrimonial sights upon. As Freddie and Eve moved away, Will wanted desperately to punch Freddie in the face. He turned to his father.

"I cannot for the life of me see what she sees in that spotted youth. Eve cannot be serious about him. And if she is, I can't believe you and mama would allow her to go through with it. He will only bring Eve misery," he remarked.

His father sipped at his wine. "He is from a good family. His father, Viscount Rosemount, I know personally to be a decent chap. It's the lad's first year in London without his father or older brother to keep him in check. I grant you he is running a little wild. But didn't we all at that age? We have to give him the benefit of the doubt and hope that he will come to his senses before he does anything stupid."

Will did not need his father to remind him that he had run off to France and become a spy at the same age as Frederick. He knew exactly how it was to be reckless and without a sense of his place in the world.

Eve's heart however, was an entirely different matter. He would not stand idly by while some fool tore his sister's heart to pieces. Charming and self-assured though Freddie may be, Will was not above setting him straight.

"What is mama doing about it?" pressed Will.

He knew his mother well. Adelaide Saunders would be well aware of Frederick Rosemount's shortcomings. She would not allow her daughter to throw her life away on a blackguard if Frederick transpired to be such a man. She would nail shut all the doors of the churches in London if that is what it took to keep her daughter from making a foolish choice.

"She is playing this out carefully. Eve has a will of her own and the last thing any of us need is for her to do a midnight flit to Gretna Green. I trusted your mother to raise the four of you, and you have all turned out well. I have full confidence that she will protect your sister from any harm," replied Charles.

Will was not so convinced. He knew Eve and if she was determined to throw herself at Freddie, she would do just that, parental approval or not.

Chapter Twenty-Three

"Would you like some cake Miss Hattie?" asked Mrs. Little. "Yes please," replied Hattie.

A happy smile appeared on the face of the Wright family's long-time housekeeper. A woman who had wept floods of tears when Hattie unexpectedly knocked on the back door in the early hours of the morning a few days earlier.

After Hattie had explained the circumstances surrounding her reappearance, Mr. and Mrs. Little had agreed to secretly harbor Hattie within the Wright family home. The housekeeping money which Hattie's father had left behind would keep the family butler and his wife fed for the time it was expected to lease out the house. Hattie was only one more mouth to feed.

What they were going to do once a new tenant took over the house was a matter for the future.

Hattie was busily wrapping up Will's greatcoat in paper. She was uncomfortable with the notion of holding onto such a personal item of his, and wanted to return it to him as soon as she could. Her main worry was how she could get it to him without Will being able to trace the source of the coat. She held the coat up to her face and took a deep breath.

The scent of Will still permeated the fabric around the collar. Her senses tingled at the memory of the smell of his body. Of his touch.

"It's a fine piece of tailoring that coat. It was kind of the gentleman to give it to you. Very kind indeed of him and his wife to take you in and see you returned safely back to England," Mrs. Little observed.

Hattie swallowed back a lump of guilt. Mrs. Little was someone she hated herself for lying to, but she could not bear the questions that would surely follow if either of the Littles discovered the truth. Mr. Little had been hard enough to win over when Hattie returned home.

The family butler had been all for marching three doors down to Edgar Wright's house, and informing him that his younger sister had suddenly arrived back in London without their parents. Fortunately, Mr. Little was kind hearted; and after gentle persuasion from his wife agreed to maintain the ruse for the time being.

If her luck held, Hattie would never have to explain the role that Will Saunders had played in her little adventure. He would remain her own secret savior. A love affair to remember in the dark of the night when she lay alone in her bed.

Where ever Will was now, she knew he would be thinking of her. Wondering just what had happened to the woman who had shared his bed and then refused to marry him.

Will was a man of means and that worried her. He was also no fool. He had family and powerful connections in London. If he was determined to find her, she was going to have to stay on her guard.

She had taken to leaving the house in the predawn to maintain her undercover existence. With one of her father's old coats to cover her skirts and a hat shoved down hard on her head, she looked at first glance like any other servant girl going about her early morning errands.

Every time she set foot outside the door of her home, she was wary. Will could be waiting for her. He could have discovered more of her true identity and eventually her hiding place. Her idea of having told him the real address of her Uncle Felix's house, no longer seemed so clever.

At the moment however, Will was the least of her problems. The

Belton Street gang was foremost in her mind. With Joshua and Baylee both now fully-fledged members, tragedy for the Mayford family seemed inevitable.

"Have you given any further thought to speaking to your brother?" asked Mrs. Little.

Hattie shook her head. The truth was she had thought of little else over the past few days. Too afraid to venture out into the streets of London in broad daylight in case someone recognized her, she had spent hours trying to decide upon her next course of action.

In times past, she would not have hesitated in seeking out her brother and asking for his assistance. The Wright family had once been close. Hattie had virtually lived between the two houses after Edgar and his wife Miranda had married six years earlier.

But in the year or so leading up to her family's departure to Africa matters between her father and her brother had reached a point where they were no longer on speaking terms. Hattie herself had said things to her brother she now bitterly regretted. Harsh words rejecting his way of the world and defending that of her parents. She had even branded Miranda a cold-hearted social climber. Her last words to Edgar had been to tell him she never wished to see him or his wife again.

"I am not sure of the reception I would receive," replied Hattie.

The only other option was her Uncle Felix, but America was such a long way away. The short journey from Gibraltar to England had put paid to her wild dreams of travelling across the Atlantic to seek out her kindly uncle.

For the time being she was stuck where she was, but at least it was home.

She took the cake and a cup of weak tea into her father's study and closed the door. Seated behind her father's desk, she opened the top drawer and took out a small wooden box.

Inside the box were the proceeds of the sale of some of her mother's smaller pieces of jewelry. Mr. Little had managed to get a fair price for most of them. The handful of notes and coins would see her through the next few months. Once winter came, she would need new boots and the house would need a reliable supply of wood. There was also the question of the Mayfords and what support she could afford to give them.

She sat and stared at the money for a moment.

"You really have not got a clue as to what you are going to do, have you?" she muttered.

It was impossible to make plans when her circumstances were so tenuous. At some point a new tenant would take the house; and the world would eventually discover that she was back in London.

Her choice at this moment was to sit by and wait to be discovered, or actively seek out those who would have a say in her life once her whereabouts became known.

Will and his demand for her to marry him was unacceptable. Their affair at sea had been the magical interlude she had craved. Marriage to Will would be a different prospect as far as she was concerned. No gentleman of the *ton* would allow his wife to walk the streets of St. Giles and directly minister to the poor. It was simply not done. Fund raising balls were one thing, being face to face with the inhabitants of the filthy underside of London was another.

Edgar on the other hand, was possibly the lesser of two evils. Blood bonded them. There was only one way to find out, and that was to seek him out. Tomorrow being Sunday, she knew exactly where her brother and Miranda would be in the late afternoon.

She put the money back into the box and locked it securely in her father's desk. Tomorrow she would make the trip to St. Paul's cathedral and test the waters with Edgar.

Chapter Twenty-Four

W ill turned up the collar of his coat as he neared the end of the steady climb up Ludgate Hill. He shivered. If England was this cold in mid-autumn, he wondered how he would survive until the following summer. A handful of days back in England and he was already pining for the sunny climes of Spain. Chilly as it was, he still knew he had made the right decision to come home and try to rebuild his life.

At the apex of the hill, St. Paul's cathedral dominated the skyline. He joined the milling crowd of evening worshippers as they climbed the cathedral's west front steps Reaching the top of the grey stone steps he turned and looked back. In front of him Fleet Street snaked its way downhill past the Fleet prison and market to meet up with the Strand.

In his younger years he had always enjoyed making the late afternoon trip from his family home to St. Paul's. Evensong attracted a different kind of worshipper from the normal morning services. Many a time he had spied the cream of London society rakes taking a seat in the wooden pews, knowing full well that within an hour of the service ending they would be out into the night and indulging in all manner of lecherous debauchery.

A promise however was a promise. His mother had pressed upon him the need for his attendance at church after his safe return to England. After all the pain and worry he had put her through he couldn't say no.

"Your uncle is coming to dinner this week and if he discovers you have not managed to set foot inside a house of worship since your return, we shall have to endure one of his lectures," remarked Adelaide.

Having an uncle who was the Duke of Strathmore was a benefit to a man of society. Having another uncle who was the Bishop of London added a different and more complex layer of responsibilities.

Will removed his hat and walked inside the cathedral. Once inside he stopped and looked up, taking in the magnificent dome.

"Ninety- one feet, top to floor" he whispered.

He, his brother, sisters, and their many cousins had spent untold hours in the nave of the cathedral listening to their uncle while he happily lectured them about the dimensions of the great church. The painted dome was Will's personal favorite.

Its eight scenes from the life of Saint Paul, were a masterpiece of art and architecture. Will had seen enough of Europe's great houses of worship to know that St. Paul's held its own.

"Better than Notre Dame?"

He turned and saw his uncle, Hugh Radley. Resplendent in his robes of office, the Bishop of London cut an imposing figure. Other worshippers arriving into the outer nave gave him a respectful wide berth.

"They both have their appeal. I would never be so bold as to make a judgement on which of the two is the best."

His uncle bowed his head.

"Excellent answer. God should only ever be the one to judge. Welcome home lad. I take it your mother sent you."

Will nodded. Little in the Radley and Saunders family circle got past his uncle.

"She mentioned that you and Aunt Mary are coming to dine at home later this week. It was made clear to me that a visit to church before then would be a prudent idea."

The bishop chuckled.

"Just once, I made the mistake of asking your mother's opinion of one of my sermons over the dinner table. Ever since then, she makes the whole Saunders family go to church before we visit. Your father has never let me hear the end of it."

"St. Paul's is always a wonderful place to visit, it feels like a second home to me. Besides, it's a good opportunity to stretch my legs. With mama haunting my every step, I have struggled to get more than four feet from the house this week," replied Will.

He hoped his mother's fervor would soon die down. Already concerned that it would not, he had spoken to his father about the need for him to find his own house. Family life was surprisingly over-bearing after having lived alone.

"I hope you will come and sit in the side aisles near the choir. I have reserved a seat for you. Just find an usher when you are ready to take a seat. Oh, and you must come to my private chambers after the service, I have an excellent bottle of wine I have been waiting to share with you," said the bishop.

After watching his uncle head further into the cathedral as the final preparations for the service were made, Will took the opportunity to wander around and reacquaint himself with the inner cathedral. Christopher Wren's masterpiece of architecture had always held a special place in his heart. His parents had been married here. He and all his siblings had been baptized at the altar font.

He was slowly making his way toward the choir area when he caught sight of something which stopped him dead in his tracks.

Across the other side of the nave stood Hattie.

Will froze. It would only take a slight move of her head and she would be staring right at him. He stood completely still. A body unmoving did not create interest to the eye.

An unexpected wave of relief crashed over him. While he was certain she had made it ashore alive, the proof before his eyes was precious. He was still angry with her, but to know that she was safe gladdened his heart. He would sleep more soundly tonight than he had done since their parting.

When finally, a small group of other evensong worshippers passed between them, Will was able to move to one side. With slow, measured steps he moved forward in the nave and out of her direct line of vision.

Now he was able to study her with greater ease. She was watching a young couple who were seated toward the large arch on the right side of the nave. It was also apparent that Hattie was locked in an internal battle with herself as to whether she should approach the couple or not. She took several hesitant steps forward, only to stop and retreat to where she had originally started.

Will watched in fascination as she did her odd little dance a half dozen times.

۶

Across the black and white checkered marble floor Hattie stood and stared at her brother and his wife.

Edgar and Miranda Wright cut a stylish couple in the milling throng. With her father having made his fortune in the mills of the English Midlands, Miranda had come to her marriage with a substantial dowry.

Theirs had been an unexpected love match. While their respective fathers had been haggling over dowries and social connections, Edgar had fallen head over heels in love with the merchant's daughter.

In the good times, as Hattie now called them, she and Miranda had been close. Miranda had viewed Hattie as the little sister she had never had. Hattie and her mother did all they could to help Miranda become an accepted member of the *ton*.

Tears welled in her eyes. She swallowed before taking another faltering step forward. They were so close and yet it felt like the floor of St. Paul's was several miles wide.

She clenched her fists. Trying and failing again to find her courage.

"Oh, come now. You jumped over the side of a ship. You can walk across the floor and speak to your brother," she chided herself.

The previous afternoon she had spent making a long list of all the provisions she would need to purchase for the coming winter. The situation was more precarious than her initial estimates had been. The money from the family bits and pieces she had thus far sold; coupled with any funds from the other pieces currently earmarked for sale would not last much into the winter.

She had discovered the true cost of living in London. Fire wood was expensive and so was food. With crop failures throughout England that summer, grain was in short supply.

Before setting out from her family home, Hattie had prepared a long and well thought out speech as to why her brother should assist her financially. It made sense for him to come to her aid in her hour of need. It was the right thing to do. She was his only sister. They had been close most of their lives.

And that was the point where her bravery failed.

In the days before the ship sailed for Africa, she had become increasingly desperate in her attempts to avoid the journey. She had written several letters to Edgar, but her father had intercepted them. As he threw the letters one by one into the fire, he scolded her.

"Your brother is wicked and does not care for our work. You have a duty to come to Sierra Leone and be Reverend Brown's wife. Now stop this nonsense."

That night Peter Brown had been allowed to stay at the Wright's house and he had visited Hattie in her bed. After that she had barely been left alone.

Only a single letter had made it successfully out of the house and to her brother. Mrs. Little at great risk of being dismissed from her employment, had ventured to the kitchens at Edgar's house and personally delivered the note to a footman. Hattie had waited all day and the next for a response, but nothing came.

The morning she had left with her parents and Peter for the ship, she had looked out the window of the carriage as they passed Edgar's house, desperate for any sign that he would come to save her. Even as she walked up the gangplank onto the *Blade of Orion* she had been praying for the sight of her brother's carriage. For him to fly up the gangplank, forgive her for all her past transgressions and snatch her from her fate.

Yet as the boat pulled away from the dockside, she saw only dock workers and sailors on the shore. Edgar had made his stance clear, he had washed his hands of his tiresome self-righteous sister.

The sound of the cathedral organ in St. Paul's began to fill the nave and choir chambers with music. Soon the service would begin and she would be unable to speak with them.

Hattie straightened her back and began to walk toward them. One final time, and she would do it.

At the same time Miranda shifted in her seat and Hattie caught sight of a small bundle in her sister in law's arms. Edgar looked down at the baby and smiled.

Hattie halted in her progress.

Edgar and Miranda had been married for just over six years. Six childless years. Yet here was a new born child. Her brother and sister in law had thought so little of Hattie and her parents that they had kept Miranda's pregnancy a secret. Even the birth of a precious child could not bring them to forgive Edgar's family.

Hattie slowly backed away.

The chasm between her and her brother was wider than she had ever imagined. She had turned her back on him until the moment she was in dire need. He in turn had firmly closed the door on the life he had once known with his family.

She turned and walked from the cathedral, all hope for a reconciliation gone.

❧

The thrill of the chase coursed through Will's body, but rather than dampen it down, he fed the flames.

By the time Hattie had made her hurried exit through the doors of the west front, the flames had built to a roaring inferno. Sensing he was on the edge of losing control, he slowed his breathing. Iron willed self-control took command.

He took a vacant seat a few seats over from the couple Hattie had been so intently scrutinizing before her hasty departure.

As he brought his temper under control, he cursed himself for not having been in command of his senses during the time on the boat. Fool that he was, he had allowed himself to be seduced by Hattie.

Before she had given him the slip, he had begun to plan a life with her. Long before that last afternoon he knew he was falling in love. Surprised at first, he had then grown to accept that she was his fate.

It burned deep to know that he had been nothing more than a plaything for her. To be tossed aside when he no longer served any useful purpose.

As his uncle began the Sunday evensong reading, Will glanced across at the couple in the same row. The woman was holding a young infant in her arms. Every so often the man looked down at the baby and smiled. Will felt the joy he saw in the man's face.

Will's initial plan had been to follow Hattie out the door, confront her on the steps of the cathedral and make her tell him the whole truth of who she was.

But he decided he would play the long game. Hattie had not seen him. He still had the element of surprise in his favor. With Lord Shale's man of business now investigating the family of Felix Wright, it would not be long before Hattie's whereabouts were uncovered.

In the meantime, he could go about the business of filling in some more of the gaps in her life story, starting with the young gentleman seated across the way from him at St. Paul's.

As soon as the service ended, Will got to his feet and made his way over to the young couple. His uncle would be expecting Will to join him for that glass of post evensong wine but it would be some time before the bishop changed out of his ceremonial robes. Time which Will could put to good use.

"Good evening," said Will.

The man rose from his chair and gave Will a friendly nod in reply.

"That's a fine young babe you have there. May I offer my congratulations to you and your lady wife."

He held out his hand.

"William Saunders at your service."

"Edgar Wright. And this is my wife Miranda."

By the time he caught up with his uncle a short time later, Will had several cards up his sleeve with which to play. In his hand he held one real and rather important one. The bishop's wine went down very well.

Chapter Twenty-Five

L eaving the Bishop of London's private office an hour or so later, Will decided a visit to Bat and Rosemary's house in Duke Street was in order. If anyone in London could help put the pieces of the puzzle together it was them.

"Edgar Wright?" said Bat.

He handed Will back Edgar Wright's calling card. Bat pursed his lips and Will sat silent while his cousin wracked his brains.

"The name is familiar, but I'm not entirely sure why. I can ask at White's tomorrow if you can wait."

Will raised an eyebrow.

"Not venturing to the club tonight?" he asked.

"I still visit it on occasion in the evenings, but I have other commitments and more compelling distractions these days," replied Bat.

A tap at the door preceded the arrival of Lady Shale. Rosemary entered the room carrying a baby.

She immediately captured her husband's attention. The sparkle in Bat's eyes served to remind Will of the joyful distraction that having a wife bestowed upon a man.

Bat rose from his chair by the fire and took hold of the baby.

"Come to your papa," he said.

Will watched the blissful domestic scene, feeling more discomfort that he had expected at such a warm and happy family home.

"So, have you made progress in the search for your missing lady?" asked Rosemary.

"Well she is not dead, which I would consider a major step forward. I saw her at St. Paul's not two hours ago. And while I was there I believe I met her brother," replied Will.

He handed Edgar Wright's calling card to the countess. She briefly examined it.

"I don't know him or his wife personally, but I do recall having met Miranda Wright once at a party. There was something odd about the family."

A look of recognition appeared on Rosemary's face, followed by a sly grin.

"There was a sister. I don't remember her name, but Eve would likely know it. I think she may have come out the same season as Eve did."

Her words sent a thrill rippling down Will's spine. The pieces of the puzzle were beginning to fall rapidly into place. It would not take much now to unravel the rest of the Hattie mystery.

Nothing was better than an unexpected breakthrough. The first tantalizing crack in an enemy's skillfully crafted plan always held a certain alluring promise. Once he saw the thin outline, Will would set to work weakening the facade of Hattie's story. Soon the whole structure she had built would come crashing down around her.

Then he would know the truth.

He sat back in the chair, shocked at the passion which had roared to life within him. The realization that this had little to do with running Hattie to ground; and nearly everything to do with her having rejected him, hit Will hard.

Bloody hell.

The emotions causing turmoil in his mind were nothing like what he had felt when on the hunt for French agents and English traitors. Even the taste in his mouth was not the same.

Hattie was not his prey.

"What I don't understand is what she was doing at Evensong. If Edgar is indeed her brother why didn't she speak to him? I watched her. She was beset with indecision. Time and time again she started to walk toward them, and each time she stopped herself and retreated."

Rosemary walked over to where Will sat and took a seat next to him. She took hold of his hand and gave it a gentle squeeze.

"This behavior is most unlike you Will. You saved this girl and saw her safely returned to England. Why then are you still so concerned about who she is?" she asked.

As a former spy, Lady Shale was as perceptive as Will was in reading the undercurrent in a conversation.

He looked at her, sensing that once the questions began, they would not stop until he had told them everything. He was tired of keeping everything in his life to himself.

"Because on the boat back to England, Hattie and I shared a cabin. Suffice to say events occurred during that time which demand a settlement of marriage."

Rosemary let out a low whistle. Will took her meaning as one of disapproval.

"I didn't ruin her. Her blackguard of a fiancé had already seen to that. And no, I didn't set out to seduce her either. In fact, she was the one who made the offer. I entered into the arrangement with every intention of marrying Hattie as soon as we got to London. I still do," he replied.

The room fell silent, apart from the gurgling of the baby.

Rosemary leaned over and playfully ruffled Will's hair.

"You my dearest Will are in love. It is written as plain as day on your face. We couldn't be happier. You deserve it."

Bat sagely nodded. When he and Rosemary were first married, he had fought tooth and nail not to fall in love with his wife. Will had been the one to convince him that he was fighting a losing battle. The earl had been madly in love with his wife ever since.

Will looked at his friends and softly chuckled. There was nothing else he could do.

Hattie had been so close to finally reaching out to Edgar, but at the last minute her courage had failed. Her long walk from Newport Street all the way to Ludgate Hill and back had resulted in nothing except sore feet and a long walk home in the early evening rain.

It had been the first time in nearly two years since she had been inside the cathedral. Once it had been her father's favourite place for Sunday worship, now he viewed it as an ostentatious display of ill-gotten wealth.

"They should tear all the fine buildings down and use the stone to build new homes for the poor." Hattie could count on her father making that particular remark every time they left the house and ventured near the finer homes close to Hyde Park.

Aldred Wright had argued the redistribution of wealth as one of the fundamental duties of the new church. Edgar however had not shared such radical views.

Week after week the arguments between her father and her brother had raged. Edgar had not taken up the new-found faith of his parents, preferring the traditional church. What had started out as a mere difference of opinion eventually became a gulf of differing beliefs.

Eventually Edgar and Miranda stopped making regular visits to the house, coming only on high days and some holidays. After the final exchange of harsh words, they stopped visiting altogether.

Reaching home in Newport Street, Hattie slumped despondently onto the wooden bench in the lower kitchen. She was grateful when Mr. Little did not bother to ask how things had gone on her trip to St. Paul's.

After a small supper of a cold pork pie, Hattie climbed the stairs and went to bed. She was out of ideas as to how she could resolve her current predicament.

Chapter Twenty-Six

C atching up with family members and sorting out affairs of business, put the issue of Hattie to the back of Will's agenda for several days. At night she came to him in his dreams. Memories of making love to her onboard the ship mixed with anger and pain created a strange cocktail of images which had him waking in the dead of night drenched in sweat and heavily aroused.

He consoled himself with the knowledge that when he did finally run her to ground, she would be even more surprised. At this moment, Hattie was living the false reality that she had managed to escape from Will.

"Looking forward to tonight?"

His father gave him a friendly pat on the shoulder. They were standing in the foyer of their home in Dover Street awaiting the arrival of the bishop, his wife Mary and two of their adult children.

"Yes, it was good to catch up with Uncle Hugh the other night after Evensong, I am looking forward to spending an evening with the rest of the family," he replied.

Gatherings within the Duke of Strathmore's extended family were always light hearted and at time raucous affairs. New Year's Eve

Hogmanay celebrations at Strathmore Castle in Scotland, were a time of late nights and never- ending snowball fights.

When the Radleys arrived, the Saunders were waiting to greet them.

"William! About time you got your foolish self back home to England."

His cousin James had never been one for mincing his words. The only boy in a family with two girls, he had forever been loud and boisterous. Always up for a laugh, but possessed with a generous soul. James Radley would give you his last penny if you asked for it, and his last pound if you did not.

Sitting down to dinner with his extended family members reminded Will of how much he had missed them all. Knowing that the war was over; and Europe was once again at peace was comfort for those long years away.

The only family member not appearing to be having a wonderful time was Eve. She sat quietly at the table, barely saying a word. Will worried for her. In falling in love with Frederick Rosemount, she appeared to have given her heart to a young man unable to see the true worth of her.

"Cheer up Eve," he said.

She gave him a small smile, one he suspected had taken a lot to muster. An odd realization dawned on him. He and his sister were both somewhat crossed in love. Freddie valued his gaming and hell raising friends above Eve, while Hattie could not see her way to find a good enough reason to marry Will.

A footman stopped at Will's chair and handed him a card. Will excused himself from the table, as Lord Shale entered the dining room.

"Sorry to disturb. An urgent matter which I need to discuss with Will has arisen."

Adelaide Saunders greeted her nephew.

"Bartholomew, how lovely to see you. Do come and join us. It's just a family gathering."

He shook his head.

"Sorry Aunt Adelaide, I have just dashed out into the night to give

Will some news. Rosemary and our son are waiting for me at home," he replied.

Will handed him a glass of wine and pointed toward the doorway of an adjoining room. He followed Bat into the room, closing the door behind them.

Bat opened his coat and withdrew a large leather satchel. With a flourish he handed it to an intrigued Will. A school boy grin was spread across his lips.

"My man of business has been busy following up on Felix Wright. While the trail ran cold with Felix now being based in America, he did manage to turn up something else. Or, should I say someone else. One Aldred Wright, who until he recently set sail for Africa with his wife and daughter, lived at number forty- three Newport Street."

Will frowned; an address wasn't much to get excited about. Bat pointed to the satchel.

"Number forty-three Newport Street is up for lease."

Will opened the satchel and took out a document, marked *LEASE*. His heart began to beat loudly in his chest. Adrenaline his old and trusted friend coursed through his veins.

"They were asking a little over market price for the lease, but it's a good house. I assumed you would want it, so I instructed my man to tell the agent you would take it. The agent will see you tomorrow at ten to make final arrangements. The house is yours until the Wright family returns," said Bat. He clapped his hands in boyish delight.

For Will this was a most unexpected, but welcome development. Moving into the house would effectively kill two birds with one stone.

He had held reservations about moving permanently back into his parent's house since his visit home earlier that summer. He loved his family and it was wonderful to be able to see them again, but the years had passed, and he was no longer a carefree young man. The house in Newport Street was close enough for him to see his parents and siblings on a regular basis, without having to live under the same roof as them.

He now desired privacy and his own home in which to reestablish his life. To create his own family.

Moving into Newport Street would also help move matters forward with Hattie. There was a good chance she was hiding out from society and her family within her parent's vacant house. If he took over the lease, she would be forced to come out of hiding and face him.

He was not looking forward to the difficult conversations which he knew lay ahead with her, but if they were at least able to speak to each other, face to face, they could make a start.

"Bat, you are a genius. Tell your man I owe him a tip for the work he has done."

He slapped his cousin firmly on the back. Then shook his hand for good measure.

The earl smiled. "I have already paid him a bonus of five pounds on your behalf. You can pay me next time we are at the card tables."

Chapter Twenty-Seven

✿❀✿

After his conversation with Bat, Will found it impossible to stay at the dinner party. He was itching to read the lease contract and see the house. After managing to make polite conversation for the next hour, he finally made his apologies and headed out into the night.

Out the front of the house he hailed a hack. It did not take long for him to reach Newport Street.

As the carriage drew to a halt outside number forty- three, he looked up and checked the windows. There was no light to be seen in the upper windows of the house. If Hattie was indeed hiding out in her parent's house she was being cautious and making sure not to draw attention to the house.

He paid the driver and got out. He waited in the light evening rain until the hack had disappeared around the corner, before walking up to the high stone wall which hid most of the house from the street. In the middle of the stone wall was an iron gate. He tested it and found to his annoyance that it was not locked. He would be making new arrangements regarding security as soon as he moved in.

At the gate, he peered inside the front garden. Black painted door.

Small, badly tended flower pots on either side of the front door. One pot broken.

With calculated stealth he unlatched the gate. He left it opened just enough to allow him a hasty departure if one was required. Who was to say that the Wright family did not have a large and unfriendly dog that they had left behind? Will was taking no chances.

The house would be his as of tomorrow, but he wanted to gain an understanding of where Hattie was in the house before he moved in. After tonight, she would be on her guard. Tonight, she still thought she had gotten the better of him.

He was looking forward to finally seeing her face when she discovered that he was the new tenant of her family home.

"You have some explaining to do young lady," he muttered.

It was frustrating to know that the woman he was so intent on throttling was the very same woman who inhabited his nightly dreams. Heated, lust filled dreams.

Breaking into other people's gardens and snooping about was beneath a gentleman of his birth. If anyone stopped and asked what he was up to, he had a convincing drunk act at the ready. Getting arrested or shot as a suspected burglar would not go down well with his family.

Reaching the back door, he slipped a set of skeleton keys from out of his coat pocket and set to work picking the lock. He stole inside and silently closed the door behind him.

He headed upstairs. The first thing he noticed as he crept about the upper floors of the house was the chill in the air. From the feel of it, fires had not been lit in the various rooms for many days.

He got to one door in the middle of the long hallway and stopped. A faint light could be seen under the bottom of the door. Someone was living in the house.

The temptation to open the door and step into the room was tempered by the knowledge that he had no legal right to be in the house. If Hattie was in residence, she would be well within her rights to shoot a late-night intruder.

He put his face close to the door and whispered.

"Tomorrow my love. Sleep well tonight."

The following morning Will caught up with his father before heading out to meet with the agent who was handling the lease of the Wright's house. There was no point in delaying the news that he was not going to be staying at Dover Street for much longer.

"Your brother and sisters will be disappointed, not to say anything of how your mother will take this news," remarked Charles.

Will grimaced. There was never going to be an easy way to inform his family that he was moving out of Dover Street and into his own house.

"I'm sorry father, but it has to be this way. I have lived too many years on my own, I find it difficult to live here. No offence intended," replied Will.

His father nodded.

"None taken."

As soon as he had arrived back in London, Will knew the days he could stay in his childhood home were numbered. In the years since Yvette's death he had become used to his own company. The silence of the house in Paris where he had lodged with Madame Dessaint had been a blessing. The calm quiet had allowed him to mourn his wife's death and attempt to find the inner peace he so desperately craved.

The near constant interaction with his family was confronting. At times he found himself wincing at the volume of the discussion around the breakfast table.

"I won't be far away. Bat has managed to find me a house in Newport Street. That's why he called in last night. Besides the sooner I have my own digs, the sooner I can look to securing a wife," he replied.

"I am pleased that you are ready to move on with your life. Not that you will ever forget Yvette."

It was comforting to know that he could now talk about Yvette without feeling that the blackness of grief would overwhelm him.

As for his parents, they had made no secret of the fact that they wished to see all their children settled in happy marriages. If Will remained at home, then Francis and Caroline would feel under no obligation to enter the marriage market. He owed it to them and himself to set up his own home.

There was another bonus to having his own home. By being away from Dover Street he could find out more about Eve's potential husband Freddie Rosemount without her knowledge. Saving his sister from an imprudent marriage was worth more than a year's lease on his new home.

Chapter Twenty-Eight

Hattie closed the garden gate behind her. While she made certain to do it quietly, the anger which flared in her mind made her want to do otherwise. How sorely she wished she could slam it shut.

"How hard can it be?" she muttered tersely.

She and the Littles had agreed that as part of the subterfuge of her living undetected in her family home, it was paramount that any passer-by considered the house to be unoccupied. No lights were to be seen from the upper floors at night. The single candle she used in her bedroom was always kept well away from the windows.

Returning to the house late in the evening after having helped Mrs. Mayford through a difficult day, Hattie was in no mood to deal with servants who could not be trusted to follow simple instructions.

As soon as she turned into Newport Street, she could see that the whole of the second floor of the house was flooded with light.

"It looks like a fairy palace."

Once inside she would be having stern words with Mr. and Mrs. Little. She stomped down the garden path, only to be met by Mr. Little who was waiting for her outside the door to the kitchen.

Hattie shot up her hand and pointed it skyward toward the well-lit windows.

Mr. Little sighed. "Now before you go getting all upset Miss Hattie, let me explain something," he said.

She gritted her teeth. From the worried expression on his face, she suspected Mr. Little was the bearer of bad news.

"Yes?" she replied.

"Someone's taken the house."

It took a moment or so for her to process his words. As much as she tried to accept what he had said, her mind firmly blocked it.

How could someone have taken the house? This was her home. Who had taken possession?

"Says he has the contract and paperwork all in order. Man, from your father's solicitor came with him earlier today. Told us we had to get out."

Hattie blinked. "He threw you out?" she exclaimed.

"He did, but the new tenant said we could stay. He said since Mrs. Little and I know the house so well, we could be of use to him."

Hattie swallowed down the lump of fear which had formed in her throat. As of this moment she was homeless. She suddenly felt a strong kinship to those whom she routinely rendered charitable assistance. Apart from her well-made clothes and comfortable boots she had little more than they did at this moment. What was she to do?

"Now we've had a bit of a chat this afternoon, the missus and I. We think we can keep you hidden downstairs until you can find your way to fixing things with Mr. Edgar," he said.

He stood back and let her enter the house, then following behind her closed and locked the door. Instinctively Hattie headed for the stairs which led to the upper levels, but Mr. Little reached out and took hold of her arm.

"Not that way Miss Hattie," he said.

She looked at the staircase. How many times had she climbed those stairs and never given it a second thought? Now she was a stranger in her own home.

Somewhere upstairs the rightful tenant of forty- three Newport Street, was enjoying his first night in his new home. More than likely sitting in her father's favorite chair or perhaps writing a letter at his desk. While she, the daughter of the house was now relegated to living below stairs.

With her schemes and plans now in tatters, Hattie followed Mr. Little down the servants' stairs and into the lower kitchen.

Mrs. Little was seated by the hearth, Hattie's pet cat Brutus curled up asleep in her lap. She held out her arms and Hattie came quickly to her side. Seated by the warm hearthstone, staring into the flames, she held back the tears for as long as she could. As she began to sob, Mrs. Little put a comforting hand to her back and gave her a consoling rub.

"It was always a slim chance the house would stay vacant for much longer. I'm sure you will be able to sort things out with your brother and everything will be set to right. He is a good man," she said.

If only it was that easy.

"I was a fool," muttered Hattie.

That final day in London, as the ship pulled away from the quay, she had frantically hoped for her brother to appear on the dockside, climb the gangplank and spirit her away. But her knight in shining armor had not appeared.

Edgar had a new family now, he did not need his old one.

Brutus leapt down from Mrs. Little's lap and came purring to Hattie's side. A scratch under the chin had the cat rumbling with contentment.

Hattie wiped away the last of the tears and smiled. Crying would not solve any of her problems.

Brutus' swishing tail brushed against Hattie's leg. She strolled from the kitchen, and headed for the doorway. Hattie watched her go. Mesmerized by the cat's swinging hips and tail, she felt her mood lighten.

She was safe by the warmth of the fireside and she still had options.

"It's a good thing the new master likes cats," remarked Mrs. Little.

She looked to the grey-haired family housekeeper. In all her self-pity she had quite forgotten that a stranger now lived upstairs.

"So, what is the gentleman like, have you met him?" she asked.

In her mind, she had an image of a silver bearded old man, retired to a quiet, solitary existence of reading books and going to bed early.

Mrs. Little smiled a secret smile. "We were introduced this afternoon. Well bred, polite and he is...".

Her gaze drifted to the fireplace and Hattie heard her whisper "lovely."

"Pardon?" she asked.

Mrs. Little stirred from her private thoughts.

"He is handsome," she said.

Handsome? In all the many years she had known Mrs. Little she could not recall her ever referring to a gentleman as being handsome. Something about the new tenant had obviously struck a nerve with her.

"You would say he was handsome would you not Mr. Little?" she asked her husband.

Mr. Little who appeared to be taking very little notice of the conversation mumbled an incoherent response. From where Hattie sat, she could see he was attempting to add several layers of pickles and meat to the top of a thick slice of that morning's baked bread.

"He looks a little like our middle lad. Doesn't he?" she pressed.

Mr. Little frowned and turned to his wife. "Who?"

Mrs. Little sucked air in through her teeth in frustration.

"The young gentleman who has taken the house. Mr. Smith," she replied.

Hattie's fingers stopped in the middle of cracking her knuckles. A chill she had never felt before in her life slid down her spine. She forced herself to remain calm. There were plenty of people in London called Smith, but something had her nerves suddenly on edge.

"Is that the name of the gentleman who has taken the lease on the house?" asked Hattie.

Giving up on the notion of being allowed to eat his supper in peace, Mr. Little sat his sandwich down on the plate and turned to her.

"Yes, Mr. William Smith. Lately of Paris, France. He is in the business of export and import whatever that is. And if you don't mind me saying so Miss Hattie, I would say he has more than two pennies in his pocket. His furniture arrived late this afternoon and he has some very nice pieces."

Hattie's father had spent months trying to get someone to take a lease on the house, yet here was this Mr. Smith taking up a full five-year lease only a matter of days after she had returned to London. The chances of this occurring by sheer coincidence seemed too slim to believe.

Which left her with one very large question to ponder. Who was Mr. Smith?

While her mind grappled with a thousand possibilities, her senses were screaming only one.

ð

Upstairs in the Wright family's formal drawing room Will stood and considered the arrangement of his beloved French furniture. It had cost him a small fortune to transport it from its place in storage in Paris all the way to London. He had tried to cull his collection of personal belongings before making the trip home, but he couldn't bring himself to part with a single piece. Every man had his soft spot, Will's was fine artisan furniture.

A small furry body crossed the floor of the room and stopped mid stride.

"Hello you, I take it you are Hattie's beloved Brutus," he said.

The cat gave him a brief look up and down before heading toward one of the priceless George Jacob chairs. When she reached the leg of the chair, Brutus stretched out her leg. Will saw a set of claws appear and his heart sank.

"Oh no you don't, you furry overgrown rat," he declared.

Before the cat had the opportunity to sink her claws into the plush silk covered cushions, Will had scooped Brutus up into his arms. He waved a finger in the cat's face.

"None of the Jacob chairs if you intend to keep living. You can claw that horrible brown leather couch over there if you need to attack anything. From the look of it you have already had quite a go at it over the years. Am I understood?"

The cat began to purr. Will relaxed. They had reached an accord and all would be well.

A piercing shot of pain stabbed into Will's hand. Sharp, unforgiving teeth drew blood.

"You bloody menace!" he bellowed. The cat dropped effortlessly to the floor as Will released her. She sped from the room.

Will looked down at his hand as blood seeped out of two puncture wounds. Pulling a handkerchief quickly from his jacket pocket, he wrapped it around his injured hand.

"First night in my new home and I'm assaulted by a feline fiend," he muttered.

He started for the door, intent on hunting down the cat and having it removed from the house. He headed slowly down the main staircase. Having been around cats all his childhood, he knew you got nowhere by chasing after them.

At the bottom of the stairs, he saw the tip of a tail as it disappeared down the servants' staircase and into the kitchen below. His hand was on the banister, ready to descend downstairs and face down his assailant, when voices drifted up from the kitchen. He stopped mid stride.

"Where am I going to sleep?"

His brow furrowed. It had been more days than he cared to remember since he had last heard that voice. A voice he once thought he would never hear again.

He whispered. "And hello to you too."

As the rightful tenant of the house there was nothing to stop him from marching down the stairs and confronting her. But that time was not yet right.

Soon enough he would make her understand that there were real repercussions to her behavior. That you didn't simply pen notes to people, and then walk out of their lives leaving them to deal with the remains of their shattered hearts. When he did finally confront her, Will fully intended that Hattie would beg for his forgiveness.

Hattie would prove to him that he meant something more in her life than a mere fool. That she too had been moved by the events of their time together. She could try and tell herself that her heart was set in stone against love, but she was not that accomplished a liar.

Will turned and headed back upstairs. It was time to come up with the next part of his plan.

As he stepped back into the warmth of the drawing room, he recalled Hattie's words. She was worried as to where she would be sleeping this night, which meant that until today she had been sleeping upstairs. Somewhere in this many roomed house were her things. Possessions which no doubt held the key to her secrets.

He rang the bell, summoning the Littles to come and clear away the remainder of the supper plates. His stomach was full, but his mind still required sating.

After citing fatigue after a long and tiresome day, he dismissed the servants and bade them both a goodnight. As soon as they were gone, he took a lighted candle from the table and began to search the upper floor.

Four doors along the hallway from his room, he found what he was seeking. The door of the room he had stood outside of the previous night now had a key in the lock. As soon as he opened the door to the room, he saw the tell-tale signs of habitation.

On the bed a clean, freshly pressed white linen gown was draped. A pale blue ribbon placed next to it. On the floor by the bed sat a matching pair of slippers.

Quickly entering the room, he closed the door quietly behind him. Confident that only she and the Littles would be in residence, Hattie had left the key in the door when she left earlier that morning.

"Careless girl," remarked Will.

At times he fancied she had the makings of a half decent spy. With training and time, she could have been a good agent.

He smiled. His plans now included taking his time to further her sexual education. As his wife she would be mistress of the house, but she would learn that he would always be master of their bed.

He locked the door behind him, but left the key in the lock. If Hattie did chance a visit upstairs, she would not only find the door locked, but her vision at the keyhole blocked by the key.

Will crossed the floor to the dressing table and set the candle down. He was in search of clues, anything which would reveal something of Hattie. Apart from a few simple personal items such as a hairbrush and a hand mirror there was little of note. He opened the drawers, only to discover they were all empty. The wardrobe and tall boy held but a few items of clothing and some old books. He considered the situation.

"Of course, she has few possessions here in London, the rest of her things are still on-board the ship bound for Africa," he said.

He was two steps short of the doorway when his sixth sense kicked in. Turning on his heel he headed back to the bed and dropping to his knees peered under it.

"There you are my lovely."

Under the bed, was a pink painted wooden box. Will shuffled further under the bed, finally getting his fingertips on the box, and slowing inching it toward him.

Satisfied with his efforts, he sat back on the floor and considered the box. What treasure would he find inside? He flipped the handle on the side but the lid remained shut. He spun the box around and saw the lock. True to form Hattie had locked it.

"Time for the tools of the trade," he said.

Reaching into his jacket pocket he pulled out a small knife and set to work picking the lock. In under a minute he had the box open. Page after page of half written letters filled the top of the box. He picked the first one up.

Dear William, I am so very sorry

Hattie had crossed out his name and changed it to Will, then crossed that out and made it Mr. Saunders. Repeatedly she had tried to write him a letter of apology. At the bottom of the pile on top of a large wrapped parcel was a folded and sealed letter. Will skillfully slid the knife under the seal and separated it from the paper.

He licked his lips, surprised to find that they were dry, as was the rest of his mouth. He could not remember the last time he had been this unsure of himself.

If he opened the letter and read it, then he would have crossed some invisible line. Breached her trust.

"You have taken over her home and are rummaging through her

things Mr. Saunders. I think we can forget about any moral arguments at this point," he chided himself.

He unfolded the letter.

Minutes later he folded it back up and sat eyes closed, wondering just how much it had taken for her to pen the words.

He put the letter to one side, he would reseal it before putting it back. From the bottom of the box he withdrew the brown paper parcel.

On the top in neat, clear writing was a card penned, Mr. William Saunders Esq London.

He did not need to open the soft parcel to know what lay inside. Hattie had wrapped his greatcoat intending to return it to him.

Unexpected relief trickled through his veins. He had doubted himself over her more than once, but now Hattie had finally begun to show her true colors.

Will opened the letter once more. Her apology was sincere, but it was the rest of the missing details which worried him. Not once in the letter had she mentioned her brother Edgar.

Something was holding her back from seeking help from her family. What had happened within the Wright family for her not to approach her brother for assistance?

The look on her face as she had watched Edgar and his wife at St. Paul's had been heartbreaking.

Edgar Wright had not struck Will as any sort of cad during the short time Will had spoken with him. Instead, he appeared to be a friendly, decent man who felt comfortable in making a fuss over his wife and newborn child in public.

He was the man whom Will would need to deal with when it came to the plan he had for a future with Hattie.

"First things Will. Find a way to talk to her without scaring her off. Then you can deal with the brother."

Chapter Twenty-Nine

Hattie slept in fits and starts. More than once she woke in the night and fumbled around for the candlestick she kept by her bedside. Instead she found only a solid brick wall.

Just before the dawn she woke and sat up. Squinting through sleep crusted eyes she could make out the shape of the kitchen window. The growing morning light through the window gave her a sharp reminder that she had spent the night downstairs in a makeshift cot.

"Good morning Miss Hattie," said Mrs. Little.

The family housekeeper placed a large kettle on the fireplace, while her husband stoked the stove with wood. Hattie poked a toe out from under the blankets but thought better of getting out of bed.

"What time is it?" she asked.

Mrs. Little chortled. "It's late. A little after five if you don't mind. All that cleaning and washing for Mr. Smith yesterday had me sleeping soundly. Mr. Little had to shake me something terrible to rouse me this morning."

Mr. Smith. Hattie had done her best to forget about the new master of the house, but visions of handsome dark-haired men chasing her through the streets of Gibraltar had filled her dreams.

"I was thinking. And I know you may think this rather strange, but what do you think about me pretending to be your daughter?" she ventured.

Mr. and Mrs. Little exchanged a knowing look. She was not the first to have considered the notion.

"We are not opposed to the idea if it will buy you a little time," replied Mrs. Little. Hattie knew what they really meant was that they still expected her to go and talk to Edgar.

"Thank you," replied Hattie.

The arrival of the mysterious Mr. Smith had thrown all her plans into disarray.

"Well then, you had better be up and about quickly, Mr. Smith will no doubt be looking for his breakfast within the hour," Mr. Little added with a wink.

Hattie dressed and set about helping Mrs. Little in the kitchen. She did not mind staying below stairs. The kitchen was warm and being kept busy stopped her from worrying about her situation.

A little after seven Mr. Little came downstairs, the morning news-paper tucked under his arm.

"Says he never takes breakfast earlier than just before nine. Also asked for coffee if you don't mind. Said if we didn't have any decent coffee beans, he knows an excellent shop up on Oxford Street which he could recommend. Bloody cheek. I've lived in this city all my life, I know where all the good shops are," he grumbled.

He caught sight of Hattie busily wiping down the table and sighed. Gentlemen who kept odd times was one thing, but the daughter of the family working as a housemaid was another thing entirely.

"Beg your pardon Miss Hattie, below stairs language can be a little more colorful than in your mother's sitting room.

"Oh, and Mr. Smith is due to go out later this morning, so you will be able to go upstairs and collect your things."

Relief flooded her mind. As she worked she had brooded over the question of being able to remove all evidence of her presence in the house. Upstairs in her old bedroom, her clothes and possessions lay in plain sight. Anyone who entered her bedroom would think the occupant had just stepped out for a moment. It most certainly did not look like the room of someone who had left a matter of weeks ago for a long stint in Africa.

There was also the problem of getting a hold of the box under her bed and finally sending Will's greatcoat onto him.

As soon as Mr. Smith left the house this morning, she would clear out her room.

Chapter Thirty

The sound of something falling to the floor and smashing to pieces, followed by the loud mewling of a cat roused Will from his late evening doze by the fire. He stretched his arms above his head before languidly rising from the comfort of the overstuffed chair.

"God, I hope it's that bloody awful reproduction Ming vase which is in a thousand pieces," he muttered.

Hattie's father had truly terrible taste when it came to the so called finer things in life. The vase in question was the work of someone who had little idea how to wield a fine paintbrush.

While Aldred Wright lacked good taste, he had clearly passed on intelligence to his daughter. Will had to admit to being impressed at Hattie's ability to remain undetected. For four days she had lived like a ghost downstairs in the servants' quarters. The only evidence of her presence in the house was the disappearance of her possessions from her room. Even his greatcoat had gone, which Will found a source of annoyance. His missed that coat.

Hattie would have been able to keep up her secret existence for a little while longer if it had not been for her cat. Brutus was her one true weakness. Brutus. True to her name she was about to become the cause of another's downfall.

Slipping into the hallway, Will closed the sitting room door quietly behind him. After waiting momentarily for his eyes to adjust to the dark, he began to make his way toward the staircase. Stopping just short of the top of the stairs, he leaned back against the wall and listened.

"Brutus, please come with me. I have to get this mess cleaned up," Hattie implored.

"Good luck with that," muttered Will.

His attempts to keep the feline menace from scratching up the cushions of his priceless chairs had proved fruitless. It was of some comfort to know that the actual owner of the cat fared little better when it came to controlling its behavior.

A loud cry from Hattie confirmed her lack of success.

"I can't believe you bit me!" she exclaimed.

Hidden from view at the top of the landing, Will bit down on his lip to stifle a chuckle. More than once he had tried to put the dratted animal outside only to have her sink her teeth into the soft flesh of his hand.

The clock at the bottom of the stairs chimed the hour of ten. It was late.

Deciding it was time to end the farce, Will pushed away from the wall and made his move. He began a silent, stealthy descent of the staircase.

In the front entrance of the house, Hattie was on her knees, her back to him. In her hand she held out what he surmised was a juicy piece of the leftover chicken from his supper.

"Come Brutus," she whispered. The cat merely sniffed its disapproval at the tasty offering.

The rising panic in her voice drew a fleeting moment of pity from Will. He did not envy her tenuous domestic situation.

As he drew close, he stopped. While she had not noticed his presence, Brutus most certainly had. The cat hissed and leapt out of Hattie's reach.

She whirled round. Upon seeing Will her eyes grew wide with shock.

He didn't have time to grab her, she made a surprisingly fast dash for a small door under the stairs. By the time Will reached it, she had it closed and locked behind her.

He shook the door handle roughly several times before finally kicking the door in frustration.

"Blast!"

For a moment he considered the door. It looked like the opening to a small broom cupboard, barely able to fit a body within.

After making a thorough reconnaissance of the area under the stairs, Will satisfied himself that there was no other way out for Hattie to escape. Pulling up a nearby chair, he placed it in front of the door and took a seat.

Brutus took up a post under the chair. Duplicitous creature that she was, for the moment she had obviously decided to stay loyal to her mistress.

"I can wait here all night," he said to the closed door.

Roused by the ruckus, Mr. and Mrs. Little appeared in their dressing gowns at the top of the servants' stair case.

"We have an intruder," announced Will.

They exchanged a look which Will made sure they thought he had not seen. A familiar game of cat and mouse was now under way.

"Mr. Little would you please go upstairs to the master bedroom and retrieve my pistol. It is in the top drawer of my bedside cabinet," he said.

"Sir?" replied Mr. Little.

Brutus appeared from under the chair and leapt into Will's lap. She began to purr and Will imagined that she was enjoying the spectacle which was unfolding.

"Didn't you hear me? We have an intruder. I have the blackguard hold up in the cupboard. Fetch my pistol."

When Mr. Little hesitated, Will urged him on.

"Oh, and do be careful handling the pistol. It's loaded."

The last words he said loud enough so that Hattie could hear. As Mr. Little reluctantly headed upstairs, Mrs. Little shifted uneasily on her slipper shod feet. Her hands were held together tightly in a twisted prayer. Desperation etched deep lines in her soft craggy face.

Will stroked Brutus while the cat appreciatively worked her claws into his leg. He gritted his teeth, determined to maintain his veneer of an outraged house holder.

"Do we have any rope? I should like to restrain the villain before I call for the Bow Street runners," he said.

"Why would you do that?" Mrs. Little stammered.

He knew full well it was wrong of him to use the loyal house-keeper in such a devious way, but Will was determined that Hattie understood the repercussions of what she had done. Under any other circumstances the Littles would likely be out on the street with no references the moment their employer discovered their role in Hattie's deception.

Will admired them for what they had done. They were no longer in the employ of the Wright family, and would have been well within the law to have refused to help Hattie. Not aware of Will's true identity, they had taken a huge gamble on hoping he would understand when their secret house guest was inevitably discovered.

It was now time for Hattie to repay their loyalty.

"Well the authorities will soon have the villain under lock and key. I dare say before a magistrate first thing tomorrow morning and on board a ship to the penal colony of New South Wales before the month is out. He won't be stealing from kangaroos while he is there," he smugly replied.

He banged his fist hard against the door behind him.

"You'd like a long sea voyage, now wouldn't you?" he bellowed.

Hattie to her credit remained silent, giving nothing away.

Mr. Little reappeared, pistol held limply in his hand. He handed it to Will.

"Is it really necessary, I mean couldn't we just talk her out of the cupboard?" he asked.

Will pushed Brutus off his lap and rose from the chair. He picked it up and made a great show of moving it to one side of the door. Then turning to Mr. Little, he fixed him with an enquiring stare.

"Her? Who said anything about our intruder being a woman?"

Mrs. Little put a hand to her mouth and then burst into tears.

"Oh, please don't hurt her Mr. Smith. She had nowhere else to go.

Miss Hattie is a kind soul, always doing the lord's work. She has been through so much. I beg of you show her mercy."

With perfect timing, the door to the cupboard opened and Hattie stepped out into the foyer.

"Mr. Saunders has already shown me more mercy than I deserve Mrs. Little. It was he who rescued me in Gibraltar and brought me back to England. I have no right to impose on his good graces any further," she said.

Will nodded. Saunders not Smith.

Hattie started for the front door. Will was still angry enough with her to be tempted into letting her make it to the front gate. A look at the tearful Mrs. Little promptly changed his mind.

"It's cold and it's late. I suggest you won't last too long outside wearing only a thin gown," he said.

Hattie turned.

"I shall gather up my things if you are agreeable and find some other suitable lodgings," she replied.

He was unsure as to how he should read her at this point. Will had seen Hattie turn on an acting display worthy of the stage when it suited her, but something in the way she held herself told him this was no act.

He puffed out his cheeks. He had achieved what he wanted, Hattie was out of the cupboard and her presence in the house was no longer a secret.

"No one is going anywhere," he firmly replied.

He gave Brutus a gentle nudge sideways with his foot. The cat who was nibbling on the edge of Will's house slipper give him a filthy look as it skulked away.

"Don't look at me like that you furry beast. If I do toss anyone out into the night, you are currently top of my list."

Mrs. Little whimpered. Hattie gasped. Mr. Little raised an approving eyebrow. Will saw a kindred spirit in the butler. It was comforting to know he was not the only one who viewed the cat in a less than favorable light.

People were the oddest of creatures when it came to pets. Brutus ruled the house like a medieval tyrant, but the thought of attempting to overthrow her evil reign had them all holding their collective breathes.

It was time to get to the issue at hand.

"Miss Wright, we have matters to discuss in private. Would you please retire to the sitting room upstairs?" he said.

"Which one?" replied Hattie.

The house, though not large by *ton* standards still had two separate sitting rooms on the upper levels, not to mention two formal drawing rooms.

"The one at the top of the stairs on the left. The one which used to have that horrid burnt orange and black striped rug. I shall be with you shortly, after I have had a quiet word with my employees."

Mrs. Little shot him a look of dismay at this clear breach of social protocol. An unmarried woman did not go anywhere with a gentleman not of her family. When Will held her gaze, she quickly joined her husband in staring down at the floor.

Good. About time someone acknowledged who it is that pays the bills in this house.

"It's not their fault I stayed hidden from you in the house. If anyone is to be punished, please let it be me," said Hattie.

Will pointed toward the staircase and watched as Hattie slowly made her way across the floor and up the stairs. Once or twice she stopped and looked forlornly back at the Littles.

She was so much like his sister Caroline, it was uncanny. In Hattie's defense, she went quietly. Caroline Saunders would have stopped at every step and insisted on pleading her case. Hattie finally disappeared around the corner at the top of the stairs.

"If you are listening at the top of the landing I shall know," he called after her.

A huff followed by the swish of skirts signaled Hattie's departure. He turned back to face Mr. and Mrs. Little.

"Now I understand why you did it, but that is not to say concealing Miss Wright in my house was the right thing to do."

Mrs. Little dabbed at her eyes with her sleeve.

"We are sorry for having deceived you Mr. Smith. I mean Mr. Saunders. We had hoped to find a solution to Miss Hattie's dilemma without you ever becoming aware of her presence. That said it was still wrong of us to have done so," said Mr. Little.

"But she is all alone without a friend in the world. We had to help," pleaded Mrs. Little.

They looked at one another, then reached out and held hands in a touching display of unity.

"If you wish us gone sir, we shall have our things out of the house at first light. Though where we will go after twenty years of service to the Wright family I surely do not know," said Mr. Little.

A lump welled up in Will's throat. The couple were the kind of faithful family servants who polite society would expect to be looked after by their employers in their old age. Only a heartless monster would throw them out on the street with no references.

"What? Oh, for heaven's sake! No one and I say this for the last time. No one is being thrown out of this house. Now if we can agree that you will never deceive me again, then we may all get some sleep tonight."

Before her husband had a chance to stop her, Mrs. Little had thrown her arms around Will. Her tears stained the front of his silk waistcoat.

"Thank you, sir, I knew you were made of fine mettle. You will take care of her," she sobbed.

Chapter Thirty-One

Hattie opened the door to her father's sitting room. It was full of many familiar things, yet it felt like it was no longer her father's space. He had taken only a few small precious personal items with him to Sierra Leone, but the loss of even those had changed the soul of the room.

She looked at the new gold, black, and tan Abyssinian rug which had taken the place of her father's orange and black striped one. She had to hand it to Will, he had excellent taste. The colors in the rug matched those of the six fine china plates which now hung on the wall.

She crossed to the plates. Expertly painted scenes of the ancient world adorned each plate. Her fingers itched to reach out and touch them.

"Absolutely beautiful," she whispered.

"Yes, and they cost me a pretty penny," said Will.

She turned to see him leaning nonchalantly against the door frame. How long he had been there, she had no idea. He could move like a silent wraith when the mood so took him.

"Am I permitted to ask what happened to the Littles?"

If Will had terminated their services she would never forgive herself.

"Mr. Little is in your old bedroom making up the fire and checking that the room is ready for you. Mrs. Little is downstairs in the kitchen boiling water so we can all have some of the hot chocolate I purchased earlier this morning at Fortnum and Mason. There is nothing better than a cup of cinnamon spiced Spanish chocolate after a trying evening," he replied.

Hattie began to shake uncontrollably. Tension and nerves, she had denied over the past days finally surfaced.

"I'm sorry, so sorry for everything I have done," she cried.

Will closed the door behind him and came to her side.

He put a hand to her cheek and lifted her head. Their gazes met. To her surprise she saw pain and anguish in his eyes.

"Oh Hattie," he murmured. She heard the rough desire in his voice.

He drew her into his embrace. His lips descended upon hers in a fiery caress. He was not tender or kind, but it was exactly the passionate kiss she knew he needed to give at this moment. She yielded her mouth to his, releasing her pent-up guilt into the encounter. He pulled her hard against him, and she felt the familiar hardness of his manhood. Her body screamed for sexual release with this man.

As their tongues tangled in a passionate embrace. Hattie submitted to Will's demands. Her hands gripped tightly to the sides of his waistcoat.

Finally, his lips softened in their touch. His anger was spent. Her lover from the sea returned slowly to her. His fingers slipped into her hair and gently held her.

When he withdrew his lips, he continued to hold her for a moment, placing a soft kiss on her hair. Then he released her from his embrace.

"Do you have any idea what you have put me through?" he asked.

She cast her eyes downward. The fingers of her right hand began to crack the knuckles on her left hand.

Will took hold of her hand. He knew enough of her to know her nervous tell when it surfaced. She looked up at him. He was still mad at her and she knew he had every right to be so. Yet she knew he would never do anything to hurt her. Protecting others was a fundamental part of Will Saunders.

"Why did you lie to me Hattie? Even after I had discovered your real name and we had become lovers, you still chose to lie to me. Why?" he said.

He was right in demanding the truth from her. Guilt was her constant and unwelcome companion. She had created enough of a web of lies to keep her tangled up forever.

"I didn't tell you the truth of my circumstances because I didn't trust you," she said.

Will's growl of frustration echoed in the room. Hattie winced. While she had learned to somewhat trust him, he did have a habit of making her feel small when she tried to confide in him.

"Do you realize that getting angry when I do try to tell you the truth is not the way to go about things? I would had told you a lot more about myself if you didn't behave like a wounded beast when I try to open up to you," she said.

Will shook his head. "How is it that you are able to turn this around to make it somehow my fault? You were the one who lied to the crew. You were the one who made sure I was drugged on board the boat. And you were the one who disappeared over the side of the ship the night before we docked in London, leaving me only a brief farewell note. Do you have any idea how I felt when I thought you were dead?"

Dead.

"I didn't know..."

"No and that is the problem. You don't think through these things enough Hattie before you undertake them. I spent a whole day with the Thames River police searching for your body. All the while I was trying to think of what to say to your uncle. How to explain to him how I had failed to bring you safely home."

He rubbed his hands over his face. When he took them away, she saw the lines of fatigue etched on his features.

The lightness she had felt only a moment or two ago disappeared under the weight of Will's revelations. After searching in vain for her, he had thought her dead. She had been the cause of his pain.

"Then I discover that your uncle left for the United States of America over four years ago. I tell you it took all my strength not to march up to you and wring your bloody neck when I finally saw you at St. Paul's."

"Oh," was all she could manage in reply.

"Yes oh. You have no idea what your lies have done. Do you?"

Fear began to burn in the pit of her stomach. If Will had seen her at St. Paul's cathedral what else had he seen? She silently berated herself for having made such an open appearance in public so soon after returning to London.

"One of the things which we will need to discuss is the matter of your brother Edgar. I spoke to him after the service."

"What did you say?" she stammered.

"Not a lot. I did not know who he was at first. I just noticed that you appeared more than a little interested in him and his wife. To be honest I suspected he might be a secret paramour. Someone who had been the real reason why you jumped ship. After all the lies you had told me, how was I to know that he was not another of your lovers. For all I knew you could have fled England, only to have changed your mind and tried to return to him."

"But you discovered the true connection?"

"Yes, I used my uncle's name as Bishop of London to make my introductions. It didn't take long for my connections to uncover the rest of your family history. My cousin the Earl of Shale found out about this house being available for lease. I broke in through a rear door the night before I signed the lease. I even stood outside your bedroom. And yes, once I moved in I went to your room and read all your letters."

The coincidence of Will taking the lease on the house was as Hattie suspected, no coincidence at all. She stood silent for a little while.

All the time she had thought her careful movements about town had gone undetected she had been under Will's secret gaze. She had never truly escaped him.

"Does Edgar know I am in London?" she finally asked.

Now that Will had enlightened her as to the truth of her situation, there was little point in dancing around the issue of her brother.

"Not at this particular juncture. Or if he does, he did not hear it from me. After watching you at St. Paul's and then putting two and two together, I guessed that there were serious difficulties between the pair of you. I determined to find out more about the both of you before confronting him. The last thing I would ever want to do would be to help save you from one heartless family member, to then place you under the protection of another who did not have your best interests at heart. Until I can be certain of Edgar and his motives toward you, your secret will remain safe."

And to hear your side of the story. He did not need to give voice to the notion. Hattie understood the inference. She would have to furnish Will with some very good reasons as to why he should not be putting her into the care of her older brother.

Most other men would have done so already.

He is not like other men.

A knock at the door interrupted the conversation. Mrs. Little appeared carrying a tray with two cups of hot chocolate upon it. She set it down on a small table to one side of the door.

"I brought up some ginger biscuits as well. I thought you might like them," she said.

She stood back, hands clasped gently together and fell silent. How much Mrs. Little had overhead upon her arrival Hattie was not certain, but it was apparent she was in no hurry to leave Hattie and Will alone again.

"Thank you, Mrs. Little. Miss Wright and I were just catching up on developments since last, we were together. It appears she has quite a few things to tell," he said.

Hattie and Mrs. Little looked at one another. As Will held all the cards, there was little they could do other than wait for him to decide how the rest of the evening would play out.

He picked up one of the cups of hot chocolate and handed it to Hattie.

"Please go and check that all is in order in Miss Wright's room. I am sure by the time you return, she will have finished her drink. Thank you, Mrs. Little."

After Mrs. Little took her leave, Will ushered Hattie to a chair by the fireside. Taking a seat in one of Will's new arm chairs, she felt ill at ease. She had spent many happy afternoons in this room standing beside her father's chair as she read passages of her favorite books to him. Much of her education had taken place in this very room.

Will took the chair opposite. Not only had he taken possession of the house, but now he was inexorably moving the memory of Aldred Wright to the background. Her family home was undergoing a meta-morphosis she had not anticipated.

The day before she had left the house with her parents and Peter, she had walked into every room and tried to paint a mental picture of what it looked like. She had not thought to be present in the house when the new tenant began to make changes.

"So, what did you do with my father's rug?" she asked.

Will sipped his hot chocolate and relaxed back in the chair. It was time to put aside his questions and for them to concentrate on smaller matters. Tomorrow was another day, one in which she suspected he intended to press ahead with his enquiries.

"I had it rolled up in a dust cover and placed in the attic. While I might consider your father's taste in furnishings to be very different from mine, I do not have the right to destroy his property. Rest assured Hattie that when your parents do return from Africa the house will be put to order once more," he replied.

Trust Will Saunders to be an honorable man unwilling to let anything befall her father's things.

"Somehow, I knew you would say that, though I would be prepared to turn a blind eye if you did happen to lose one or two items. I could give you a list," she offered.

If Will broke her father's collection of puzzle jugs she was certain she could see her way to forgiving him. She could even be trusted to hide the pieces. Her own mother had developed the gift for acciden-tally swiping one or two of them from the side board onto the floor.

The last two jugs her father purchased had been stored on the top shelf of a high cupboard, safely out of harm's way.

A yawn escaped her lips and Will followed suit. He set his cup down.

"It's late, I suggest we defer our discussion to the morning. Though when we do continue our discussion, there are one or two things I will ask of you Hattie," he said.

"Yes?"

"I need you to start being honest with me. I am sticking my neck out for you by allowing you to remain under my roof. Your honesty in dealing with me is a fair price to ask. You may not hold a lot of value to your reputation, but I do. I also have my own reputation and that of my family to consider. My Uncle Ewan is the Duke of Strathmore and my Uncle Hugh is the Bishop of London. They are both powerful and well- respected men. I would never wish to lose their good opinion of me."

He left her with little choice. Her agreement was already a foregone conclusion.

"And the other thing?"

"A promise that when we have managed to sort through things you reconsider my marriage proposal."

☙

After making as elegant a retreat as she could, Hattie headed to her old room. Mrs. Little soon joined her.

"Well that turned out so much better than expected. I tell you I was certain he was going to throw us all out at one point," she said.

Hattie picked up her nightgown from off the bed. It had been neatly folded. She gave a glance at Mrs. Little who was busying herself with arranging Hattie's hairbrush and mirror on the top of the dressing table.

Will's words continued to rattle around in her head. She was now at his mercy. There were no more ships for her to leap over the side of, he had her right where he wanted her.

"Nice man that Mr. Saunders. So, he is the one who rescued you in

Gibraltar. Funny how things worked out and that he was the one who took the house. I wonder what his family is like."

Mrs. Little was kind in her gentle rebuke. She had been with the family long enough for Hattie to feel terrible about lying to her. For someone who constantly protested about falsehoods and mistruths she had become far too ready to use them when she felt the need.

Mrs. Little came to her side and gently prised the gown from out of Hattie's fingers.

"It's alright my dear, I understand why you felt you couldn't tell me the truth. You are back home safely, and that is what matters. I am sure Mr. Saunders was the perfect gentleman while he brought you home."

Hattie felt her cheeks burn. If Mrs. Little had any inkling as to what she and Will had done during the long afternoons and nights on the boat, the housekeeper would be out of the house and knocking on Edgar's front door demanding an audience.

She quickly changed into her nightgown and bade Mrs. Little good night. Sitting on the edge of her bed, she pondered this unexpected turn of events. She had expected at some point to encounter Will once more. What she had not expected was for him to be living in the very same house. And for him to still be insistent on his demand for them to marry.

Placing a fingertip on her lips, she remembered the fierce way he had kissed her. Will still lusted for her. His kiss also held the promise of something else. He cared deeply about her.

When he held her in his arms, her hunger for him had stirred within once more. She longed to be naked in his bed as his skillful fingers worked their magic on her heated body. She ached for him to be deep within her once more, claiming her body as he brought her to the pinnacle of sexual pleasure.

But to have him once more as her lover, she would have to agree to his demand for them to marry. Marriage meant Will having a major say in her life, and her work. London society wives did not walk the streets of St. Giles unchaperoned and they most certainly did not spend their days cleaning churches.

As she slid beneath the warmth of the blankets, Hattie allowed her mind to drift once more to Will and the kiss they had shared. When her mind began to touch on the point of examining her feelings for him, she pushed away. Allowing her heart to give itself over to Will was folly. Heartbreak could only follow.

Chapter Thirty-Two

H attie left the house just before sunrise the following morning. It had come to the notice of the rest of the household that Will was not an early riser. Most days he would not come down for breakfast until well after nine.

"Continental hours, he calls them," Mr. Little noted.

Whatever they were, Will's desire to remain abed late each day meant Hattie had the run of the house to herself in the morning. It also meant she could slip out of the house without him asking her where she was going.

As part of her need to make amends not only with Will, but with the world, she knew the time would come when she would have to face returning to St. John's parish church. As she dressed this morning she knew that time was now.

One of the unexpected outcomes of her work at St. John's parish was her parent's acceptance of Hattie moving freely between their home and the church without an escort. This decision had been the cause of the first of many rows between her father and Edgar.

"I know these streets better than either of them," she muttered.

Rugged up against the chill of a mid-Autumn morning Hattie set out. She made good time along Long Acre Street and up Drury Lane until she reached Holborn.

When she got to Holborn she stopped on the opposite side of the street from St. John's. She had spent many days inside the simple stone church, helping London's poor and needy.

The plain watery broth she prepared in the church kitchen when she was able to source ingredients, was often the only meal the church's parishioners got.

She pushed back her shoulders, then crossed the street and climbed the steps to the front door. In a matter of minutes, she would know whether she was welcome to return or not.

Closing the door behind her, she stood in the dimly lit church and breathed in. Placing a hand over her heart, she whispered. "Home."

As expected, nothing had changed since the last time she had set foot inside the plainly decorated nave. It had only been a matter of a month or so, but it felt like half a lifetime.

There were no beautiful lead decorative windows in St. John's, only glass. The floor was a functional grey tile. The little money the parish had, was spent on charitable works. Two vases either side of the altar were the only concessions to color. Filled with red and white roses from the bequest of a deceased benefactor, they gave heart to the soul of the building.

The hacking cough which was the signature tune of Father Retribution Brown announced his arrival.

"Here I go," she whispered.

As the minister slowly made his way through the side door entrance, Hattie waited.

"Father Brown?"

He turned and screwed his eyes tight as he tried to focus on her face. His initial look of recognition, was swiftly replaced with shock.

"Hattie? Good lord child where did you come from?" he exclaimed.

He looked to one side of her. Hattie shook her head.

Her, "Only me," was met with a frown. Father Brown shuffled closer and took a hold of Hattie's hand.

"So where are your parents and Peter? Has something terrible befallen them?"

It was the question to which she had spent most of the morning constructing a suitable response.

"My parents and your nephew are likely still at sea and somewhere off the coast of West Africa. They should be in Freetown by the end of the month. I chose not to go with them," she replied.

Hattie waited. She had agreed with Will that the lies were to cease. The truth was, she was here in London and the others were not. There was not much else to say.

Father Brown's aged weathered hand squeezed hers gently. He sucked air loudly into his lungs and then began to laugh.

By the time he let go of Hattie's hand, he was well into a rough cackle. She stood watching him, dumbfounded.

It was not the reception she had been expecting. Anger perhaps, even open dismissal would not have come as a surprise, but laughter was most certainly not something she had entertained in her thoughts. She found it rather unsettling.

Retribution Brown was a man Hattie had never been able to see clearly. He was more softly spoken than his nephew, but she had never felt at ease in his company. His name had always given her reason for pause.

"I don't understand," she finally said.

Father Brown's laughter dimmed to a smile.

"That's because you have not fully accepted God's purpose for you. Though the fact that you are here, and not on your way to becoming a missionary's wife, tells me he has spoken to your heart," he replied.

Her parents were black and white when it came to their role in the church, Peter even more so. They had a calling to preach and convert, so therefore must she. Her role was well defined as far as they were concerned.

"I told that thick headed nephew of mine he had no right to force you into marrying him. He of course in his usual stubborn way would not listen. Your parents should never have encouraged him. I told your father the very same thing the week you left."

She was taken aback by his words. Someone had seen her despair and she had been blind to it. Father Brown of all people had pleaded her case. If only she had known, so much of the pain which had followed could have been avoided.

"You grew a spine Hattie Wright, and I am certain that our heavenly father had a hand in it. He needed you for the church's work here in London. Come," he said.

Hattie followed him back through the door from which he had come. Soon they were in the small stone cottage adjacent to the church.

"The lighting of the candles can wait. No one will be at prayer this early in the day," he said.

While Hattie took a seat at the kitchen table, Father Brown pulled two cups from the shelf and busied himself about the place. Once a week one of the parishioners would come to clean the house and restock the small larder, but other than that Father Brown was content to take care of himself.

"Has your brother taken you in?" he asked.

At her lowest point, Hattie knew she would never have lied to a priest. She was glad to be back on the road to being her old open book self.

"I have made other arrangements for the short-term. My brother does not know I am returned to England, but I shall seek him out when I am ready," she replied.

Father Brown handed her a cup of pale, weak tea. The tea leaves were reused many times before being thrown out onto the small kitchen garden patch at the back of the vicarage.

"I see. So, my dear. Have you come back to continue your work with me?"

"Yes please. I would love to come home," replied Hattie.

Father Brown scratched the scraggly strands of white beard on his chin. He pointed to a small wooden pail sitting in the corner. Hattie had carried that very same pail to and from the market more times that she could recall.

"Well I suggest you get to work on the measly carrots I managed to get from Covent Garden this morning. The traders are not as generous with me as they were with you. I think some of them might be angry with me for letting you go. Once you are done with them, I would be happy to hear your confession."

Hattie wiped a tear away. There was nowhere else in the world that she would rather be than seated on the broken step outside the church peeling carrots.

She would take her time with the carrots. She had a long list of sins to compile for confession.

⸎

Hattie's happy mood at being back at St. John's and receiving Father Brown's blessing lasted until she arrived back at Newport Street. Will's reaction to discovering she had ventured unaccompanied from the house was not so pleasant.

"I thought we had agreed you would be honest with me," he said.

His words while delivered in an even tone, contrasted with his right hand which was tapping loudly on the breakfast room table.

"I didn't lie to you. I simply went out without telling you. You cannot expect me to wait around the house until you rise. Half the morning would be gone," she replied.

After the unexpected joy of discovering Retribution Brown was more than happy to welcome her back into the fold, Hattie refused to allow Will's bad temper to get the better of her. He was welcome to be as angry as he liked.

It was not as if it was the first time she had made the trek across to Holborn on her own. And it wouldn't be the last if she had any say in the matter.

The thought did however give her pause. She pulled a chair out and took a seat at the table, unwilling to argue her case like a recalcitrant child made to stand before its displeased parent.

"I am sorry you were not aware of the arrangement which existed in this house before you took possession. I regularly make my way on foot to St. John's and St. Giles," she explained.

"Unaccompanied?" he replied.

And there it was, the reason for his wrath. He feared for her safety.

As she wracked her brain for a suitable response, one which would not further invite his ire, Hattie observed Will. It was intriguing to watch a man such as Will work to control his emotions.

It was clear he did not enjoy his display of bad temper. She wondered if he felt ashamed of his apparent inability to control that part of himself. He was most certainly a man who liked to be in complete control of any given situation.

The tapping on the table ceased.

"I am not at all pleased with the notion of you wandering the streets of this city alone, especially when your care is my responsibility," he added.

His voice was as calm as before, but she caught the hint of anger still simmering just below the surface.

"What would you have me do? I can't drag either of the Littles from their work about the house," she replied.

"I could hire you a maid."

Hattie's hands met tightly together beneath the table. She cracked the first knuckle.

"You know that is bad for your fingers," said Will.

A rush of heat filled her cheeks. How many times had her mother instructed her not to crack her knuckles?

"I don't know, I haven't observed any particular problem which may be caused by it. I have tried not to, but it is as you have already noted, a nervous habit of mine," she replied.

What Will didn't know, to Hattie's secret pleasure, was that cracking her knuckles was also something she did when she was happy.

If she had a maid in tow, there was a good chance she would be recognized. Questions would then be asked. It would not be long before the scandalous truth of the domestic situation at forty-three Newport Street became public knowledge.

The Bishop of London's widowed nephew living with an unmarried gentle society woman under his roof would be the talk of the *ton*. Worst of all her brother would find out and then there would be the devil to pay. Will would be able to pressure Edgar into accepting his offer to marry Hattie. She would not stand a chance of saying otherwise.

"I need to be able to continue my work. It is the reason I came back. A maid will make things difficult for me in the rookery. It will make me target."

Her reply was slow and measured. She was not foolish enough to try and tempt the protective beast that lived within Will. She had to address her message to the other man that he was, the man who had a secret past. One she knew in her heart included living with danger.

That man would understand the need for her to move unseen among the streets of St. Giles. A maid would only bring unwelcome attention from the villains who also lived within the rookery.

He resumed strumming his fingers on the table. Hattie remained silent.

"I am not the least bit comfortable with this situation, but until I can convince you that this is not the life you should be living, I am prepared to go along with it. But, I reserve the right to change that decision if I feel that either your body or your reputation is under threat. Are we agreed?" he said.

Hattie nodded. "Agreed."

She had been prepared to threaten to move to the vicarage at St. John's. Will however, was not a man who took kindly to threats. She had won this round of the battle, and she knew not to push her luck.

Chapter Thirty-Three

Will woke with a start. He had been reading a book in his study after supper and had dozed off.

His ear was ringing. If a platoon of Scottish pipers had been playing in the room it could not have been louder.

Something was terribly wrong.

Some people were gifted with premonitions that warned them of danger, for Will it was his left ear. Whenever someone he cared about was close to danger a sudden high-pitched ringing would begin.

He had thought as a young man that he was going mad when it first began to happen. Heading home from a late afternoon stroll in the park with his sisters, the noise had filled his head. He stopped, shaking his head in a vain attempt to drive the maddening sound away.

His sisters Caroline and Eve had continued walking along the street, oblivious to his absence. They had gone no more than five yards ahead of him, when out of a nearby lane, a daring food-pad had emerged and attempted to violently relieve Caroline of her reticule. The would-be thief had received several swift thumps to the head from Will for his trouble and been handed over to the authorities.

It was only when the ringing happened a second time that Will began to see a possible link. Over the years he had learned not to ignore the obvious message from the gods.

"But who?" he said.

He pulled out his pocket watch from his waistcoat. It was after the hour of eleven. Who did he know that could be out on the streets of London at this ungodly hour and finding themselves in mortal danger?

A cold chill crossed his heart.

Hattie.

She was of the habit of leaving the house early and then returning late. He had not seen her since the previous night.

Opening the top drawer of his desk he withdrew his trusty cudgel and pistol. He checked the pistol. It was loaded.

In his left hand he held the thick cudgel, his weapon of choice for dealing with the vile scum who preyed on the innocent.

It had a comforting heaviness about it and fitted his grip perfectly. From the years he had walked the dark streets of Paris, he knew it would allow him to hold off most assailants. Those who offered a fight with a knife or bare fists were no match for such a deftly wielded blunt weapon.

Reaching the bottom of the stairs he found Mr. Little in the foyer.

"Has Miss Hattie returned home this evening?" he asked.

"No Mr. Saunders. She did say she would be late tonight. She was going to see her friends, the Mayford family after she finished at St. John's. Mrs. Mayford is slowly dying from the consumption. Hattie has been very worried about her," replied Mr. Little.

"Do you have an address?"

The butler shook his head. "No, just Plumtree Street."

Seeing Mrs. Little approaching up from the lower kitchen stairs, Will stifled the curse he was about to utter. Hattie could be anywhere in the filthy maze of overcrowded houses in Plumtree Street. It would be near impossible to find her if anything had happened.

He had just put on his greatcoat and was heading for the front door, when Mrs. Little stopped him.

"Oh, thank god," she huffed, reaching the top of the stairs.

Behind her trailed a young man, no more than sixteen. He was dressed in filthy clothes. Will shifted the cudgel in his hand, ready to use it if necessary.

"This is Joshua Mayford. He is a friend of Miss Hattie. She is in the garden."

Will raced for the stairs. The others followed close behind.

"Over there," said Joshua, as they stepped out into the garden.

As his eyes became accustomed to the dark, Will was able to see a shape leaning doubled over against the high brick wall at the back of the garden. When Mr. Little arrived holding up a lit lantern Will caught his first look at Hattie.

Her face was a bloodied mess.

He stood for an instant, rooted to the spot. Memories and images of that fateful night in Paris with Yvette crashed through his mind. He reached out a hand, desperate to touch the ghost which consumed his vision.

"Hattie?" he stammered, as the spell broke.

"Yes, it's me. Or at least what is left of me," she replied through gritted teeth.

Will raced to her side and after slipping two strong hands under her arms tried to help her to stand upright.

"Ow, ow. Let go you are hurting me!" she cried.

"Where does it hurt?" he asked.

Hattie gasped for air.

"Everywhere. I think he may have broken some of my ribs."

She took hold of Will's hand and with great effort managed to finally pull herself away from the wall. They walked toward the house, stopping every few feet while Hattie got her breath back.

Joshua followed behind.

Once inside Will gently sat Hattie down on the steps which led up to the ground floor of the house. Mrs. Little went into the kitchen and came back with fresh rags and a bowl of warm water. Mr. Little was sent out to locate and bring back the Saunders' family doctor.

Will took one of the clean cloths and wiped the blood from Hattie's face. She winced when he got to the source of the blood, a nasty cut high on her forehead. From the look of it, a blade had cut cleanly across her head. The wound would require stitches.

"Hold this firmly to the cut on her head," he ordered Mrs. Little.

He turned to the lad who had brought Hattie home and summoned him over.

"What happened?" he asked.

Joshua looked at Hattie, but she was too busy trying to breath to give him any answers.

"The Belton Street Gang. They don't like people who try to help in the rookery. Miss Hattie stood up to Tom, my boss, tonight and he beat her. It was supposed to teach her a lesson about coming onto his patch without his permission," replied Joshua.

Will fixed his gaze hard on Joshua.

"Your boss?"

Joshua took a step back. His shoulders slumped. Will thought the boy close to tears as he watched Mrs. Little change the blood- soaked cloth on Hattie's forehead.

"I have a sick ma, and a family to look after sir. When Miss Hattie left for Africa the gang were the only people who offered to help us. I had no choice."

"It's not Joshua's fault," said Hattie.

Will held his temper and his tongue. Now was not the time to reprimand Hattie for having been so stupid as to have gotten into a fight with a criminal gang. He would wait until after her face had been stitched and the doctor had seen to her other injuries before taking her to task.

⁂

"The situation is untenable."

Hattie opened her eyes and turned her head in the direction of the voice. As her eyes gained focus, her gaze settled on the figure seated in a chair by the door.

"Will?" she said, in a voice still full of sleep.

He rose from the chair, but as he did another figure in the room stirred and caught her attention.

Seated by the fireside Mrs. Little yawned and stretched. Seeing that Hattie was now awake, she hurried to her bedside.

"How are you my sweet girl? We were so worried when Joshua brought you in last night. I must confess when I first saw him, I feared the worst."

Hattie attempted to sit upright in bed, but a stab of sharp pain in her left side, quickly made her think otherwise. Placing a hand to her chest, she felt the bulk of bandages which were wrapped around her ribs. She lay back on the pile of pillows.

"The doctor says you have bruised at least two, possibly three ribs. It will take a few days for the swelling to go down before we know if any of them are broken. To be honest, I have never found the broken ones to be that big of a problem, it's the severely bruised ones which always take the wind out of me," said Will.

"Oh," Hattie replied, remembering the events of the previous evening.

Things at the Mayford home had escalated quickly. One minute she was helping to give Mrs. Mayford a bed bath, the next she was facing the angry boss of the Belton Street gang.

Members of the gang had accompanied Joshua and Baylee home; and decided that watching the invalid Mrs. Mayford while she was semi naked was good sport. When Hattie asked them to respect Mrs. Mayford's privacy she quickly found her entire field of vision taken up with the sight of a ruddy face and a mouth filled with broken teeth. The Belton Street gang boss screamed a tirade of abuse at her before setting upon Hattie with his fists and heavy boots.

"I was annoyed that he felt he and his thugs could treat Mrs. Mayford with such little regard for her dignity. What I didn't realize until it was too late was that I had openly challenged his authority."

Fists had rained down on her until she was finally knocked unconscious and left on the floor. With the sport of beating a defenseless woman over, the gang soon tired of the Mayford's house and left.

When Hattie regained consciousness she was genuinely surprised to discover she had survived the attack.

"Joshua then helped me to make it back here. It took us quite some time because I kept passing out."

Mrs. Little busied herself about the room, adding more wood to the fire and smoothing down the bed covers. After looking around for any other minor task of which she could occupy her time, she came and stood near to Will.

"I think Mr. Saunders is right Miss Hattie. You cannot go on like this, something even more terrible than last night is likely to befall you without the protection of your family. There are others in this world who do not appreciate your fine efforts," she said.

Will nodded, in obvious agreement.

Hattie closed her eyes and wished them both gone from the room. The pain of her injuries now seeped into her bones. She ached all over.

When a rustle of skirts signaled Mrs. Little's departure Hattie slyly opened one eye.

"No such luck. I'm still here," said Will.

He pulled up a chair and took a seat next to the bed.

"I want you to listen to me. To put your stubborn pride to one side for a moment and think upon your current situation."

Considering the pain, she was in, coupled with the heavy bandages, Hattie had little choice other than to lie back and listen to him. She lifted her fingers from the bed clothes in silent acceptance.

"Good," he said.

Will rummaged around in his jacket pocket, and pulled out a piece of folded paper.

"I made a list while you were sleeping."

Hattie groaned in a mixture of pain and undisguised disgust. Will waved her protests away.

"First thing. I will contact your brother. That is non-negotiable. By living under the same roof unchaperoned we have done enough to cause a major scandal."

Hattie frowned. She cared little for society, and doubted they gave a tinker's cuss about her and what she did. Will snorted.

"You may not care about your own reputation, but I have one to maintain. Lord knows the damage it would do to my chances of securing a seat in parliament if news of this scandalous domestic arrangement ever became public."

"And the rest of your list?" she replied.

Whatever else he had planned, she doubted it could be worse than having to deal with Edgar.

Will screwed the piece of paper up into a tight ball and tossed it into the fireplace.

"Actually, that was my list. I reason that once your brother is made aware of your presence in London, whatever other plans I may have had for you will be overruled by him. From that point on I shall have to negotiate with Edgar," he said.

Hot tears formed in her eyes. An encounter with her brother was eventually bound to happen, but until now she had been the one to dictate the time and place. Ever controlling Will, had decided to take that decision out of her hands.

"Do we have to involve my brother? Couldn't I just go away somewhere and send you a note letting you know of my safe arrival?" she offered.

Will cleared his throat.

"I shall need more than a less than subtle suggestion of leave well enough alone to dissuade me from talking to Edgar. A solid and truthful reason would perhaps assist in your cause."

Hope flared.

If she did tell Will the truth of her family schism, he may be convinced of her need to find another solution to their problem. To her mind at least, the current arrangements were more than satisfactory.

Will was the perfect tenant. He kept a well-run house. The larder was always full of food. And apart from his ongoing disagreement with her cat, Brutus, domestic harmony reigned. She was all for the status quo.

"Alright, I will tell you what happened between Edgar and myself. Once you have heard me out, you may be more inclined to consider helping me find another solution."

She made a few adjustments of the pillows and then took her time to get as comfortable as her injuries would allow. Will meanwhile sat silent. Waiting.

Hattie looked into his eyes. They were warm, welcoming pools which beckoned her to let go and fall into them. He gave her an encouraging smile.

For ever after she would mark this moment as the exact time in her life when she knew with her whole being that she was in love with Will. Small flickers of emotion had been stirring from that first day at the market in Gibraltar. On the boat she had fought tirelessly not to fall in love with him. But as she looked at Will everything she felt for him coalesced into something powerful. Love was no longer a concept, but an undeniable reality.

She yearned for him to take her in his arms like he did that day and kiss her once more.

Will sat forward in the chair, hands gently clasped together. Outside, the first light of day was breaking. Will was traditionally not an early riser, so she knew he would not have any appointments until later that day. He acted like he had all the time in the world to listen to her, and she was grateful.

He was allowing her to take the reins. She could set the pace of their journey to the truth. She welcomed his trust, knowing it was hard won after all she had said and done to him.

"It's a long story," she offered.

"I'm not going anywhere and neither are you," he replied.

She started to laugh at the ridiculousness of the situation, but her badly bruised ribs swiftly put an end to her mirth. She wondered if she would ever feel whole again.

There was nothing else to do but tell him the truth and hope that he would understand.

❧

"When my parents first became followers of Reverend Retribution Brown, Edgar and I were shocked. We both thought it a temporary fad. Another one of Papa's long list of fleeting fancies," she said.

Will had seen enough of the many collections of objects, papers and furniture dotted throughout the house to understand what Hattie meant. Aldred Wright it was clear, was possessed of the very English trait of eccentricity. Why else would anyone want a collection of ceramic eyes.

"It was odd that Mama went to the church meetings with him. She had never been one for more than a dusting of religion on a Sunday morning," she said.

Will nodded. For many, including his own mother, Sunday mass was an opportunity to meet with friends and share glad tidings. Worship was simply a part of the tapestry of their lives.

The conversation was interrupted at this point by the return of Mrs. Little bearing a tray with a teapot and two cups. She sat them down on the bedside table.

"Would you like some breakfast my dear?" she asked Hattie.

It mattered little that Will was the master of the house and her employer, Mrs. Little's loyalties clearly lay with Hattie.

"No thank you, but I am sure Mr. Saunders must be hungry," replied Hattie.

"Oh, I know he will be, his breakfast is already baking in the oven," said Mrs. Little. She gave Will a happy smile.

Will's already good opinion of the housekeeper lifted. Perhaps there was hope for him to become master of his own home.

After Mrs. Little left, he leaned over and poured a cup of hot tea from the pot on the bedside table. He offered it to Hattie, but she waved it away.

"My stomach is still not the best," she replied.

"That would be the laudanum we had to give you in the early hours. It was the only way the doctor could get you to stay still long enough to stitch your face. For an invalid you certainly put up a good fight. He was most displeased when you attempted to elbow him in the nose."

He sipped the tea, reminding himself to speak to Mr. Little about finding a decent supplier of coffee beans. Making the journey to the coffee house in Oxford Street each day just to get a palatable cup of coffee was a chore. Tea was a poor substitute for the silken black of South American coffee beans.

"You were saying about your mother," said Will.

He needed to get the truth from Hattie if they were ever to move forward with their relationship.

The thought pulled him up short. A relationship did exist between him and Hattie. An odd and at times uncomfortable one, but a relationship none the less.

Defining and solidifying the true nature of that relationship would depend greatly on resolving their current domestic situation. While Hattie continued to reside under the same roof as him, Will knew she would never let her guard down long enough for him to have a chance to capture her heart.

He set the cup down. A calmness now warmed his soul. He did want her heart.

"My mother fully supported my father's desire to do good. She was the one who suggested we should work with the poor and indigent of London. Prayer was not enough. We had to do something in this life to right the injustices of the world. I suppose that was what eventually brought me over to their way of thinking. I grew up with the finest of everything. My father's family comes from landed gentry. I have never in my life had to want for anything."

Her words were encouraging. Her story thus far made sense with all that Hattie had told him, and what his agents in London had been able to uncover. He sensed however that she was dragging out the tale to further delay the discussion of her brother.

"Hattie, does Edgar pose a threat to you? When he discovers that you are in England, will he seek to put you on the first ship to Africa?"

Experience had taught him well that dancing around a difficult subject was not a good idea. Getting to the truth of the matter meant that any resultant pain was dealt with more quickly.

Hattie shook her head and Will's hopes lifted.

"No. Edgar would never do anything to harm me. And I can assure you that he would be the last person to send me after our parents. He was the one person I had hoped would save me from going," she replied.

Will did his best to dampen down his enthusiasm. He knew he

was getting close to the heart of the matter. He decided to venture closer.

"But he didn't save you, did he? He didn't arrive on his white charger. The fact is your knight in shining armor failed you. If it were me, rather than avoid him, I would want to know why. If he knew you didn't want to go to Africa, then why did he abandon you?"

Chapter Thirty-Four

"This is the right thing to do. The only thing," Will muttered to his reflection in the mirror.

Day by day the barriers were coming down between Hattie and himself. Small but sure steps of progress were being made in his campaign to win her heart. Today he would take the first big step on the path he now saw set out before him. Today he would do as he and Hattie had agreed. He would meet with Edgar Wright.

Contrary to his usual habits he was up early and ready to leave the house well before midday. Before heading to White's, he planned to stop by his usual coffee house on Oxford Street and fortify himself with two strong cups of their best Brazilian coffee.

Slipping out of the house, he made a point to avoid Hattie. He didn't need her changing her mind at the last minute. She was recovering well from her injuries and only last evening had broached the subject of when Will thought she might be well enough to return to St. John's.

At White's club, Will checked with the day attendant. True to his sources, the man confirmed that Edgar Wright was indeed in attendance at the club just before luncheon.

It would have been simple enough to have called upon Hattie's brother at his home, but Will decided their first meeting should be in public. He had no way of knowing how Edgar would react to the knowledge that his unwed sister was living under the same roof as a young widower.

He penned a note and asked that the club attendant pass it on to Edgar.

While he waited, Will took a seat in an alcove. Seated facing the front door, he recited the first few words he planned to say. A well-rehearsed initial greeting always helped to establish control at the beginning of a meeting.

The attendant soon returned and escorted Will to where Edgar Wright was seated.

"Mr. Wright?"

Edgar looked up and Will saw the look of recognition cross his face. Hattie's brother rose from his chair and offered Will his hand.

"We meet again. William Saunders at your service sir," said Will.

Once seated in the chair opposite to Edgar, Will took a minute to undertake a closer study of Hattie's brother. They were quite similar in looks. They shared the same warm brown eyes and light straw-colored hair. He was pleased to note that Hattie did not have the same long, almost equine facial features as did Edgar.

"You sent a note asking to see me," said Edgar.

Will took in a long slow breath and fixed him with a steely gaze.

"I have come about your sister," he said.

Edgar's eyes narrowed, mistrust evident in them. Their meeting at St. Paul's cathedral had not been the sheer chance he had been led to believe.

"If my sister has been troubling you or the members of your household for donations, I apologize. Rest assured that she will not be bothering you again for a very long time. If ever. My parents have taken her with them on a mission to Africa."

Will noted the tone of anguish in Edgar's voice. He did not expect to ever see his sister again.

"No, I have not come about her philanthropic work. What would you say if I told you that Hattie is in London and that she is living under my protection?" replied Will.

Edgar's demeanor immediately changed. He leapt from his chair and stood over Will. His hands were held out in front of him ready to strike.

"What have you done with her you blackguard? If you have hurt her I will end your very existence," he said.

The sideways glances from other members of the club set Will's nerves on edge. He did not like being the center of attention, even parties made him uncomfortable.

"Please resume your seat Mr. Wright you are causing a scene. Until you do I will not continue this discussion. I have come here in good faith and with only the guarded blessing of your sister. If it were up to her, I would not be here at all. Now sit down," said Will.

The look on Edgar's face was one of shock. He was clearly not a man used to having another speak to him in such a fashion. He snorted at Will's command, but did as he was told.

"Well?" said Edgar, resuming his seat.

"Hattie is safe and living at your parent's house. I have recently taken over the lease and reside at that same address."

Considering Hattie's recent injuries Will knew his statement regarding Hattie's state of health to be a misrepresentation of the truth. But since Edgar would discover the truth about Hattie soon enough, Will decided he didn't need to cloud the discussion with that piece of news.

The first thing he needed to do was to establish trust.

Will then spent the next half an hour or so retelling the story of how Hattie had jumped ship in Gibraltar, and how he had brought her back to London. Several delicate aspects of that tale Will decided it was best not to mention. It would not aid his cause if Edgar Wright thought Will had taken scandalous advantage of his vulnerable sister.

"And she had been living downstairs all that time, unbeknown to you?" asked Edgar.

Will adopted his best disinterested air. "Yes. It was quite a shock when I discovered her deception," he replied.

As soon as the words left his lips he watched closely for Edgar's reaction. Edgar sat back in his chair and took a deep breath. A simple move, but one which spoke volumes to Will. Hattie had just been called a liar and Edgar was making ready to defend her.

Good. About time someone in your family gave a damn about her.

"Though I fully understand her reasons. Hattie has explained the difficult situation which arose within your family before your parents left for Africa. She felt she could not approach you, and so took shelter with the two most trusted servants of the family," added Will.

His last words had the effect he desired on Edgar. Edgar's shoulders dropped and his gaze fell to the floor.

Sitting watching as the saddest of emotions played out across Edgar's face Will knew he had the true measure of the man. Edgar was exactly the kind of brother he had hoped he would be for Hattie.

"Will she see me?" Edgar finally asked.

Will stifled a self-satisfied smile as his plan played out before him.

"That can be arranged. But firstly, we need to resolve the situation regarding her place of residence. As you can understand it is entirely inappropriate for her and I to dwell under the same roof while we are not married," replied Will.

Again, he chose his words carefully. Planting the first seeds of thought in Edgar's mind.

"Of course."

"I was hoping you would take her into your home. It would allow the courting of your sister to be conducted in a more socially acceptable manner. We were forced to share a cabin on the boat back to England, and so I feel a deep obligation to offer for your sister's hand in marriage," said Will.

Edgar looked Will up and down. Will knew when another was trying to take his measure. He silently granted his approval of Hattie's brother. She needed a champion on her side, someone who did not have motives of self-interest such as himself.

"If you wish to court my sister I would need to know more about you Mr. Saunders. As you may be aware, Hattie was engaged to the young man who was accompanying my family to Africa. Something tells me that she may be a little warier of a second betrothal. It may take some convincing on your part. Hattie has at times been known to stubbornly stand her ground," replied Edgar.

Will chuckled. "You don't say. Anyone would think you considered your sister to have a will of her own."

Edgar scowled. "You are a brave man, I grant you that. But tell me William Saunders, are you intending to court Hattie just because you feel honor bound to offer for her hand, or do you hold genuine affection for her? She deserves to make a good marriage. I will not have her forced into a match not of her choosing."

Will decided his future brother in law deserved to be told as much of the truth as was possible. He hoped the discussion would not end with him having to face Edgar at dawn on Hampstead Heath with pistols drawn.

"I do hold great affection for Hattie. You should also know that we shared a bed on the boat and matters of an intimate nature took place between us. That said, I did not ruin your sister. Reverend Brown had already forced his attentions on her before they left London. Unlike the situation with the reverend, it was Hattie's decision to embark on our affair. It was also her decision to end it before we arrived back in London."

It was unseemly and disgusting to talk of Hattie in such a way. Will felt he was betraying her trust by informing her brother of such private matters.

"I had already decided to offer for your sister before matters developed further between us. I did at first feel honor bound. Now I find the idea of making her my wife something which I look forward to doing. Which is why it's imperative for her to move out of my house and into yours," replied Will.

Edgar sat silent for a time. Will's revelations were enough to give pause to any man who valued his sister and her reputation.

"Answer me this William, do you intend to bring Hattie back into the fold of the *ton*? My sister deserves better than to spend the rest of her days working in the filth and degradation of St. Giles."

Will nodded. If he had his way Hattie would never set foot in Plumtree Street again once they were wed.

At those words, Edgar rose from his chair and offered Will his hand once more.

"You do realize we are going to have a fight on our hands. Hattie will not want to move out of forty-three Newport Street, even if you are still residing there. As for her work among the poor, I don't know how you will find a workable solution to that problem."

He called an attendant over.

"Let us seal our agreement with a bottle of White's finest, after which you shall accompany me back to my house in Newport Street. I wish you to speak with my wife. If anyone can help with our mutual cause, it is Miranda."

Chapter Thirty-Five

Hattie stood outside the closed door of her parent's formal drawing room trying without success to calm her breathing. Her knuckles ached from being repeatedly cracked.

She looked down at her dress, there were no more invisible creases to smooth out.

"You look fine my dear," said Mrs. Little. She patted Hattie gently on the shoulder.

When the door opened and Will stood on the threshold, Mrs. Little gave her an encouraging smile. Will held out his hand.

"Come, Edgar is waiting," he said.

Hattie stepped into the room. The heartfelt speech she had spent the better part of the past day rehearsing sat ready on her lips. Edgar stood hands clasped in front of him by the window.

His gaze immediately fell on the still healing deep cut on her forehead and he sighed. The Saunders' family doctor had done an excellent job of close stitches, but Hattie would always bear a scar.

They both took a tentative step forward toward the other.

"Ed," she barely managed. He put his arms out, ready to pull her into his embrace, but she stopped him.

"I had an encounter with some unpleasant people recently. Much as I would love to wholeheartedly embrace you, it must be a gentle clasping of arms today."

He looked to Will.

"What is this? You did not mention that my sister had been injured."

Will walked toward the door. They had agreed that Hattie would tell Edgar the story of what had happened to her at the hands of the Belton Street thugs.

"I shall leave the two of you alone to get reacquainted," said Will.

"It's alright Edgar. I shall explain. Thank you Will," she said.

Once Will had closed the door behind him. Brother and sister stood several feet apart staring at one another. Neither had hoped for this moment, for this miracle of reunion.

"Oh H, thank god you are safe. Every day since you left has been a waking nightmare. Miranda has cried herself to sleep so many nights. I have torn myself apart with guilt."

Hattie stepped forward and gingerly put her arms around him. Edgar held her softly in his, as he would a small child. The tears Hattie had managed to hold back, finally won. Edgar meanwhile ruffled the top of her hair in the same affectionate way he had done when they were children. Hattie sobbed ever harder at every stroke of his fingers.

When he finally released her, and stepped back, she saw tears shining in his eyes. One of his huge, lopsided grins formed on his lips. She snuffled back the tears and chortled.

"Anyone would think you were pleased to see me," she said.

"You have no idea," he replied.

They repaired to the comfort of the big floral couch which sat close to the window. A couch on which they had spent many hours seated side by side in the years before Edgar married and left home. She was grateful that Will had seen fit to keep it.

"How is Miranda? I saw the two of you at St. Paul's not long after I arrived back in London. Will tells me you have a son."

Edgar took hold of her hand and held it so tightly in his that Hattie feared he would never let go. Regret over not having sought him out that day at the cathedral brought more tears to her eyes.

"We have been granted two miracles in a year. Long after we had given up hope we were graced with a son. He is the most perfect thing I have ever seen. Miranda cannot wait for you to meet your nephew," he said.

"What was your second miracle?" she replied.

"You of course. Hattie, we never expected to see you again."

Edgar sucked in a deep breath.

"Sebastian was born the day you sailed for Africa. Miranda and he both nearly died in childbirth. I had received your message and intended to confront papa the morning you were due to leave. But I could not leave Miranda's side. It was only later that day when my wife and child were both safe, that I was able to finally leave the house in search of you. I rode like a madman to the dockside but your ship had already sailed. I cannot begin to tell you how many tears I wept at the dockside thinking I had lost you forever."

Hattie brushed a hand on her brother's cheek. Edgar had been faced with a terrible dilemma. He had done the right thing in putting the safety of his wife and child first.

"I didn't abandon you Hattie. Even after you said those cruel things to Miranda about her being too concerned with her looks and money, we never gave up on you. We always knew you were not meant for the life of a missionary in the African jungle. I am beyond grateful that you realized it as well before it was too late. That was an incredibly brave thing you did in Gibraltar."

She smiled softly. There would not be too many other young women in London who could lay claim to that feat of daring.

"He is a good man, your Mr. Saunders," said Edgar.

Hattie blinked, taken aback by the sudden change of topic.

"He is not my Mr. Saunders," she replied.

"Really, I don't think that is how he sees things. He was deliberately vague about the details of what transpired between the two of you onboard the *Canis Major*, but I know enough to have agreed to Mr. Saunders' request to court you. Hattie, you need a husband and knowing the family that Mr. Saunders comes from, you would be hard pressed to do better. There are some realities which you are going to have to face up to and marrying William Saunders is one of them."

She rose from the couch. She had been half expecting this position from Edgar. Will was no fool, he would see Edgar as the means to press his case for their marriage.

"What is to happen now?" she asked.

"Well Mr. Saunders and I have agreed that you shall move into my house. But before that happens, I need you to explain to me what happened to you. Why can't I hug you as much as I desperately need to, and what happened to your face?"

"I crossed the boss of one of the criminal gangs in the rookery in Plumtree Street. He gave me a beating which left me with this angry scar and a number of badly bruised ribs."

The shock and anguish which appeared on Edgar's face matched that of Will the night Joshua had brought her home. The young women of their social circle led protected lives. Strapping footmen and trusty maids ensured that vagabonds did not get close to them.

Young unmarried women of the *haute ton* would be hard pressed to point to St. Giles on a map, let alone be willing to set foot in its dangerous streets.

He was about to open his mouth and Hattie knew a pronouncement about her charitable works would soon be on his lips. She had her own speech well-rehearsed.

"I am prepared to come and live with you and Miranda, but I will not give up my work."

Edgar huffed. "You cannot expect me to accept that condition."

"Father Brown needs me to help him at St. John's. In return for letting me undertake my daily visits to the church and Covent Garden market I will agree to stay out of the rookery. I shall live under your roof until my future can be determined."

Edgar considered her words for a moment.

"And you will rejoin society and allow William Saunders to court you?"

Hattie sighed. She had little other option but to accept those terms. They did however fit in with her plans. By joining society and spending time with Will among the rich and powerful of London, she would be able to show Will how ill- suited they were.

The more Will pushed for her to marry him and give up her work, the harder she would resist. Edgar would not stand idly by and let her be browbeaten into an unhappy marriage. It was therefore only a matter of time before she was able to convince Will that a union between them was a terrible idea.

"We have an accord," she replied.

Chapter Thirty-Six

Despite her protests, Will and Edgar agreed that Hattie's personal effects were to be moved to number thirty- seven Newport Street that very day. There was a slight tussle over where Brutus would reside, but Edgar insisted that the cat was part of the chattels of the house and therefore covered under the lease. Brutus would be staying at number forty-three.

Hattie stifled a laugh when she saw Will holding his feline nemesis as she walked out the front door of her family home. She knew Will well enough to know he would be mighty peeved at being left with Brutus and her two sets of silk tearing claws.

Miranda Wright embraced Hattie's return with gusto and within days of Hattie's arrival had arranged an entirely new wardrobe of clothes for her sister in law. She would have happily thrown out Hattie's other plain clothes but Hattie insisted she needed them for her work at St. John's.

Hattie was left humbled when Miranda accepted her heartfelt apology with good grace.

"You are family. Edgar and I never stopped loving you," said Miranda.

Hattie kept her side of the agreement with Edgar. She stayed away from Plumtree Street. Little Annie Mayford came by the church every few days and picked up some fresh fruit for Baylee which Hattie had specially set aside.

Hattie quickly slipped into a comfortable routine. In the morning she would make her way to St. John's to help Father Brown, in the afternoon she would come home and spend time with Miranda and baby Sebastian.

She had just returned home late one afternoon when Miranda caught her at the front door.

"Quickly my dear, head upstairs and change. That coffee colored gown with the dark blue stripes will be perfect. I have had your maid lay it out on the bed," said Miranda.

Hattie frowned. She had been working at the church since just after dawn, and her feet hurt. She had no wish to go out and spend another afternoon shopping with Miranda.

"Mr. William Saunders is here to pay you a visit. Your maid is waiting in your room to fix your hair. Hurry."

Miranda gave Hattie a gentle push toward the staircase.

Hattie headed upstairs. Will had given her a few days peace, but she knew he would be impatient to move things along.

When she entered the formal drawing room a short while later Will rose from his seat and greeted her with a formal bow. He was dressed in a dark blue jacket with matching striped trousers. The subtle charcoal grey of his waistcoat was stylishly offset by the pure white linen of his shirt and cravat. Not a hair on his head was out of place.

Her heart skipped a beat. Mrs. Little had been wrong in her estimations of Will, he was more than handsome. The very sight of him stirred something deep within. She knew it to be longing.

"Hattie, it is a pleasure to see you again. You look lovely."

She looked to Miranda who was seated on a nearby chair sporting a social smile. Her sister in law would be thrilled with Will's visit. Hattie suspected she already had a wedding guest list hidden somewhere in the desk of her private sitting room. The moment Hattie accepted Will's suit the wedding invitations would be out.

The whole scene was a tad farcical knowing what had already

occurred between her and Will, but she had given Edgar her word and knew she had to go along.

"Mr. Saunders has offered to take you to the pleasure gardens at Vauxhall. Isn't that wonderful?" said Miranda.

Hattie took a seat next to Miranda, who took hold of her hand and gave it a gentle pat.

"Oh. Thank you," replied Hattie.

She wondered how much Miranda had revealed to Will of Hattie's old life. Will would no doubt have been gently pressing her for clues of how he could gain Hattie's favor.

The pleasure gardens had once been her favorite place to visit. The trip across the river by boat to the south bank of London was a summer highlight of her younger years. Miranda would know full well how much a visit to the gardens would mean to Hattie.

"Yes, my sisters and brother will make up the rest of the party. They are especially keen to meet you. I think you may remember my sister Eve from your debut," said Will.

"You need to get out, socialize with some people of your own age and have some fun" added Miranda.

A little bubble of excitement started in Hattie's stomach. She could not remember the last time she had gone out in search of entertainment, let alone fun.

It was later in the year than she was used to attending the gardens, but if she wore warm clothes the journey across the river and to the gardens could be enjoyable. An evening out with Will and his family would be interesting at least. She vaguely remembered Evelyn Saunders, but did not know either of Will's other two siblings.

"Thank you. I would love to join you," she replied.

"Oh, do come on Hattie!" Edgar called impatiently from the bottom of the stairs.

He shook his head in disbelief.

Hattie appeared at the top of the stairs, her cloak tucked over her arm. She had been ready for quite some time, but Miranda insisted that she make Will wait.

"Never appear too eager to please, even after you are married. Keep to the rule that making them wait creates a certain tension. A flustered man is far easier to bend to your will than one whom you hurry after."

The more time Hattie spent with Miranda, the greater understanding she had of why her brother so loved his wife.

Reaching the bottom of the stairs Hattie handed her cloak to Edgar, who promptly handed it to Will standing beside him.

"Have a wonderful time," said Edgar, giving her a kiss on the cheek.

A chill went up Hattie's spine as Will lay his hands on her shoulders and draped the cloak around her. It was the closest they had been since the night he had last kissed her. Her body ached for his touch.

The scent of his cologne filled her senses, reminding her of how good it had felt to be in his arms. To know the pleasure of his body loving hers. His sexual presence was tattooed on her mind.

As they left the house and stepped out into the early evening chill, Hattie did not feel the cold. The singular touch of Will's hands had her blood heated with desire.

A footman opened the carriage door and Will helped Hattie to climb aboard. He climbed in after her.

She was met with the sight of three smiling, welcoming faces. A tall young man, with a shock of white hair called out her name as she sat down.

"Hattie, finally we meet!"

He reached across and offered his hand.

"I'm Francis. This is Caroline," he said pointing to the young woman seated beside him. Will chuckled, as his younger brother shamelessly stole his thunder.

Caroline was a stunningly beautiful young woman. She was graced with pale blonde hair and porcelain skin so flawless it would make an artist weep. When she smiled her deep green eyes drew Hattie in.

"Hello Hattie, lovely to meet you," she said.

"Oh, and I think you know Eve from your first season," said Francis.

Hattie took a moment as memories of her half-finished coming out season two years earlier resurfaced in her mind.

"Now I remember you Eve. You had a pale purple gown at the first of the balls and I was desperate to find out where you got the fabric from. I had never seen anything like it before, and I must confess to having been jealous" said Hattie.

Eve smiled.

"My mother had the fabric smuggled in from France. It was terribly wicked of her and papa was furious. I remember the row they had when he found out. Still mama was adamant that the dressmaker was going to use it."

Hattie looked at Will, but he did not react to his sister's words. Will it appeared had decided that he was going to adopt a social face when he was in public with Hattie. She suspected that his siblings had been told very little about her, other than that their brother saw her as a potential bride. He was playing the courting game by the rulebook.

Eve and Caroline both seemed lovely girls. Any other young woman would be pleased to have them as sister in laws. From the way they had greeted her, she knew they would be disappointed when they discovered that she would not be marrying their brother.

Her own disappointment came with the discovery that instead of taking a boat across to Vauxhall as her parents had liked to do, the Saunders carriage crossed over the Thames at Westminster Bridge. Will to his nature read her mind.

"I did enquire about taking a boat across, but the river is icy up this far and none of the small pleasure boats are making the trip across at this time of the year. My apologies to you all," he said.

A short while later they reached the pleasure gardens which were situated not far from the South bank of the Thames. A crush of carriages and people made finding a place to alight a difficult prospect. Finally, a frustrated Francis opened the door and made a clearing in the road for the others to step down.

At the entrance to the gardens, Will paid the entry fee and Hattie took his offered arm.

"Ah there he is," exclaimed Eve.

Picking up her skirts, she raced ahead of the group and threw herself into the arms of a young man who was standing to one side of the entrance path. They then proceeded to indulge in an all too passionate kiss for such a public place.

"Steady on girl, your brothers are watching," said the young man, finally releasing Eve. His words noted protest, but the smug look on his face said otherwise.

Hattie felt Will's grip on her arm tighten. She was sure he cursed under his breath.

Eve took a firm hold of her male friend's hand and brought him over to the group.

"Sorry, I forgot to mention that Freddie was going to join us tonight. I am sure it is alright with you all," she announced.

From the way Will was grinding his jaw, Hattie knew Will was far from pleased.

"Oh, and who is this?" said Freddie, rudely pointing at Hattie.

She had been away from polite society for some time, but Hattie knew well enough that both Eve and Freddie were behaving poorly in public. From the look of disgust on both Francis and Caroline's faces they were not impressed with such common behavior.

Will stepped in.

"Miss Harriet Wright, may I introduce the Honorable Frederick Rosemount. Frederick is the second son of Viscount Rosemount."

Suddenly reminded of social expectations Freddie dipped into an elegant bow.

"At your service Miss Wright. You may call me Freddie. All my friends do."

He was immaculately dressed, his coat cut to fit snuggly against his shoulders and chest. His bright red waistcoat which was finished with gold buttons screamed for everyone's attention. As she observed him Hattie noticed he kept shifting his stance. It was clear he was trying to find the best pose with which to impress the other members of the party. The only person who seemed to think he was anything but a pompous ass was Eve, who inexplicably hung on his every word.

He was a tad too polished and smooth for Hattie's liking. If he wasn't the son of a viscount, she would have picked him for a conman.

The group walked on through the crowded park. Everywhere she looked there were different forms of entertainment to entice and delight.

Hundreds of lamps which hung from trees and poles lit the way. The soft light they threw out gave the entire gardens an almost fairy land appearance. Hattie was enchanted.

"This reminds me of when we visited St. Michael's cave. It is like another world," she whispered to Will.

He looked up into the trees and then looking down at her smiled.

"Yes. Let us hope there are no monkeys."

They stopped for a few minutes and watched a juggler who managed to have five supposedly loaded pistols in the air at the one time. As the juggler caught the last of the pistols, he fired it into the air. The crowd gasped and then loudly applauded.

"Do not try that at home Francis," said Will.

Francis caught his brother's jest and laughed.

"Lord no. Far too dangerous. I shall only use three pistols."

They walked on following the flowing crowd as it moved along the main path. Finally, they reached a large grassy clearing. Dotted around the edges of the clearing were a series of private boxes. Will retrieved a ticket out of his pocket and led them to the private box he had booked.

The women retired to a soft overstuffed couch and got settled. Will meanwhile, beckoned to a nearby waiter. After a short conversation, the waiter headed off. He returned a few minutes later carrying a tray filled with glasses of champagne which he set down in front of the group.

Will picked up a glass and handed it to Hattie. Their fingers touched as she took a hold of the glass. The sensation of touching his skin reminded her as to why Will had invited her this evening. He had plans for them to be forever touching skin.

Hattie blushed when she saw Will lick his bottom lip. She remembered all the wicked things that tongue and lips had done to her body.

As she took her first sip of the champagne, she smiled. Miranda was right, it had been too long since she had had any fun. No matter how things eventually ended with Will, tonight she would make every effort to enjoy herself. It would be a night for making pleasant memories.

Eve downed two glasses of champagne in quick succession, earning herself a brotherly rebuke from Francis. Freddie, Hattie noted, stood to one side, and let her do as she pleased. When she called for a third drink, Will reached over and took her glass out of her hand.

"I think you should take it a little slower Eve, the night is still young," he cautioned.

Hattie was surprised to see a pout appear on Eve's lips. She seemed determined to take her brother to task over some unknown slight.

"Don't think that just because you have come back to London that you have any right to tell me what to do Will. I am a grown woman. I shall decide if I want another glass of champagne, not you," replied Eve.

To Hattie's surprise, Freddie stepped in at this point and attempted to calm things down.

"Now Will my good chap, how about I take Eve for a turn around the gardens. The fresh air might return her to good humor. Rest assured we shall remain in full public sight on the main paths."

Hattie knew the look on Will's face all too well. It was his, "*I would love to punch you in the throat, but society won't let me*" look. They all knew he was being played, but Eve and Freddie were masters of getting their own way.

"Fifteen minutes no longer, or Francis and I shall come looking for you," Will ground out.

Eve's demeanor immediately changed and she took hold of Freddie's arm, half dragging him out of the supper box and toward the nearest path.

Hattie knew enough about Vauxhall to know that there were other paths that lovers could take which took them off the main walk. Those paths were not well lit and all manner of scandalous behavior was known to take place in the bushes which were dotted along them.

"So, Hattie, where did you first meet Will?" asked Caroline.

Will came and sat beside Hattie.

"At St. Paul's, she was there with her brother," he said.

Hattie took another sip of her champagne, as she quietly absorbed Will's lie of how they had met.

It was quite some time before Eve and Freddie finally returned to the group. As they approached, Hattie caught the look of frustrated anger that Francis and Will exchanged.

"We got lost, must have taken a wrong turn," explained Freddie, unconvincingly.

Releasing Eve's hand, he stepped away. A grinning Eve came and sat next to Hattie and Caroline.

The look Will gave Freddie would have melted the sun, but he said nothing. Freddie was no doubt relying on the fact that they were in the company of others to save his skin.

At some point before the evening was over, she suspected Freddie and Will would be having a private, but unpleasant conversation.

"You need to be more careful," whispered Caroline.

Caroline pulled a leaf off the back of her sister's cloak, and another one from out of her hair. She flicked the leaf away, but not before Hattie and Eve had both caught sight of it.

"Oh," Eve murmured, blushing.

Caroline made a quick, but not too obvious inspection of the rest of Eve's hair and clothing. Whatever had taken place between Eve and Freddie during their walk, it was clear things were progressing toward an inevitable wedding.

Hattie was surprised at her own reaction to Eve's indiscretion. The

Hattie of a few months ago would have frowned upon such behavior. She would have viewed Eve as a lush to permit a young man such liberties with her person.

Now that she knew the raw pleasure that came from being with a man she viewed things very differently. The heat which flared within her body, revealed her own longing to be touched and possessed.

She chanced a look at Will. He had quietly retracted his claws, returning to the well contained persona he had adopted for the night.

Disappointment flared. There would be no chance of Will dragging her off into the bushes to take liberties with her body. She stifled a snort. Where had that wicked notion come from?

From knowing that you want him.

And there it was. The indisputable fact that she did want Will. That she ached for him to take her in his arms and kiss her senseless. Whatever liberties he demanded of her, she would willingly give.

This was another of those moments when she wished they were back on the ship and lying naked in one another's arms. Things were simpler then. She knew exactly what she wanted. A brief affair and no ties.

He turned and gave her a smile. It was as if he could read her mind. She smiled back, helpless to resist the lure of his charm.

Ending things with him would shatter her heart into a thousand pieces.

§

The mood of the party was strained. Eve and Freddie had selfishly put everyone in an uncomfortable position. If Will had called a halt to the evening at that moment Hattie would not have been the least bit surprised.

Francis to his credit had also read the mood. He clapped his hands loudly together and announced. "Righto, time for some dancing. I am not leaving until my feet hurt. Come on Caro you shall be my partner."

Caroline wasted no time in getting to her feet and taking her brother's arm. They headed out toward a nearby space in which a small orchestra was playing. Eve and Freddie followed quickly behind.

Hattie and Will were left alone in the box, the first time they had been alone in over a week.

"Shall we?"

Will offered Hattie his hand. She took it, feeling a tremble throughout her body, as he closed his strong fingers about hers. As he pulled her to her feet, Will slipped his hand around her waist and drew her close.

"Unfortunately, the only movement you and I can do together tonight is that of the socially acceptable type. I just wish we could be somewhere that would allow us to indulge in the dancing we shared on the boat. Of course, if we were married, that would be easily accomplished at the end of this evening."

Will was keen to press his need for them to marry. She was dreading the moment he asked for permission to speak to Edgar.

"Let's not. It has been a long time since I danced. The last time was after I had been presented to the Queen. That was over two years ago. Even then my dancing was adequate at best," she replied.

If Will was disappointed with her reply, he hid it well.

"Well then, how about we take a short stroll instead and see what other entertainment is at hand?"

"But what about the others?" she replied.

"They have made it abundantly clear that they are old enough to take care of themselves. They do not need me to shadow their every move. Besides I am here tonight for you."

The crowds in the gardens had built to a peak. There were hundreds of people all pushing and jostling to find the best places to watch the entertainment.

Towing Hattie behind him, Will weaved his way through the throng. She held on tight as he cleared a path for them.

Eventually they managed to find an area where the crowd thinned and they could stroll together. A line of small booths selling trinkets was set up along the side of the path. They walked slowly, hand in hand, along the line of booths content just to be in one another's company.

At one booth Will bought Hattie a small silver pin adorned with a lion's head. She happily pinned it to the bodice of her gown.

When Hattie yawned a short while later, Will took his cue and led her back to where they had left the rest of the group. They found Eve seated on a chair her head in her hands, while the others milled around.

"I think the champagne has caught up with her, so it might be time for us to take our leave," announced Francis.

Caroline helped her sister to her feet and the group slowly made its way to the main gate. Hattie walked alongside Will, lost in her own thoughts.

Outside the gate to Vauxhall, beggars crowded the path. The rest of the group ignored the outstretched hands, beggars were aplenty in this part of London. Hattie saw a young woman standing to one side under a tree holding a small child in her arms.

She stepped away from the group and went to the woman's side. Other beggars followed and soon she was surrounded. She looked back over her shoulder briefly, but Will and the others were lost from sight. She opened her reticule and pulled out a handful of coins, handing them to the woman.

"May you be blessed," said the woman.

As Hattie leaned in to offer the woman some words of comfort, the child made a grab for Hattie's lion pin. At the pull on her gown, Hattie moved forward to save the pin from being torn through the fabric.

A concerned Will forced his way into the group.

"Hattie!" he bellowed.

People scattered at the sound of his voice. In the ensuing scramble, someone pushed against Hattie's back and she fell hard into the woman and child. All three of them tumbled to the ground. The child screamed in pain as her small fingers caught the sharp edge of Hattie's lion pin.

Will came over and helped Hattie to her feet. Picking up the child he handed her to her mother. The woman took one look at Will in his fine evening clothes and quickly fled.

He attempted to put a comforting arm around Hattie, but she angrily pushed him away.

"Why did you do that?" she said.

She watched as the group of beggars disappeared into the London night. In her reticule sat the rest of the coins she had intended to give to them. Finally, she turned to Will.

"Please take me home."

Chapter Thirty-Seven

The journey home in the carriage was a long silent one. In the corner Hattie sat and stared at the lion pin which she now held in her hand. She was angry enough with Will for having made a mess of things with the beggars, but she reserved the center of her rage for herself.

When the carriage stopped at her brother's house, she did not wait for Will or Francis to help her down. As soon as the footman opened the door, she rose from her seat, gave a perfunctory *good night*, and climbed out. She went inside Edgar's house without looking back.

Knowing Miranda would want to know how her evening had gone, Hattie waited inside the front door until the Saunders' family carriage had gone. She then walked the short distance back to her old home and took a seat in the back garden.

A short while later Will appeared from out of the house, carrying a lantern.

"Mrs. Little said you were sitting out here, mind if I join you?"

She got to her feet.

"I'm sorry, old habits die hard. This was always the place I came as a child when I was out of sorts. Forgive me if I forget that this is no longer my home," she replied.

She began to walk toward the garden gate. Will took hold of the edge of her cloak, and pulled her back to him.

"But it could be your home. It should be your home. You just have to say that you want it to be. I can speak to Edgar tonight?"

Tears threatened, but Hattie knew she had to hold herself together this time. To make Will understand.

"I cannot marry you Will. I have had my doubts all along, but tonight the truth was made clear to me."

He sighed.

"I'm sorry if you think I was a little heavy handed with the way I went about rescuing you from that group of beggars. But, you should not have wandered over to them on your own. It was a rash thing that you did. You were without my protection, anything could have happened to you."

In the dark moonlit garden, Hattie found it hard to read Will's expression, but she knew her own mind.

"And therein lies the problem," she replied.

He searched her face, while she saw only confusion and hurt written upon his own.

"I give up, I can't fathom you. Am I not allowed to give a damn about your safety? Tell me Hattie. Make me understand," he pleaded.

For a moment she was at a loss as to what to say. But Will was right, she had to make him understand. She pressed on.

"The first time we met I was trying to escape a life where my husband would control my entire existence. My heart tells me that if I married you it would be the same. The second I accept your proposal you will be telling me what to do. And just as importantly what *not* to do. Which is exactly what you attempted to do tonight. You barreled into that group of people without a thought for them. You were single minded in your need to drag me away and back into your world," she said.

The spark of bravery she had felt that sunny morning off the coast of Spain reignited within. With her back straight, she raised her head and met Will's piercing gaze full on.

"So, you are saying I am a controlling male?" he ground out.

As a huff of disgust escaped her lips, she saw anger flash in his eyes.

"Yes. You are a gentleman of a certain class and I am yet to meet one of you who does not think women exist to do your bidding. You cannot stand me attending to my mission. Will, you don't seem to want to understand that the poor and destitute of London are my life's work. I have walked into crowds of beggars many times before, each time bringing them a little hope. Tonight however, was the first time I have brought fear and pain. Fear and pain that came because of you."

Hattie swallowed her own lump of fear.

"I'm sorry. I lost sight of you and I panicked. I worry about your safety and wellbeing Hattie, that is all. And yes, when we do marry I expect you to listen to me when it comes to your safety. You clearly don't see danger when it is in front of you," replied Will.

"I don't understand this overwhelming need to protect me. I've been working my mission for a long time. Longer than I have known you. And yes, sometimes things do go awry, but that is the risk that comes with my work. I understand that and I accept it."

Will raked his fingers through his hair, and sighed. He held out his hand to her.

"Hattie, please come inside the house. I think it is time that I told you the truth of Yvette's death," he said.

❧

Hattie followed Will inside and into her father's old sitting room. Will poured them both a brandy. He took a seat in the chair opposite to her and sat silent for a time.

"For many reasons, some of them being a matter of national security, I cannot tell you the whole story. When we marry, you will have to accept that there are some things of my time away from England, that I can never share with you," he said.

Hattie ignored his stubborn statement about their future marriage. There was not point starting that argument again. If they could not get past their differences, no matter what Will demanded, there would be no wedding.

"During the war, I was a spy for the British government. I spent three years living undercover in Paris working to help bring Napoleon down. After the mess he made attempting to invade Russia, the British government and its allies were hopeful that his powerbase was weak enough for an attempt to topple him. I volunteered to go to France."

Hattie sat and stared at her brandy glass. She had never fully believed the story that he was in the import trade, it didn't match what she did know of him to be true.

His having been a spy made far more sense. His need to constantly check and double check details. His need to sit facing the door. His need for control.

"Yvette was a French agent, part of an undercover team working with a number of foreign governments, including Britain to bring Napoleon down. I met her not long after I arrived in France. Being married was a good cover for us. Eventually our marriage of convenience, became a real one. We fell in love."

His gaze remained fixed on the carpet. A deep line was etched in his brow. Hattie wondered if Will had ever had this conversation with anyone else.

"Being a spy is a dangerous game. One false move and you can find yourself on the wrong end of a blade. Yvette went out on her own to meet with an informant. It turned out that the informant was actually one of Napoleon's agents and he murdered her."

Will screwed his eyes shut as tears began to roll slowly down his cheeks. Hattie remained in the chair, instinct telling her that pity was the last thing he needed at this moment. She ached to reach out and hold him.

He wiped the tears away. "She was so much like you, at times it takes my breath away. You talk of knowing the streets of London, well Yvette knew the lanes and rooftops of Paris. She was fearless, as are you. I have never doubted your bravery Hattie. But there is one thing you do have in common with her that scares the life out of me. You don't sense danger until it is too late."

Hattie could not argue with Will on that point. She had done some foolish things and barely gotten away with them. The beating she had received at the hands of the Belton Street gang had been a lesson painfully learned.

"But, I am not her. You cannot compare us on such a simplistic level. She was a spy, that comes with an entirely different set of risks from that of working with the poor in the rookery."

"Yet, if I ordered you not to go to Plumtree Lane, you would still go, wouldn't you?" he replied.

A creeping worry entered Hattie's mind. Did Will somehow blame himself for Yvette's death; and was this where his need to dictate the terms of their relationship stemmed from? She sensed they were close to the truth. She decided to gamble on asking the right but fearful question.

"Where were you when Yvette died?" she asked.

It was cruel and the second she uttered the words Hattie wished them away, but she knew if they did not address the issue of Yvette's death, they would never get passed it. The poor girl who had suffered such a terrible and premature death would forever stand between them.

She felt nothing but utter sadness and grief for the young woman she would never know, yet somewhere deep in her heart she would always have a place for Yvette. They shared a bond which no one else could.

They both loved Will.

He put a hand over his face and went silent for a long time. Hattie sat with her hands softly in her lap, rolling her two thumbs in a circle over and over.

Will finally got to his feet.

"Are there events in your life that you wish you could go back and relive? Moments that at the time you did not understand their impending significance, but which changed your life forever.

I have relived that day in my mind a thousand times. How different our lives would have been if she had followed orders. If instead of getting drunk and passing out in some tavern miles from Paris, I had listened to my instincts and gone home to make sure she bloody well did as I had told her. But by the time I sensed that something terrible was about to happen, it was too late to save her. She was already dead by the time I got back to Paris."

Hattie swallowed back tears. Her worst suspicions were now confirmed. Will did blame himself for Yvette's death. The guilt he carried, clouded his every thought of Hattie.

She had to make him see that loving someone meant accepting them for their faults and mistakes. It also meant allowing them to make their own choices, even if he did not agree with them.

As she rose from the chair, their gazes met. She held firm as Will searched her face, his look of pleading was heartbreaking.

"Thank you. I cannot imagine how hard it must be for you to finally confide in me. To share the truth. Now that I know what really happened to Yvette, I have a clearer understanding of your motives regarding myself. In a way, I also feel that I know her a little better now. Her mission to save her country meant a great deal to her, as does my work with the poor."

She reached up on her toes and kissed him. When Will attempted to deepen the kiss, Hattie pulled away.

"What needs to happen now Will, is for you to make a choice. You must decide if you can live with a wife who is exposed to danger as part of her work. I love you Will, I do with all my heart. But not even for you, will I give up my life's calling."

Will walked Hattie home to Edgar's house, ignoring her protests of being safe for the short distance between the houses. After he returned to number forty-three, he went back to the sitting room and poured himself another brandy.

It was apparent to Hattie's mind, that they were at an impasse. For Will, while it had been a challenging evening, he was able to see that they had made unexpected progress.

Hattie now knew the truth of Yvette's death. That secret no longer lay between them. There was an odd sense of relief in having passed that point in their relationship. While Hattie did not agree with Will's need to protect her, she at least now had somewhat of an understanding of his motives. She knew what lowering his guard had once cost him.

He set the glass down on the table, and pondered the other unexpected, but welcome development of the night.

She loved him. She had spoken the words.

The decision he now faced was what to do with that new knowledge. She wanted more than his wealth or social connections could give, she wanted a true partnership. A marriage where she would be able to make her own choices. Where he would have to let go of the need to control.

The challenge now lay in how they could find a way forward. How they could forge a future together where both could be happy.

The problem he faced was the sure knowledge that he would never be happy having his wife working in the dangerous streets of St. Giles.

The clock in the sitting room chimed the hour of twelve. He was tired, but his mind was too restless to consider sleep.

Hattie had made it clear that if she was ever to consider living back in his world, then she would have to be able to keep her work.

"Fool", he muttered.

Grabbing his coat, he headed downstairs and hailed a hack outside.

"St. John's church, Holborn, please," he instructed the driver.

Chapter Thirty-Eight

There was a certain sense of déjà vu the following morning when Hattie and Edgar argued over her refusal to take a maid with her when she left the house. The very same argument she had had with Will only weeks earlier.

"I have walked the streets of St. Giles alone many times with our parents' approval, I do not need a chaperone. You agreed to let me keep doing my work as long as I stayed out of Plumtree Street," Hattie firmly stated.

The males in her life, seemed incapable of accepting that she was no feeble female. She was more than capable of looking after herself. Hattie was determined to hold out against Will and he was far more stubborn than Edgar.

Attempting to keep matters cordial between them and avoid another family schism, Edgar finally conceded defeat. He did however make his displeasure known.

"You cannot expect to continue this life indefinitely. I expect William Saunders to make an offer of marriage to you any day now. As he is a good man, with wealth, and a first- class background I will be most inclined to approve his request. You need a husband to keep you in check."

Hattie wrapped her scarf around her neck and shoved her hat down over her head.

"Yes, brother I hear you," she replied.

She was in a hurry to get out of the house and away from Edgar. She needed a morning of being away from men who were trying to tell her how she should live her life.

As Hattie passed number forty-three, she glanced up at the windows of the upper floor of the house. The curtains of Will's bedroom were still fully drawn.

It was still odd to think of it as Will's home. She had been born in the house. It would forever be her home.

She hastened her steps to pass by the front door. Even if Will was his usual late abed self, she knew he would have eyes watching the street, looking for her.

"Bloody over protective stubborn man," she muttered.

Hattie's day progressed much the same as most others since her return to St. John's. She spent time helping to clean the church. Reverend Brown, however was in an odd mood all day. He was not his usual self. From his constant yawning, it would appear he had not gotten a full night's sleep.

After completing her work at the church, she headed over to Covent Garden markets and collected the vegetable scraps with which to make soup for the poor who would be attending the church later that day.

It was late by the time she finished preparing the soup and feeding the parishioners. She was washing out the last of the large soup pots when little Annie Mayford appeared at the door to the church kitchen.

"Hello sweet heart, you are out late," said Hattie.

She quickly finished with the pot and dried her hands. She gave Annie a hug.

"How is your mother? I am sorry I have not been to see her."

Tears formed in the little girl's eyes.

"Joshua says you shouldn't come and visit because of what the gang did to you, but."

"But what?"

"Mama is dying. She hasn't eaten anything for the past few days. All she does now is cough up blood. I'm frightened," sobbed Annie.

Hattie put her arms around Annie and held her close. She had always known that there would come a time when Mrs. Mayford's health would eventually fail. Annie would then be left in the care of her two gang affiliated brothers. It would not be long before Annie was drawn into the world of the Belton Street gang. Life in the rookery had a certain predictable pattern to it.

She was torn as to what she should do. Only last night, she had told Will she didn't knowingly walk into dangerous situations, and this very morning she promised Edgar she would stay out of Plumtree Street.

On the other hand, if Mrs. Mayford died and Hattie had not been able to see her before her passing, she wouldn't be able to live with herself.

"Is Joshua home?" she asked.

Annie nodded.

The news was encouraging. If Joshua and Baylee were home, then it meant the gang did not need them any further for the night. If she was careful she could slip into the rookery, visit the Mayfords, and the Belton Street gang would be none the wiser. It was worth the risk to be able to say one final farewell to Mrs. Mayford.

"I shall come with you. Let me get my coat and hat. I have some apples which I think Baylee would like."

The climb up the long, thin staircase of the slum house in Plumtree Street was never easy. Entire families lived on the landings of each floor. Their meagre possessions only allowing a small gap in which a visitor could pass by on their way up to the next floor. Annie ran ahead of Hattie and knocked on the door of her family's lodging.

Joshua opened the door. Seeing Hattie, he stepped out onto the landing and checked to see if anyone had noticed her arrival. He closed the door quickly behind him once he was done.

"You took a huge risk coming here Hattie. But I am grateful. Mama does not have long for this world."

When she looked at him, Hattie felt nothing but pity. He had aged in the short time he and Baylee had been members of the Belton Street gang. Gone were the youthful looks of his mere sixteen years. In their place was a grey pallor and bloodshot eyes.

"Oh Joshua. What have they done to you?"

He laughed. "Nothing, I'm fine. Baylee and I are having a whale of a time. It's great to be out with the lads every day."

His gaze fixed on little Annie and his mother both seated on the bed in the corner. Hattie took the subtle hint. They did not need to know of all the terrible things which the boys were forced to be involved in when out with the gang.

Taking her cue from Joshua, she opened the small sack she had brought with her and placed the handful of apples on the table. Upon seeing the apples Baylee swiftly snatched one up. Hattie laughed as he bit into the apple with unrestrained relish.

Hattie then went and sat with Annie and her mother. Mrs. Mayford managed a weak smile. From the tired look on her face and her labored efforts to breathe, Hattie knew it would not be long until she was gone.

"Could you please tell us another of your travel stories Miss Hattie?" asked Annie.

The youngest of the Mayford children delighted in Hattie's tales of her adventures in Spain. She especially loved hearing about the tall, dark stranger who had helped to rescue Hattie from the sea.

She had just begun to tell Annie about the wonderous cave of St. Michael when there was a loud rap on the door of the lodging. A booming voice came from outside on the landing.

"Open up!"

"It's Tom, my boss!" whispered Joshua.

Hattie went cold with fear. Finding her at the Mayford home for a second time would not go down well with the gang leader. He had warned her that the next time he caught her in Plumtree Street he would do much worse than give her a beating. He had boasted of tossing her into the Thames and holding her under until she drowned.

Hattie silently rued her stubborn nature. Will would be livid if he knew where she was right now and the danger she had placed herself in. It would be cold comfort for him to know that he had been right about Yvette and herself not taking their own safety as seriously as he did. And especially not when there was a good chance she was about to share Yvette's fate.

"What are we going to do? Tom will find you here. He thinks some of the lads are holding onto stolen goods and not giving him his cut. He will check both rooms in case we're hiding stuff from him," said Joshua.

Hattie took a deep breath, and tried to calm her mind. She remembered how Will had checked their surroundings when they were being threatened by the market crowd in Gibraltar. She now did the same.

"Can you climb safely down to the ground from here?" she asked.

When Joshua went to argue, she took a firm hold of his arm.

"Listen to me Joshua. You are the only one who can help me right now. There is nothing we can do to stop Tom and the gang coming through the door and taking me. I need you to go to my old house in Newport Street and find William Saunders. You remember him, you met him the night you brought me home. Tell him where they will have taken me."

There was a second and more violent bang on the door.

"Oy! Open up inside!"

Joshua raced to the window and clambered out onto the tiny ledge before disappearing. Hattie gave a silent prayer of thanks for the fact that the family lived on the second floor.

Turning to the others, she held a finger to her lips.

"Not a word any of you about Joshua. Don't even look at the window."

She took a deep breath and opened the door.

Chapter Thirty-Nine

"Are you sure Hattie won't be joining us this evening?" asked Caroline.

"No, she has some other personal matters to attend to tonight," replied Will.

After the events of the previous night, Will was in no mood to go into the finer details of Hattie's absence from the party. He would call on her at Edgar's house in the morning and discuss the plan he had agreed to with Reverend Brown. If she agreed to his terms, he would ask Edgar for his sister's hand in marriage.

He prayed she would agree. He was fast running out of options.

Stubborn Woman.

In the aftermath of his fight with Hattie, Will had forgotten entirely about his promise to accompany two of his younger siblings to a small gathering at a family friend Harry Menzies' house; only remembering when Caroline sent word earlier that afternoon.

Having spent so many years away from home, he owed it to them to step into the role of big brother now that he was permanently back in London. He could never give them back the time he had been absent during their younger years.

"Do you like my new gown, mama says it makes me look quite regal?"

Will looked at Caroline, but his mind was elsewhere. His every waking thought of the day thus far had been about Hattie. She wanted him, he had always known that much. Now he knew she loved him.

But was love enough for her to take her place by his side; of that he was not so sure.

"Well?"

"You look delightful sis. I'm sure all the gentlemen whose favor you wish to hold tonight will notice. Dull of mind older brothers being an unfortunate exception," said Francis.

Will stirred from his musings at the clear rebuke from Francis.

"I'm sorry Caro. Yes, your gown is beautiful, as are you. Forgive me for my woolgathering I have a lot on my mind this evening."

He focused on his youngest sister. Caroline was a true beauty. One of the diamonds of the *ton*. Behind her astonishingly deep green eyes was a sharp mind. Heaven help the man who sought to marry her just for her looks.

They headed out to the mews at the rear of the Saunders town house in Dover Street. Charles Saunders preferred the French mode of coming and going discreetly from home, rather than the grand show the English made of departing from the front of their houses.

Will waited until Caroline and Francis were on board.

"Could you give me a minute?" he said.

He walked away from the carriage. From his pocket he withdrew a small cheroot and a nearby footman lit it for him.

Leaning against the side of the carriage, he tried to clear his head. He had sent word earlier in the day to call on Hattie, but had received a short note stating that she was working at the church and would not be back until early evening.

The beginning of what he thought was a headache had been forming in his brain for the past hour or so. His hearing was also off cue. A long low whistle was ringing in his ear.

One of the kitchen maids appeared from the kitchens, with a large wooden bowl in her hands. She headed over to the rear of the garden and out through a side gate.

Adelaide Saunders had grown up in Scotland with fresh eggs delivered every day from the Strathmore estate chickens. She flatly refused to have eggs bought from the markets of London, and so the family kept a dozen chickens in a small garden at the rear of their house.

The chickens came racing over to the gate as soon as the maid opened it. The flap of wings and excited squawks stirred the night air as the chickens jostled for position to gain access to the supper leftovers. Will watched as the chickens made short work of the carrot and potato peelings.

Will drew back on his cheroot. There were always hungry mouths to feed. The chickens in his parent's garden likely ate better than most of Hattie's friends in St. Giles.

He threw the barely smoked cheroot down and crushed it with his boot. After the gathering tonight, he would call at Edgar Wright's house and speak with Hattie.

Will climbed aboard the carriage.

❧

"So, who is at this soiree tonight?" asked Will.

The carriage was headed toward Bedford Square where Harry Menzies' family owned a fine new mansion.

Caroline huffed. "Mr. Menzies has invited a few of his business connections, how terribly boring. Harry has his hunting pals, so I expect we won't see Francis all evening. I was hoping cousin Lucy and her new husband Avery were going to attend, but they have cried off. So that leaves a few stray folks such as you and I to mingle together for the duration. Such a pity Hattie could not come tonight. After last night, I am keen to talk to her about the work she does with the poor. She seems so noble about it."

The low whistle in Will's ear began to rapidly escalate to a loud ring. He found it hard to hear anything else. A sense of utter dread filled him as he realized that his senses were screaming for his attention.

"Would you mind, if we turned the carriage around and it took me back home? I don't think I am going to be very good company this evening," he said. He knocked on the roof of the carriage, and the coachman slowed the horses.

An increasingly uneasy Will, was about to suggest that he get out and find his own way home, when Caroline suddenly screamed. A riding crop was smashed violently against the side window nearest to her.

"What the devil!" exclaimed Francis.

"Halt! Halt I say!" a voice cried out in the street.

Will leapt to the other side of the carriage and pulled down the window. He put his head out, only to be met with the terrible sight of a frantic Edgar Wright riding at full tilt alongside the carriage.

"Pull the bloody carriage over! Stop!" Edgar bellowed.

Francis and Will both banged furiously on the front wall of the carriage, signaling the driver to stop.

As soon as the carriage came to a halt, Will jumped out.

"Wait here Francis and keep Caroline safe," he said.

Edgar reined in his horse. At that point Will got a glimpse of a figure tucked up behind Edger on the back of the horse. A figure whose face was a mask of fear.

"Joshua?"

Chapter Forty

"The Belton Street gang have taken Hattie, they are going to kill her!" cried Joshua.

Will saw the look on Edgar's face. A look which Will had prayed he would never have to see again after the war with France. A look of unrestrained terror.

"I was at your house looking for Hattie, when this lad arrived. Your butler told me you were headed this way tonight. Thank god we've found you," explained Edgar.

Will turned and to his relief saw that the Saunders' family coachman was already in the process of unhooking one of the horses from the carriage.

"Where have they taken her?"

"Down to the river, near the new Waterloo Bridge. The gang have a hideout there for shipping stolen goods up river. They also do a trade in dead bodies," replied Joshua.

Will felt a deadly chill run down his spine. These were not a simple gang of pick pockets he was dealing with tonight. The Belton Street gang were known even in polite society as vicious thugs.

Edgar leaped down from his horse and handed Will the reins.

"We were on our way there when we saw your carriage. If you are the man rumors at White's say you are, you should take Joshua and my horse," added Edgar.

To Will's surprise and bone deep relief, Edgar produced a pistol and a knife from out of his coat. Will quickly took them. He leapt up on the horse, pulling Joshua close in behind him. Edgar meanwhile headed over to where the other horse was being separated from the carriage.

"Go! I will be but a minute behind you," he said.

Will dug his heels into his mount and it leapt away. Joshua gripped on tight to Will's evening coat.

Hunched low over the reins, Will urged his horse on. The streets were filled with carriages heading both ways. Several times they came to a halt as pedestrians stepped out in front of them.

"Get out of the way!" Will screamed.

The startled Londoners jumped back onto the pavement, waving their fists angrily at Will and Joshua as they sped away. Down Drury Lane, Will managed to make up precious time.

He looked over his shoulder as he turned left into the Strand. Edgar Wright was right on his tail.

"Surry Street," cried Joshua.

As he turned the horse's head into Surry Street, Will caught sight of Waterloo Bridge. He was grateful to have Joshua on board. The bridge was recently built and Will would never have found it on his own.

At the end of the street, he reined his horse in and jumped down.

"Where?" he asked.

Joshua pointed toward the river, where Will saw a small fire had been lit on the beach.

"They come down here all the time to look for bodies. They search them for anything they can sell and then offload the body to the body snatchers," said Joshua.

Will turned as his ears picked up a familiar sound. Edgar had had the good sense to bring along a second pistol. He had it loaded and cocked. Will pulled his own pistol out of his coat and did the same. Joshua produced a badly battered pistol from out of his pocket. Will feared it wouldn't fire straight but said nothing.

Bile rose up in his throat. He had not had the need to kill a man in some time, but the memory of the stench of death came close behind, whenever he saw a loaded and readied weapon. He had seen hundreds of bloodied and dead men on the battlefield at Waterloo. No one ever became immune to the agonizing cries of a dying man.

He turned to Edgar. If he was about to walk into a fight to the death to save Hattie, he needed to know the caliber of the man beside me.

"How useful are you with a pistol Edgar? And don't be vain about it. Your sister's life could very well depend upon it."

He did not need to mention that all of them were currently in great danger. For himself, he would be relying on years of experience and muscle memory.

"I train regularly at Manton's shooting gallery in Davis Street. The pistols are well maintained. Other than that, you are going to have to trust that I am prepared to do everything within my power to save my sister. That includes shooting any blighter who gets in my way."

Edgar's words were exactly what Will needed to hear. They moved down the street, closer to the water's edge, keeping to the shadows to avoid being seen. As they crept closer Will was able to make out the shape of a half-dozen figures standing around the fire. To one side was a small hand cart.

"The tall one with the battered top hat, that's Tom, he's the gang leader. See that cart over there, we use it to carry bodies around. I would bet all my coin that Miss Hattie is in the back of that cart," said Joshua.

Will prayed that Hattie was still in the cart.

Still alive.

❧

A roar rose up among the gang as a fight broke out. Tom grabbed hold of what appeared to be a young boy aged about ten years old. He slapped the boy about the face several times. When the lad begged for mercy, he was punched cruelly in the face. The boy fell to the ground and lay still.

Will and Edgar looked at one another. They knew that when they headed into the fight, there would be no mercy shown to them.

Tom began to strut about, howling into the night air. When he reached the cart, Will's heart sank.

"Time to go lovey! I'm sure the fish will love to hear your bible preaching," he bellowed.

Several of the gang rushed over and dragged a sack out of the cart. It landed heavily on the muddy river shore. A muffled sound came from within the sack. Hattie was for the moment, still alive.

The gang members began to drag the sack to the water's edge. Will turned to Edgar.

"Do not hesitate if you get a clear shot. You won't get a second chance."

As the sack containing Hattie reached the water, Will made his move. Brandishing his pistol in one hand he raced out onto the mud flat of the river. A gang member stepped out, waving a large military sword. Will shot him as he drew close.

Will then made a bee line for Tom who was now rolling the sack into the water. Cries from his crew alerted him to the arrival of Will. Edgar was in close pursuit.

With one last heave, Hattie went into the water and disappeared. The gang leader put his boot on top of the sack, holding Hattie under. In a matter of minutes, she would drown.

Will launched himself at Tom, knowing if he did not take him out, none of them would be leaving the river side alive. They fell into the dirty brown water.

In the sinking river mud, he and the gang leader struggled to their feet. They were now between Hattie and the shore, cutting off any hope that Edgar may have had in trying to reach his sister.

In the dim light, Will saw the flash of a blade. He dived out of the way.

Out of the corner of his eye, he caught sight of Joshua waving his pistol in the direction of the remaining gang members. Fortunately, none of them were stupid enough to attempt a move to save their boss and Joshua was spared having to fire his weapon.

Coming up, Will grabbed hold of Tom's legs and tried to knock him off his feet. Tom raised his arm, in readiness to stab Will. Will saw the blade as it began its deadly descent. When it landed he would take the blow fully in his back. He braced himself for the knife's heart stopping impact.

A shot rang out in the night and the blade went wide of its intended mark. Tom's hold on Will was suddenly gone. Will looked up to see the gang leader, stagger backward on his feet. A large bloody hole was now in the middle of Tom's forehead. He fell back and disappeared under the murky waters of the Thames as Edgar lowered his pistol.

The remaining members of the gang scattered in all directions.

Will got to his feet in time to see Edgar and Joshua both wading into the water. He reached them as they managed to drag the sack back to shore.

Joshua cut the sack open and Hattie spilled out onto the muddy beach. She rolled over and struggled up onto her hands and knees. She sucked air into her lungs in large gulps.

Utter relief washed over Will. She was alive.

"Oh, thank god," he muttered.

Edgar pulled his sister to her feet and for a moment she stood and stared at him. The look of shock and anguish on her face, showed that she had not expected to survive her trip into the river.

She took two steps forward and flung herself into her brother's arms.

"You came for me. You came!"

Edgar and Will exchanged a look of relief. They had done it. As Will reached their side, Edgar released Hattie.

"Of course, I came for you. I will always be here for you. But Will is the one who really saved you. That blackguard was going to hold you under until you drowned. It was Will who fought him. I just put a bullet in his head."

She turned to Will with tears streaming down her face. In the chill night air, she began to shiver.

"I swear to you Will, I didn't seek the gang out. I did everything I could to avoid them."

He nodded in the direction of Joshua.

"I know. Joshua told me what happened. You did exactly what I would have done. You read the situation and you made the right choice," he replied.

Edgar let go of Hattie and pushed her gently in the direction of Will.

"Go to him. He is where you belong. I will always be your brother, but Will Saunders is your future."

She got to within a foot or so of Will and stopped. He sensed her hesitation. Will reached out and pulled Hattie into his arms.

"Come here my girl."

She wrapped her arms around his waist and held on tight. Will sent a thousand prayers of thanks to the heavens. She was alive. He had saved her.

A carriage drew up at the end of the street and Francis jumped out. Edgar and Joshua walked toward him, waving.

On the beach, Will and Hattie held tightly to one another. As the others walked away, she looked up at him. He bent down and kissed her tenderly on the lips.

"You taste of the river," he murmured.

"Yes, I need a large brandy to wash my mouth out. I always thought the Thames looked filthy. Having now drunk at least a pint of it, I know for certain."

He ruffled what he could of her wet and tangled hair, and kissed her once more.

"Promise me this will be the last time I have to go into the water to save you. I would rather you didn't make a habit of it."

"I was doing just fine in Gibraltar as I recall, but yes, I promise this will be the last time," she replied.

Will put his arm around her and they began to walk toward the carriage.

"When we get home, I have a plan I wish to discuss with you."

Chapter Forty-One

Mrs. Little washed the dirty river water out of Hattie's hair while Hattie scrubbed her skin in the bath. She had only been in the water for a matter of a minute or so, but she feared she would never get the stench of it out of her pores.

When a travel trunk with Hattie's clothes arrived from her brother's house, Mrs. Little was too busy weeping to notice the obvious. Edgar had decided that Hattie was moving back into number forty-three permanently.

Finally, dried, dressed and with her hair tied up in a soft chignon Hattie went in search of Will. She was keen to hear his plan.

She found him in the main drawing room seated on her favorite floral couch. It was comforting to know that her favorite room in the house, was also Will's. He greeted her with a devilish grin, then held out his hand. Hattie took it, letting out a playful squeal as he pulled her into his arms.

He took her mouth in a surprisingly soft kiss. She could sense he was doing everything he could to keep his passion at bay. The time for love making would come later. At this moment, they had the serious issue of finding a way to make their impending marriage work.

Will released Hattie.

"We need to talk first," he said.

His words did nothing however to dim the spark in his eyes from the reflection of the fire's glow. He wanted her as much as she wanted him right this very minute. The heat between them rivaled that from the well stoked fire.

"Before I ask you the question which this moment requires, and of which Edgar has already given his approval. I have something to discuss with you. A plan for you to be able to have the best of both worlds. Would you care to hear it?"

Hattie clasped her hands softly together, and nodded. Her nerves betrayed her and she was soon reaching to crack her first knuckle.

"I shall pay you a farthing every time I get you to stop doing that," he said.

She gave him a sultry look and licked her bottom lip. If he wanted her to quit her habit she would only take payment in one form. Will raised a knowing eyebrow.

"I went to see Father Brown after you left last night. He and I discussed the work you do at the church. He agrees that it has always been dangerous for you to venture into the streets around St. Giles. After tonight, you would have to agree that it is no longer safe for you."

Hattie nodded. Even with Tom dead, the Belton Street gang would have her marked for death if she ever set foot in Plumtree Street again.

She gasped.

"What about Joshua and his family? They won't be safe either."

"Which is why they have been moved elsewhere. Francis went to see my man of business as soon as he got home. You didn't think I would let the Mayford family stay in Plumtree Street another minute, did you?" he replied.

Hattie looked down at the floor, embarrassed to have doubted Will and his ability to see all the needs of a situation. He lifted her hand to his fingers and placed a tender kiss on her finger tips.

"Do you know what Father Brown and I discussed to the early

hours of this morning? A soup kitchen is what is needed at St. John's church."

Hattie frowned. At least she now knew why Father Brown had been so tired and grumpy all day, but Will's plan was nothing new.

"Father Brown and I already hand out soup to the poor," she replied.

"I mean a real soup kitchen, funded by us and our friends. One that is stocked with fresh vegetables, barley and some meat. With an oven for baking fresh bread. A soup kitchen that runs every day. Something that will feed dozens of the needy of St. Giles. I remember what you said about your father and that his mission was all about numbers. With a proper kitchen which you could manage from St. John's your work will continue and it can grow."

Her heart flipped. Will had been earnest in his endeavors to find a solution to their impasse. He had spoken to Father Brown and found the one area where they could make the biggest difference in people's lives.

She would never need to venture back into the rookery. The people she wanted to help could come to her at the church.

"And I take it that in return I shall have two burly footmen with me at all times. And I will keep you informed of my daily schedule and send word if I am to return home late?"

It went without saying that those were Will's terms, but she needed to give voice to them.

"Yes. And I think you would agree that a couple of useful lads could be put to work around the church, doing repairs etc. Father Brown is not a young man. They can also help with peeling and chopping vegetables."

"Thank you for finding a way. If anyone could, it was you. My answer is yes," she said.

She had not dared to dream that her deepest desire to have the best of both worlds could come true. That Will could actually be hers.

Hattie licked her lips, teasing him. Will growled. She leaned over and planted a soft, but enticing kiss on his lips. Their bodies were close, intimacy beckoned. She had given him the answer he needed, now she would allow him to claim his reward.

The shackles of polite social behavior were tossed aside, in its place was a deep hunger which demanded to be slaked. Will claimed Hattie's lips with a kiss which brooked no misunderstanding.

She gave into her deepest desires. As Will's strong arms pulled her tightly against him, her hands searched for his hair. She speared her fingers through his dark brown hair offering him her unspoken encouragement. They both knew where she would be sleeping this night.

As they finally ended the kiss, Hattie realized she still had one question which needed answering. She knew Will wanted her, but she did not fully comprehend why. Somewhere in the deep recesses of her mind there was still the worry belief that he felt compelled to marry her.

"Before you ask me the question that we know is coming. I need to understand why you want me. For many women it would not matter, but since I fled a betrothal to someone who didn't want me for me, I would like to know."

Will kissed her once more.

"I want you because I love you. I love the Hattie Wright who is before me. The Hattie Wright who made the decision to claim her role in the world. The instant I saw you drop over the side of the ship and into the harbor you became the woman for me. The girl who Peter Brown took by force is long gone. In her place is you, a woman who makes choices about her life, and about whom she wishes to love. I can only hope and pray that it is me," he said.

She cupped his face in her hands.

"I have done everything I could not to fall in love with you. I ran away because I knew I would never be able to resist you if I stayed. You have held a power over me from the very first day.

Believe me Will, when I say I never saw you as something to use and then throw away. I wanted our affair on the boat to happen because I knew you were someone whose love, even if it were held for only a short time, would be worth it. To tell you the truth, I was frightened of how you made me feel. When we made love, I felt reborn. You touched a part of my soul I thought no longer existed, something I didn't know if I wanted to reclaim."

"So, what you are saying is that you love me?"

She chuckled.

"Of course, I do. Any woman who does not fall for your charms is made of stone. I love you Will Saunders. You have rescued me, and I promise to spend the rest of my life making sure I stay that way," she replied.

She kissed his forehead. He smiled when she kissed his nose. As she pulled back to take in his handsome face, she saw the light of passion ignited in his eyes.

"So, you do me the honor of becoming my wife?" he asked.

"Yes."

"Thank god."

The sense of relief in his voice had her on the verge of tears. No one had ever wanted her purely for herself. In Will she had found someone who valued her for just being Hattie. Joy mixed with over-whelming humility left her speechless.

"Which now leaves the question of what to do with you tonight," said Will.

It would have been easy enough to ask Mrs. Little to make up Hattie's old bed. But sleeping anywhere else but in Will's arms tonight, was out of the question.

"I won't force you to do anything against your will. Ever," he said.

They had come so very far from the day they had met. She trusted him and her heart felt fit to burst knowing that he trusted her.

"I have gone half mad missing your touch. I need you inside of me. I need to hear your roar when you come," she murmured.

The growl of need and desire which came from deep within him gave her the answer she craved. He had missed her too. Knowing he wanted her, filled her with the furious need to be naked and under him. To seal the connection that was no longer in any doubt between them.

He rose to his feet, pulling her up with him.

"Come to bed."

She mewed disappointment, and looked at the couch. The couch was the right height; and had a soft enough back that he could easily take her while she was bent over it.

He shook his head.

"The bedroom. This will not be a quick coupling. I intend to take my time. As soon as I have you naked on the bed I am going to slip my tongue inside you, and then hold you down while I take you to the brink. Rest assured my love I am not going to spare you this time. You can forget about sleep."

Once inside his bedroom, Will pulled Hattie to him. She responded with a kiss that would make any grown man weak at the knees. She had learned a great deal from their time together on the ship. Will quietly congratulated himself on being such an excellent tutor.

"I want you. I want you now and forever," she said.

He heard the hunger in her voice, echoed in his brain. Hattie unbuttoned the top of her gown and let it fall open. He whistled his appreciation of the fact that she was naked underneath.

'Naughty girl,' he chuckled.

She kicked off her slippers. Will stood watching as she slowing let the rest of her gown fall to the floor. She was now completely naked before him. He felt himself go rock hard.

He came to her and knelt on the floor before her. With hands held on the top of her thighs he pulled her toward him.

Hattie whimpered as Will slid his tongue inside her heat. He held her steady as he began to tease her. When he flicked the outer edge of her clitoris she shuddered. She placed a gentle hand on his head, spearing her fingers through his hair when he delved his tongue deeper inside.

"Will," she whispered.

He took his cue, knowing he had roused her to a state where she would be ready for him.

He rose to his feet and guided her to the bed. He playfully threw onto the bed, where she lay watching as he quickly rid himself of his shirt and trousers.

"How do you want this?" he asked, climbing onto the bed.

She bit her lower lip for a moment. His cock twitched. He was desperate to sink deep into her and bring them both to completion.

Hattie clambered on to her knees and pushed Will onto his back.

"I was watching the riders in Hyde Park yesterday with Miranda. I think I should like to go riding right now, Mr. Saunders," she replied.

Will lay back on the bed as Hattie threw one leg over his hip and sat on top of him. As she moved into place, he guided his hard shaft into her slick, wet passage.

"Oh sweet…" he murmured.

She placed her hands on his shoulders and began to rock back and forth. Her feet gripped tightly to his hips as she increased the pace of their coupling.

Will pulled her head down to his and caught her lips in a searing kiss. Tongues tangled together as their bodies met one another in a thrusting rhythm.

When Hattie whimpered, he knew she was close to the end. He flipped her over onto her back and thrust deep into her, knowing this was the best position for her to reach maximum pleasure when she came.

"Will. Oh god." A long low groan escaped her lips.

He kissed her as the wave of her orgasm ebbed. When she finally focused on his gaze, he knew she was ready to give him the submission he craved.

Will withdrew from her body, but he was far from finished. He arranged her with her knees bent and facing away from him. He stood on the floor and pulled her to the edge of the bed. Her long dark blonde hair which had been piled up in a soft chignon, was tussled to a perfect state.

He leaned forward and slowly entered her once more. With hands gripped tightly to the side of her hips, he began to thrust slowly in and out. He closed his eyes and let his need for her take control.

In the room the only sound was that of Hattie's soft sobs of pleasure.

As Will quickened the pace of his thrusts, he took hold of her nipples and squeezed them hard. Hattie groaned.

"It's been so long since I took you like this," he murmured in her ear.

To have her at his mercy, to make her give herself to him completely, was his deepest desire.

"Don't be gentle with me, Will. I need you to take me hard. I need you to mark me, to possess me," she begged.

He did as she asked, thrusting harder and deeper than he had ever done before into her willing body. Her cries urging him on until he finally came in a fiery rush. His roar of completion shook the night.

Chapter Forty-Two

"All set?"

Hattie gave Edgar an encouraging smile. "Yes," she replied.

Her long white gown took up a good deal more of the carriage than she had expected. Initially she had opted for a simple design for her wedding gown, but Miranda had convinced her otherwise. There was only one time a woman walked down the aisle at St. Paul's cathedral to be wed.

The crowd outside the cathedral when the carriage drew up had her heart thumping in her chest. As she stepped out onto the pavement, she could see many friends who had been pushed away from the family over the past few years.

Standing alongside them was one who she now also called friend. Reverend Retribution Brown stood among the well-wishers, his hands calmly by his side holding his beloved bible. She released her hand from Edgar and went to him.

"Thank you for coming. This means a great deal to me," she said.

He kissed her hand. "He is a good man your Mr. Saunders. You have chosen well," he replied.

"Joshua sends his apologies for not being able to make your

wedding. He did not want to leave his mother. He asked me to give this to you."

He opened his bible and took out a piece of folded paper which he handed to her. Tears formed in Hattie's eyes as soon as she unfolded the paper and saw Annie's simple drawing of a tree and a house.

"Mr. Saunders has found them a place in the country. Somewhere they can all live safely. Mrs. Mayford can spend the remaining time she has left on this earth happy in the knowledge that her family has a future. Joshua is to be apprenticed to a local blacksmith, so he will be able to provide for Annie and Baylee in the years to come."

Hattie folded up the piece of paper and tucked it into the sleeve of her gown. She knew she would never be able to save all the poor of London, but with the Mayford family she had succeeded in giving at least one family a better future.

"Will you come inside and see Will and I get married?" she asked.

Reverend Brown looked up at the towering magnificence of St. Paul's cathedral and grimaced. St. John's church was nothing like London's grandest cathedral.

"Well, I don't expect anything untoward will come of it. Besides you are about to marry the Bishop of London's nephew, you might be able to put in a good word for me."

Hattie took Edgar's hand once more.

"I am ready to take another leap into the unknown," she said.

Hand in hand her brother led her up the stairs and into the cathedral to where Will and a new life awaited.

The End

Epilogue

Dearest Harriet,

Your father and I are standing here in our modest cottage in Freetown, holding one another and thanking God that you are safe and home in London. Your letter was the greatest gift we could have ever received.

Daughter you do not need to beg our forgiveness for having jumped from the ship, it is we who should offer our most humble apologies for trying to force a life upon you which you clearly did not want. The fact that you were driven to undertake such a dangerous endeavor, only showed us the depth of our failure as parents.

The grief we felt during those long months believing you were dead, made us question many choices we had made. Please believe that when we do return to England it will be with loving hearts and the hope that you and your brother can find it in your hearts to forgive us.

We shall write again soon telling you more of our work and lives here, but I wanted to make sure this note made the ship which leaves for England today.

Your loving and much relieved mother and father.

PS: You may also wish to know that Peter Brown married your maid Sarah Wilson. They make a sensible and suitable couple. He does exactly what she tells him.

Coming Soon

Lord of Mischief: June 2018
Eve and Freddie's story

The Duke of Strathmore Series

Book 1: Letter from a Rake
Book 2: An Unsuitable Match
Book 3: The Duke's Daughter
Book 4: A Scottish Duke for Christmas (novella)
Book 5: My Gentleman Spy

www.sashacottman.com

About the Author

Born in England, but raised in Australia, Sasha has a love for both countries. Having her heart in two places has created a love for travel, which at last count was to over 55 countries. A travel guide is always on her pile of new books to read.

Her first published novel, *Letter from a Rake* was a finalist for the 2014 Romantic Book of the Year. Sasha lives with her husband, daughter and a cat who demands a starring role in the next book. She is always on the look-out for new hiding spots for her secret chocolate stash.

On the weekends Sasha loves taking long walks while trying to nut out the latest plot point in her writing.

www.sashacottman.com

Printed in Great Britain
by Amazon

81155158R00161